The *Disappearance* of Douglas White

By

MaryJo Dawson

Also by MaryJo Dawson

The Death of Amelia Marsh
(First Sally Nimitz Mystery)

The Strange Situation at Emlee
(Third Sally Nimitz Mystery)

MaryJo Dawson

The *Disappearance* of Douglas White
(Second Sally Nimitz Mystery)

The *Disappearance* of Douglas White
Copyright© 2013 MaryJo Dawson
Revised by MaryJo Dawson 2016
Revised by MaryJo Dawson 2021

Published by
MaryJo Dawson

Also published in ebook form by Elderberry Press.

Cover Photo: William Dawson

Published in the United States of America

ISBN 978 1 494 26758 2

Acknowledgements

I would like to thank Robert A. V. Jacobs and my husband, William Dawson, whose invaluable assistance made the publishing of this book not only possible, but a better read.

Prologue

As my second adventure is put into print I want to clarify the time period of the story. Years have passed since these events took place, and technology has made leaps and bounds since then. For example, having a cell phone would have changed everything. If you realize how different communication was in the mid 1990's, you can understand why the situations developed you are going to read about.

Chapter One

It is interesting how different it is being in the hospital as a visitor, rather than showing up as an employee. Hospitals have been a part of me for more than half of my life. I have walked endless miles in their corridors. They have become a part of who I am. It is secure and friendly walking up and down the halls of an obstetrical ward, listening to the sounds, smelling the familiar odors of the cleaning solutions, the coffee brewing in both the staff and patient care lounges. Gone are the days of the unpleasant odors of ether and strong disinfectants. The pain and anxiety of childbirth gives way to the lusty cries of the newborn. Hospital obstetrical units have been my second home.

But this was not a birthing unit, not even the hospital where I was employed, so I was like any other anxious person waiting to hear how someone they love is doing. Here no one knew me. I was politely but impersonally directed to the surgical waiting area on the second floor, which was basically deserted because it was a Sunday morning. That meant there were few surgeries going on and that the emergency room here had been relatively calm on Saturday night. This was pretty remarkable since this was a holiday weekend, Memorial Day weekend.

Getting up out of a too soft chair I gazed at the pictures on the wall without seeing them, and thought back to remember other times I had been in this position. Not often, thankfully. When my husband died he had been dead on arrival in an emergency room.

In that horrific scenario the staff had shown me every courtesy and consideration. Everett's tonsillectomy did not count, nor did the fifteen or twenty stitches in my daughter Janelle's knee. Being the mom had given me special status and the worry factor had been minor. Only my mother-in-law and my own father had been hospitalized for any period of time, both in the terminal stages of their illnesses, and both had eventually died at home.

There had been sadness and concern then. Now the emotion foremost in my mind was anxiety. I admitted it and took a very deep breath as the second step in getting control over it. Everett was returning with our coffees, I could see him getting off the elevator at the far side of the corridor. He didn't need me to lose my grip.

It was our beloved Judy, Everett's wife. We were waiting to hear how she was doing. Judy, who had not only lost her baby, but could now lose her own life. Everett might not realize that, but I knew it.

Only two weeks earlier they had called me to share the news they were expecting another child, a brother or sister for Joel. They were excited and happy and so was I. The baby would have been due at Christmas time.

Another phone call last night had not been so happy. Judy was bleeding and they wanted some advice. Should they go to the emergency room? I advised them to do so if the bleeding continued, or if Judy was in a lot of pain. We all knew it meant she was having a miscarriage. A few hours more put them on the road for the forty-minute drive to the hospital, with a quick drop off of a sleepy Joel at Judy's grandmother's house. At five-thirty Everett called me back, as frantic as I had ever known him to be. Judy was in surgery, but what had begun as a minor procedure had become complicated.

"The doctor just came out here to talk to me," Everett said tersely. "He says they are having trouble stopping the bleeding and he asked for my permission to transfuse her. He said something about a tumor in her uterus. I don't understand this, Mom. Could you come?"

As a rule I am not easy to wake up at that time of the morning, but I had my clothes on and was headed to the hospital in record time. The state police patrolling the highways between

2

Hanley and the medical center in Terre Haute must have been at breakfast or I would have been pulled over for speeding, no question about it.

Since I had been looking up at the clock in the surgery waiting room or down at the watch on my wrist every few minutes, I knew it was about eight-thirty. Afraid to leave in case someone from the operating room came to give him an update, Everett had been waiting by himself for what must have seemed like an eternity before I arrived.

"She was bleeding a lot by the time we got here," Everett told me when I joined him. "It was three-thirty or so. They took her right in and let me stay with her. You know how it is; they asked a lot of questions and started giving her fluids by intravenous. The emergency room doctor called her own doctor and in an hour or so she went to surgery." He talked quietly, the worry showing in his bloodshot eyes and tense posturing. "But Dr. Paulden said it was an uncomplicated procedure and she should be in recovery in half an hour. Instead, he came out just before I called you." He repeated what he had told me on the telephone, not knowing anything more to say.

I persuaded him to take a little walk and bring back some coffee for us. There was only a drinking fountain available in the corridor outside of our waiting area. The coffee bar usually set up during the week on a shelf underneath a photograph of the original hospital, built in the last century, was clean and empty.

In a more normal situation my son would have returned with donuts or pastries to go with the brew. The fact he didn't only confirmed how frightened he was. He had no stomach for sweets this morning and had not even thought I might be hungry. Anxiety had shut down my own hunger pangs for now.

Taking the disposable cup he held out to me we both sat down again. "You been praying, Mom?" he asked unexpectedly, after we had taken a few sips of palatable coffee.

"Yes," I allowed. "And you?"

"Yeah," he managed a small smile. "I'm scared, Mom, and you probably know it. Losing Dad was bad enough but the thought of losing Judy..." He swallowed hard and lowered his head to keep me from seeing his face.

I put out a hand and stroked his hair. When I arrived he had

3

showered me with questions, hoping I could give him some answers. I urged him to wait for the doctor to come back, assuring him they would do what they had to for Judy, reminding him she was young and strong, and also reminding him Joel's birth had been quite easy. I did not tell him what they might have to do if they could not control the hemorrhage. There was no point in alarming him if it did not come to that.

"I'm surprised Liz hasn't found a way to get in touch with you," I said just to make conversation, but the point was a pertinent one.

Everett raised his head and nodded. "She's probably working on that. But I wanted to have something to tell her, and I don't want the whole family barging in here right now."

I knew it was only a matter of time before Judy's grandmother would make an appearance. It was inevitable her sisters would also come when they heard Judy was in the hospital.

"Joel's probably sleeping in after being gotten up in the middle of the night," was my guess. "That will keep her there a little longer."

We both heard footsteps in the hall and stood up as a tall and portly man entered the waiting room. There was no question who he was. His surgical attire spoke for him before he opened his mouth. Dr. Paulden and I had met when Joel was born but I was sure he would not remember me. His face looked as weary and spent as Everett's, but his posture was still straight and he had a sympathetic little smile for my son as he met his eyes.

"She'll be all right, son," he said, getting blessedly right to the quick. His thinning gray hair and the fairly deep lines of his face put him in the above fifty category, giving him the privilege of the familiarity. He motioned for us to sit down again, indicating he had more to say.

Everett courteously introduced us and we nodded at each other as he took a chair directly across from ours.

"You're a nurse, aren't you?" he surprised me by asking.

I must have looked surprised because he added, "Judy reminded me as she was going under the anesthetic." His face relaxed into a small grin. "She said you would hold me accountable if I didn't take good care of her."

That personal note was too much for my son. He let out a

jerky sob, no longer able to stifle it. "So did you?" he gasped, meaning no offense.

"She didn't make it easy." The good doctor ran a hand over his weary face and leaned back in his chair. "If this is a little confusing for you, Everett, I'm sure your mother will go over it again. I have bad news for you, too, I'm afraid."

I knew then what he was going to say, and he knew I understood as his eyes held mine for a brief second. "Go ahead Dr. Paulden" I said quietly. "As long as Judy is going to recover, I think we can bear the rest."

****

After the happy frenzy of the Christmas holidays there were five months of cheerful routine back in my life. It was business as usual, with twenty-four hours a week of hospital work, helping my friend Barbara get her gift shop ready to open again in the spring, and every few weeks getting together with Everett and his family to spend time with Joel. I had no problem filling the time between with my hikes, my home, and whatever else came up. Judy's crisis ended that.

Even though there was no correlation between her miscarriage and Detective David White's visit to my home two days later, it is intriguing how events often seem to pile up. Life seems to be a series of ebb and flow, or sometimes a tidal wave.

The doorbell rang about four-thirty and Joel ran to answer it. I was right behind him as he opened the door with no hesitation whatsoever.

"Hello," he chirped cheerfully, looking up at our visitor.

"Hello yourself," replied the visitor pleasantly. "Who might you be?"

"Joel Warren Nimitz," my grandson volunteered proudly.

"Nice to meet you." With a grin Joel took the offered hand and shook it vigorously.

"Would you like to come in?" Joel further extended his hospitality.

"No inhibitions here," David White directed this remark over Joel's head at me. "Your grandson? I bet he doesn't live in New York City."

"Right on both counts," I casually waved him in although I was very surprised to see him. He was wearing blue jeans and a brown Henley shirt, so Joel had no idea he was a police officer. Knowing would have increased his exuberance.

"I apologize for showing up unannounced like this. If this is not a good time we can arrange another." He leaned back on the living room couch as Joel scampered off into my second bedroom to play the Tonka truck program on my computer.

"Late afternoon is a very good time," I assured him truthfully. "It's too soon for dinner preparations, and making a meal for the two of us doesn't take very long."

I eyed him speculatively.

"Having your grandson visit you for a bit?" he asked redundantly. "Or are his parents here, too?"

"Just Joel," I answered politely, allowing him time to warm up to what he had come to say. "He came home with me on Sunday." I almost added a few of the details but decided not to. Paying me an unannounced visit on his own time, Detective White obviously had something on his mind. He would listen politely and express sincere concern, but he didn't know my family.

"He loves that Tonka truck program," I added, "and should be happy for a little bit. Would you like a soda or a cup of coffee? You didn't just drop in to see how I was, and I don't think we have any loose ends from last year, do we?"

He admitted we didn't. He would take a coke if I would have something.

It only took a moment to fetch two sodas, but Joel heard the refrigerator door open and ran in to get some refreshment for himself. I poured six ounces of orange juice in his sippy cup and he trotted back into the spare bedroom. During that time I made small talk, asking my visitor how his wife and own children were.

They were fine. He accepted the cold drink, took a long swallow and sat back on the couch again. He was trying to be casual but he looked ill at ease.

I settled into my favorite chair across from him, took a sip of my own caffeine and sugar free beverage, and said, "Okay, go head. I'm very curious. You have waved to me once or twice from your cruiser, but otherwise I haven't seen you in months, which doesn't surprise me. We don't move in the same circles and your wife hasn't had another baby."

He grinned and relaxed a little. "No, she hasn't. We have all we can handle with the three we have now." He took another swallow of his drink and began. "Okay, here it goes. I have a problem, a personal problem. For a while now whenever I try to figure this out you keep coming across my mind. I talked to Debbie and she agreed it wouldn't hurt to tell you about it and see what you think."

I waited, more intrigued than ever.

"It's all about my brother, Doug. He's the oldest, I'm the youngest." He paused a moment to consider his presentation. "You'll have to have a bit of family history to put this together. Bear with me."

I nodded encouragingly.

"There are five of us, four boys and one girl. I was the surprise, nine years after the other four. Doug always took a shine to me and looked after me, even more than my sister. We stayed close even after I grew up, but now I haven't heard from him since Christmas.

"Doug is fifty-one. His wife died about a year and a half ago from breast cancer. She was three years older than he, but she was still young. They were married almost thirty years. We used to kid her she robbed the cradle, but they had a good marriage. There were two kids but they didn't turn out too well. They both live in California, and since their mother died no one has heard from them. My brother still lives in Wisconsin where we grew up, or at least he did. Our folks are still alive there; they're in their seventies and he kept an eye on them.

"He did, but he doesn't now?" I found myself asking, breaking my intention to just listen.

"Not since right after Christmas. None of us, my brothers, my folks, or my sister, have seen him in five months."

After a pause the detective continued. "You must think it strange for me to come here and tell you this. Here I am a police officer and I'm telling you, a lady I don't know very well, about the disappearance of my brother."

"That's about it," I agreed mildly. "If he has disappeared you have all sorts of means at your disposal to find out what's happened to him."

David White sighed. "That's part of the problem. He hasn't exactly disappeared; there have been a couple of messages." He leaned forward, put his pop can on the coffee table and his large hands on his thighs.

"He's been in touch with our folks a couple of times by mail, just a note to tell them he's okay and not to worry. He's also withdrawn money from his bank account. He has money, he owned a successful business, but a few months after his wife died he sold his interest out to our brother, Marty. He stayed on as a regular employee and sort of as a consultant for a while but last December he ended that, too."

"So, about the time of the first anniversary of his wife's death he just packed it in and took off," I summed up.

"Right. And that would have been okay for a few weeks or so. But now we're getting worried, except for Janice. My sister Janice says to give it a little more time and he'll show up."

"But you don't agree."

My guest leaned back again and rubbed the back of his neck. "That's what I keep telling myself. But every year, and I mean every, Doug has remembered my birthday. I turned thirty-five three weeks ago and nothing, not even a card. Last year he was still grieving pretty bad and very lonely. He still came to town and took me out for a steak."

I nodded agreement this was odd.

"The thing is, Sally, he can't be classified as a missing person. I have no evidence of foul play and I'm sure he wrote those cards to Mom and Dad. I've talked to a sergeant on the police force in his hometown and he told me what I already knew. Professionally, there's not much I can do."

"Where were those cards postmarked from?"

"Chicago, both of them."

"That would rather be like looking for a needle in a haystack. And the last time he sent one?"

"April fourth was the postmark on the second one. It arrived in three days, about two paragraphs. He said he's fine and hopes all is well. I had Dad forward them to me and I've read them a dozen times. There's no hint to his whereabouts.

"But you said you are sure he wrote them," I reiterated.

8

"Absolutely. He has a very distinct handwriting."

Joel, who had come quietly into the room and draped himself over my knee, interrupted us. I lifted him into my lap and he whispered loudly into my ear, "I would like to go for a walk."

"So would I, "I whispered back. "We can go in a few minutes, okay? You can go find your shoes and bring them here."

He obligingly went in search of his shoes. I looked back at David White.

"You can guess I'm wondering what help I can give you. This is very intriguing but why come to me?"

"Last fall you showed yourself to be a very good judge of character. You noticed things and your hunches paid off. That's why I thought of you. I'd like to know what you think."

I drummed my fingers on the side of my chair and considered what he had told me.

"I think, from what you say, if I were in your shoes I would be concerned too. Your sister may be right but this birthday thing… Darned if I know what you can do about it, especially from this far away. Doesn't anyone in your family have a clue? What about his friends? Surely they've been asked."

"They have been. Everyone seems as puzzled as we are. I tracked down his kids and talked to them on the telephone, but they say they don't know where he is and frankly, they don't sound like they care too much."

"That," I said sincerely, "is a shame." I thought my two children would be very upset if I dropped off the face of the earth and I was very glad. David White surmised what I was thinking.

"Yeah. My wife and I hope ours turn out better. Both of Doug's are in their twenties but maybe they'll grow up someday. I do believe them, though. I'd bet a paycheck they don't know where he is."

Joel trotted in with a shoe in each hand and plopped himself down on the floor in front of me to put them on. My visitor tilted his soda can to his lips and polished off the rest.

"What are you going to do?" I looked up at him as he rose from the couch. "I feel like I haven't helped you at all."

He grinned. "No, you've been a good listening ear. What I haven't told you is I have to decide if I'm going to take some time off and go up there to pursue this. Running this by you was an

9

idea to help me make that decision."

"What does your wife think?"

"She says it's up to me," he said wryly. "No help at all, not that she isn't right."

"Maybe you could go up as a family," I offered, "sort of a vacation. Couldn't they relax and visit while you mix business and pleasure?"

"Maybe," he countered, but not too enthusiastically. I guessed Debbie wasn't too keen on going to Wisconsin.

I walked him to the door. He started to apologize again for intruding but I brushed him off.

"Would you mind if I thought about this a while and got back to you? I do better after contemplating something over a little time. Your little problem is going to nag at me. Not," I added hastily, "that I resent it. Really, I'm flattered you thought of me."

We agreed that he would call me if he had any more information he thought would be useful and that I would leave a message at his desk when I was ready to offer more.

"I guess there's no way of knowing if haste is needed since we don't know what's going on, but I'll get back to you in a few days," I promised, but not telling him I was taking Joel home on Wednesday and wouldn't be back until the day after that.

Chapter Two

There had been no picnics or parades for us Memorial Day weekend. On Sunday, a few short hours after Dr. Paulden came out of surgery, I scooped Joel up from his other grandmother's house. He felt just as comfortable with me as he did with his parents and gleefully helped me pack his things and settled into his car seat for the ride, no questions asked. He chirped a goodbye to Everett on the phone, promising to be a good boy, and sent kisses to his mother. He was told she did not feel very good but would call him soon.

Grandma Liz had grudgingly given him up because she trusted me and because she soon figured out she would have both Joel and Judy with her for several days after Judy was released from the hospital. As we had known she would, Liz made her appearance in the surgery waiting room. By then Everett was visiting his wife in recovery so I had to deal with her. Miffed with Everett at first, she forgot all about it in her concern for one of her darling girls.

Liz would be termed a colorful character. I thought she must be about sixty-five, although I didn't know for sure. That was the age I came up with by my calculations from what I did know. She had married young, had four children within the next eight years, and never forgave her husband for then having a very innovative procedure called a vasectomy so there wouldn't be any more. He had stuck around for another decade before removing himself from the picture. Liz didn't seem to miss him very much. As soon as her own grew up she started raising grandchildren. Judy's mother had been her oldest child. She had married the high school star athlete before her twentieth birthday, and in the family tradition had babies immediately, three daughters, before deciding she wasn't so keen on being a wife and mother. It was easy to leave Judy and her little sisters with Liz and go on a permanent vacation to Florida. Judy's father waited for a year before divorcing her, but he allowed his daughters to stay with their maternal grandmother. Privately I doubted there were many men up to the challenge of taking Liz on in the fight to take them away. I had met Judy's father, a very nice but mild mannered fellow, and was sure he wasn't up to it. Instead he married again and had another family.

You get the idea I'm sure. Liz was short and buxom with ramrod straight posture, dyed black hair always pulled back into a bun, and the habit of wearing black slacks and brightly colored shirts. She arrived that Sunday in an orange Hawaiian print. She listened intently while I explained what had happened.

"No more babies," she gasped. In Liz' book not too many things rated worse than that.

"No," I repeated. "They had to remove her uterus to stop the bleeding. There was a tumor in there as big as a large fist, silently growing since Joel was born. The hormones surging with this pregnancy made it a monster. The whole thing is a little complicated, Liz, but there was no way to take just the tumor and stop the bleeding. They tried."

"But she's all right? She'll be all right?" Liz's brown eyes were like saucers. Her hands were clutching the handbag she had in her lap.

"Yes, praise God, it looks like it. She's young and she's strong. They've given her blood. Dr. Paulden said she was stable and awake. Everett and Dr Paulden are going to tell her what they had to do to save her life."

Liz's mind was obviously awhirl. "Do they think its cancer?" She had the next question out before I barely answered the first one. If possible the hands were clenched even tighter.

"No, they don't. We'll know for sure in a couple of days when the pathology report comes back. That's the laboratory studies of the tumor."

"I want to see her. When will they let me?"

"Only Ev is being allowed in the recovery room, Liz. The rest of us have to wait until she is released to a regular hospital room. That's probably another hour or so."

It was plain she didn't like this one bit, but after opening her mouth to protest she closed it again, knowing it was no use to complain to me.

"My poor baby," she whispered instead, her lips quivering.

I put my hand on her arm. "It's hard," I said softly in my best professional manner, deciding this was the best approach, "but Joel needs his mother and Everett needs his wife. We have to think of that."

She nodded numbly, reached into her bag for a tissue, and blew her nose. I offered to go to the cafeteria and get her something to drink, knowing she wouldn't budge until Everett came out, and she accepted, requesting hot tea.

When I got back, having also taken a bathroom break, Everett was with her. He took each of us by an arm and steered us back to the elevator.

"They're cleaning her up and getting her ready to transfer to a regular room," he explained. "She'll be in room 312 in about 40 minutes. I'll buy you both breakfast and tell you how she is. Come on," he added as Liz began to ask a question, "you must both be hungry and I'm starved."

My son was back to his normal self. He was no longer afraid so his visit with Judy must have reassured him. That certainly reassured me.

****

Three and a half days later Joel napped in his car seat as I drove him home. We had both enjoyed his visit immensely, and he had been blissfully unaware of what his parents were dealing with. His mother called from her hospital room to do what mothers always do; she told him to be a good boy. She thanked me for taking him home and generously added she wouldn't have to worry about him now.

It was after I had a chance for a brief visit with Judy that

13

fateful Sunday morning that Everett asked if I would take Joel with me. Of course I would.

"I'll deal with Liz," he said. At that moment the lady named was crooning over Judy and the two of us were in the corridor outside the room. "You know where she lives, just go over there and get him. He'll go with you, and you know how to get into our house so you can get what he needs. I'll stay here today but I have to work tomorrow. I want to know he's not being handed around to all of Judy's relatives or spending too many hours here. A hospital's no place for a little kid unless he's sick."

It was a marvel Liz and Everett got along as well as they did. He was not the pushover most of the men in Liz' life had been.

Judy's hospital recovery went well. She would be discharged in time to greet us when we arrived. Everett had taken the day off to be there for discharge instructions and to bring her back to the house she grew up in. I knew they both wanted her back in their own home, but she was not strong enough to run after a lively preschooler or do the housekeeping. Everett was in the middle of a large remodeling job, and now more than ever they needed the money that would provide. It was a godsend, really, that Judy and Joel could spend at least a week with her accommodating grandmother.

I grinned to myself. Not that there wouldn't be a price to pay. Staying at Liz' was rather like bunking out in an airport terminal. People came and went constantly. Liz loved it. I hoped Judy would be able to climb stairs and retreat to her old bedroom when she craved some privacy. It was too soon to know how she would respond to the irrefutable fact she could not bear more children.

During a phone call to check on Joel, Everett had made his position very clear. "I love kids, you know that, Mom," had been his words. "But we have Joel at least. Who knows, maybe someday we can adopt or something. We'll worry about that later. Judy just needs to get better."

Trying to be tactful, I told him Judy might find it harder to accept. "When she's stronger and home again, this might be a big blow for her. It could be rough for awhile."

Everett conceded that was so, and that he had been warned about this by Dr. Paulden. His philosophy was in line with his usual practical approach, crossing that bridge when it came up.

Everett was more emotionally based than his sister, but we were all of a practical nature.

My mind was switching gears back to the visit on Tuesday by David White, when a voice piped up from the car seat behind me.

"I need to go potty and have a snack."

"You don't say?" I glanced at the car clock. We still had over an hour to go.

"I know a place coming up where they have bathrooms, and ice cream. Can you wait ten more minutes?"

"Ice cream! Maybe I could. What kinds do they have?"

****

Twenty-four hours later on my solitary drive home, my mind once again got back to the disappearance of David's older brother. What would make an ordinary middle-aged man decide to withdraw himself from everyone who knew him? Could there have been foul play? Could someone be forcing him to write those notes, and why would they? No, that was really too far-fetched.

But as soon as I got back to my condo in Hanley I phoned the police department and asked to leave a voice message for Detective White. That's not necessary, I was told, he's in and taking calls.

"What I want to know is why your sister is not as concerned as everyone else is. Also, have you asked anyone if they know how much he took when he left, and did he make any long term arrangement to have his house taken care of, the utility bills paid, that sort of thing."

"Since I'm one up on you on the last part of your inquiry," replied the police officer, "I'll answer that first. Doug moved his wife to a smaller home in town as she got sicker, and they leased the larger one. He didn't sell their first house until late last year and I thought it was interesting the sale went through just days before Christmas. It made me wonder if he was waiting for that to happen before leaving. He owns the smaller place outright. I'm told it's all locked up. My Dad goes over there and mows the lawn. To be honest, I don't know if the power and the water are still turned on. As to how much luggage he took with him, no one seems to know."

15

"Did he make any arrangements for anyone to pick up his mail?" I continued.

"He had it held at the post office until further notice. They told my family they would do that for six months. Until then they won't release it to anyone but Douglas or with written permission from him. It's still sitting there; the six months won't be up for four more weeks."

"That sounds like he planned to be gone a long time."

"Agreed," the voice on the other end of the line sighed. "I just don't think anybody thought it would be this long. Maybe we should sit tight until the end of June."

"Maybe you won't have a choice. But what about your sister?"

"Janice," David White considered her. "I haven't really thought of it the way you seem to be. I just assumed she's being laid back. You think she might know something the rest of us don't?"

"Is it possible? Would your brother confide in just one of you, and could it be her?"

"I would like to think it would have been me," he said honestly. "Still, they get along. She lives about sixty miles west of where Doug and my folks do."

"You said one of your other brothers bought Doug's business?"

"He did; Marty. But Marty moved the home office to Michigan where he lives. It's a supply business for foreign parts for vehicles."

"Oh."

There was a few seconds pause as the idea of Janice knowing more than she had come forward with was considered.

"If Jan has let us all worry like this I'll wring her neck."

"Not a good line coming from an upholder of law and order," I reproved.

He chuckled. "Okay. But I think I'll call her tonight."

"I can see from what you are telling me," I observed, "that there is a lot you can't find out for certain being this far away."

Another long sigh, then he confided, "I know. The problem is, I only get so much vacation time and I owe it to Debbie and the kids to take it with them. She puts up with a lot, being married to a police officer. As a detective I'm pretty much on-call twenty-four seven. We're only allowed to take two weeks of time off through the summer. You get my drift?"

"Absolutely. You have a problem."

"Any advice?"

"Sure. You don't have to live with your brother, even if he turns up. You have to live with your wife."

"Point well taken and that's occurred to me, too. She doesn't like the idea of a working vacation."

"You can talk to your sister and see what comes from that. I don't have anything else to suggest."

Detective White expressed his appreciation for my input, said he would let me know if any new information came up from a conversation with Janice, and rang off.

Almost a week went by. I put my house in order on Thursday and went back to work on the weekend. Being a night nurse on twelve-hour shifts, that left only enough time for sleeping, eating, and personal hygiene, until Sunday afternoon. My daughter called, wondering why she hadn't been able to reach her brother. A long conversation ensued where she was brought up to date on as much as I knew. I hadn't heard from Everett or Judy in three days myself.

"He should have called me!" Janelle wailed. "How awful for them!"

"Could he have tried?" I asked casually. Janelle is notoriously hard to get up with.

"Well, maybe," she allowed sheepishly. "It's been a so busy since Memorial Day, and I went to Maine Friday night with Robert, to his parents' cabin for the weekend."

"We're his parents there too?" I asked casually.

She laughed. "Yes, mother, if you want to know, they were. It was a nice time. We took Libby and Chase up with us."

These were Robert's children by his first marriage. My reservations about my daughter becoming involved with a divorced man had weakened after meeting him in person over the New Year's Eve weekend, when Janelle had brought him with her from Boston to meet her family.

"When I saw Judy on Wednesday," I provided information, "she was very sore, very pale, and very tired. There was nothing wrong with her physically that time and rest won't cure."

Janelle picked up on my stressing the physical part. For twenty minutes we discussed our concerns about Judy and Everett recovering from the loss of the baby they had hoped for by the end of the year, and accepting the long-term loss as well.

"I want just one baby," confessed my daughter. "When Robert and I get married, and Mom, you must know we plan to sometime, he agrees to have one more. But Judy, well, I think she wanted two or three. What do I say to her?"

"Say what comes naturally," I advised. "She knows you well enough to know if you're trying too hard. I'm sure they'd both like to hear from you."

I gave her the phone number for Judy's grandmother's house. We talked amicably for fifteen more minutes about her personal life before saying our goodbyes.

Hmmm, I thought. Perhaps there would be a wedding in the fall. I fantasized happily about the possibilities as I did a work out on my walking track. Out of the shower and towel drying my hair, I heard my phone ring and the answering machine kick in. The detective's voice was leaving a message.

"Feel free to call me back if you get this before five," he said, "otherwise I'll be at the station tomorrow morning."

He left a number, presumably for his home phone. Since there was still fifteen minutes to the deadline and I was curious, I called.

"Hello, Sally," he said, picking up after the second ring. I didn't at all mind one of the local cops feeling comfortable calling me by my first name.

"Caller ID?" I inquired.

"Affirmative."

"You sound very cheerful. Does this mean your talk with your sister went well?"

"It did, and you deserve to know it. She said Doug told her he would be away for quite some time; maybe months, but he wanted it hush-hush. She says she talked to our folks about it yesterday since he hasn't turned up yet, but she didn't realize I was that worried."

"Did she share any details?"

"She says she doesn't know any. Doug went to see her in

18

December. He made it clear he wouldn't be in touch and didn't want to explain, but there was nothing to worry about."

"So," I said slowly, "you aren't worried now?"

"Not so much," he admitted. "I think he'll explain himself when he comes home." There was a pause. "I feel a little stupid, like maybe I jumped the gun. Police officer paranoia."

"The situation is a little unusual. Often siblings don't keep up with each other for weeks or months at a time even if they get along. That's my family experience, anyway. But they're usually available when you want them."

"Yeah, well, I'm sorry I bothered you with this. Thanks, though. If you hadn't given me the idea to call Janice I'd still be brooding about it."

"Now you can take your family on vacation without guilt," I suggested.

"That too"

I sensed his smile.

Chapter Three

But Douglas White did not turn up. I discovered this when his brother and two fellow officers decided to have an early lunch at the diner where I was having a late breakfast.

It was early July. There were no parades for me over this holiday, either; I worked the 4th and the 5th. The trade off was several days off afterward. One of those following weekday mornings was the day David White and I saw each other again in the café.

When the three police officers entered the restaurant there was a sudden lapse in the hub-bub. The quiet jarred me unconsciously from my chapter in a Dorothy Sayers novel about Lord Peter Whimsey. Because I was in a small booth in the back none of them noticed me, but fifteen minutes later when I got up to leave I had to pass their table and I caught the detective's eye. He gave me a courteous nod and a greeting so I paused. You can do that - linger at a table where three law officers are sitting - when you have a totally clear conscience and no police record.

"Hello, Sally. How are you?"

I replied that I was just fine and asked deliberately, "And how are you?"

He knew what I was really asking and he shook his head slightly, making it very clear this was not the time to go into that subject. The others might not even know about their companion's dilemma, and it certainly was not my place to make them aware of it. In any case, Detective White made sure I had no opportunity.

"This is Sally Nimitz," he introduced me. "We became acquainted four years ago with the birth of my daughter. She's a nurse at the hospital." He named his two fellow officers, one older, balder, thinner, the other one younger, blonde, heavier.

They nodded politely and the younger said thoughtfully, "Weren't you involved in that business last fall with the death of the elderly lady at The Hedges?"

I admitted that she had been my neighbor and yes, I had been involved.

"I read the reports," he said. "Very interesting how that all turned out."

"Very," I agreed. "Enjoy your lunch, gentleman." As I started to go on I looked at David and added, "I'll call you soon, Detective, to get your advice on that matter we talked about."

"Okay," he replied neutrally.

Strolling down the street toward home I thought, so, big brother hasn't turned up. Now that I had been invited into the situation it was not in my nature to leave it alone.

In fact I never did leave it alone.

****

Before I could make that call to the detective he got in touch with me first. It was Thursday night and when I got home from running errands my message machine was beeping.

"Sally, this is David White. I'm very busy right now and will be through the weekend. I'll get up with you next week, I promise." There was a pause and I thought he was finished but he added, "I'm not putting you off. I will talk to you next week. Take care."

It was tempting to take my weekend off and go back to visit my son and his family, but I nixed that idea for several reasons. First, I had promised Barbara I would work Sunday afternoon at her gift shop. Second, I hadn't seen my long time friend George Thomas in several weeks, and we had agreed to have breakfast together on Saturday morning. And third, I didn't want to go back to see Everett and Judy until I was invited.

We spoke on the telephone every week and their lives seemed to be getting back to normal. Judy was home. Everett had completed his remodeling project on an upscale home and told me he was starting another job for a friend. I'm always leery of depending on your livelihood with doing things for your friends but I didn't say so. Some things you have to learn for yourself. Hopefully it would work out. Joel was always chatty and cheerful. He liked staying at his grandma Liz' house, he told me, because there was always someone to play with. But he was glad to be back he had missed his dogs and his neighborhood buddy. I knew the whole family attended a neighborhood block party and barbeque to celebrate the Fourth of July. By all appearances everything seemed fine and I hoped it was. Judy assured me her blood count was almost back up to normal and she felt much stronger. No one talked very much about how Everett and Judy were adjusting to their losses. The subject came up only once.

"Liz made the mistake of being a little too nice," Everett said drolly in a conversation we had after he moved his family back to their own house. "Finally Judy said, 'for heaven's sake, Gran, you have four kids, eleven grandkids, and three great-grandkids at last count. It will be all right.'"

We both laughed and agreed Judy knew her grandmother very well. I knew Judy well enough to wait for her to talk to me about her personal feelings. So far she had not done that. Our chats were always about what to expect physically as she mended, or other typical subject matter, like Joel.

I wandered into my living room, sat back in my recliner, and looked absently out of the front window. It was a warm, beautiful evening. It would be light outside for almost three more hours. The weather forecast for the days ahead was more of the same and I wasn't scheduled to work again for a week. Sally, I thought, just enjoy it. There would be time for hiking, gardening, housekeeping, and scheduling my car for servicing. I could do it at a nice leisurely pace. I might even call my mother in Arizona.

I would do all of those things. But my mind was on Douglas White.

****

It was good to see George.

"Miss me?" he grinned as I joined him at another of my favorite breakfast spots.

"Yes, I did," I admitted with a smile back. "You must have spent a lot of time on the boat."

"Oh? How do you know?"

"You've got an even deeper tan than usual. In fact you're practically sunburned." George's arms, neck, and face, were weathered by years of outdoor employment. But now his skin had a ruddy cast over the brown.

He looked smug. "We got out on the lake three days running. I've got a freezer full of trout and bass."

I congratulated him and thought, please, do not offer me any! I like fish; I just hate to cook it.

"I know you like fish," he continued, as I tried to keep a look of dismay off of my face, "and thought maybe I would cook some out on the grill one night and you could come over. I've already invited my neighbors on the south side. She doesn't know how to cook fresh fish and he loves it. They offered to bring bread and dessert if I'd do the grilling."

"Wonderful." I said in sincerity and relief. "Just pick a night when I don't have to work. I can bring watermelon and an appetizer."

I encouraged George to tell me a little more about his vacation. He had gone to northern Minnesota with his son Robin and his brother-in-law. He stayed at a remote cabin where the fishing had been sublime. The only thing more plentiful than the fish were the bugs, but everyone coped.

"What did you do with your animals?" I asked idly, my mind partially on the menu in front of me.

"Oh, the neighbors, same ones I just mentioned, looked after the cat. We took the dog with us."

"You did? How did she behave on that long drive?"

"Great. He was happy in the bed of the pickup most of the time. I left that little window between the bed and the extended cab open and she'd stick her nose in once in awhile to look at us. We let her in the back seat one rainy spell and she stayed in the seat with her nose out of that window." George took a sip of his orange juice and commented, "She was the only female within ten miles of the cabin."

"She was the only female who could have stood being within ten miles of that cabin," I said dryly. "How often did you guys take a shower?"

"My lips are sealed," he replied righteously.

"That's what I thought."

The server stopped at our table and we ceased conversation to order our food. As George relished a day of someone else fixing his morning meal and ordered the sunrise special with a side of pancakes, I observed my old friend with sentimental recollection. He had been a life long friend to my late husband. They had grown up together, joined the Navy in the same month and amazingly, seen a couple of the same duty stations before George decided a career in the military was not for him. Their friendship endured through the changes the years had brought and came full circle when my Michael retired back to Indiana. Michael and George had gone on several fishing trips together. Sometimes they took Everett and Robin. George's wife Jill and I didn't have much in common except we both knew we were not cut out for these fishing getaways.

Now George had been divorced for almost four years and I had been a widow for almost two. We were two middle-aged people who found peace in our lives after the pain had eased. For myself there was a good measure of contentment and I was pretty confident that was true for George, too. He was not that hard to read.

Now he was scowling at me.

"You didn't hear what I said," he accused. "Where are you?"

"Sorry. I was taking a little stroll down memory lane. What did you ask me?"

"How's that little old lady friend of yours? Anne."

"Miss Carey?" I called her Anne, too, but thought of her more often as Miss Carey. Her decades as an educator made it difficult not to do that. It was strange hearing George use her first name. He never addressed her that way; she was still the school marm to be respected in his book.

"Of course Miss Carey. How many of your elderly friends do I know?" The words would have sounded rather sarcastic coming from me, but they sounded mild out of his mouth. He eyed me curiously. "Where is your mind today?"

I sipped my coffee before replying. "I'll answer that in a minute, after answering your first question. To keep the record straight she's your friend too, you know."

"Point taken," he allowed, "but I've only seen her once or twice since last Christmas. How is she?"

Miss Anne Carey, George, and myself, had made an impressive trio – we thought – the year before when doing our own search into the death of a close friend of Anne's, who happened to be a neighbor of mine. When that was settled we all went back to our own lives.

"As far as I know she's just fine. We try to get together for coffee or something once in awhile. Now it's been weeks because she's been traveling. I got a postcard about two weeks ago from the Monterey coast. She sent her regards to you."

He grinned. "She's a game old gal, isn't she? How old is she, do you think?"

"Late seventies. Some people have good genes. It wouldn't surprise me if she has ten or twenty years to go."

"If she's back why don't you bring her along for the fish fry?"

I said I would ask her. He asked politely but not without sincerity about my family. Our breakfast came while I was answering him.

"That's a rough break," was his comment when I finished telling him about Judy's surgery.

"Yes," I allowed, "but not the end of the world. Some people only have one child. Some have none. I think they'll handle it." I picked up my knife and added blackberry jelly to my toast. "You did."

"Had to," George commented between mouthfuls of eggs and pancakes. "Jill only wanted one and she made sure that was all we had."

I didn't response to that at first because I had a hard and fast rule about not talking down George's former spouse. It wasn't a hard rule to stick to because George seldom mentioned her.

"Did that bother you a lot?" I asked cautiously now.

George stabbed his pancakes again and chewed another generous forkful before answering me.

"For a while," he admitted. "But she wouldn't budge, and I wanted her to be happy. I also wanted peace in my house."

We ate in mutual contentment. When the plates were cleared and we each had a fresh cup of coffee I moved back to deeper territory.

"George," I began, "can I ask you something rather personal?"

He smiled slightly. "You can ask. I reserve the right to decline to answer."

"Fair enough. When Jill left, were you ever tempted to do anything really drastic?"

"Like what? Take a shotgun to the guy?"

I laughed. "That's not exactly the angle I'm thinking of. Did you consider making a change in your own life? We haven't ever talked about this because Michael was alive then and you could relate to him if you needed someone. What I'm trying to say is, were you ever so depressed you thought about chucking everything?"

"Sure. Didn't you?"

My situation had been different, as George well knew. My husband died in a tragic accident. Our relationship had been wonderful so I had countless good memories. Although George didn't realize it, my grief could be more closely compared to Douglas White's. The difference was in our gender. My late husband told me once men and women deal differently with grief.

"Most of us men don't want a shoulder to cry on all the time," he said. "We don't think it will do any good so we don't see the point."

"Not seriously," I got back to George's question.

"Why are you asking?"

"You don't have to elaborate if you don't want to, but it might help me."

He leaned back in his chair and rubbed the side of his nose. "Okay. But you will tell me why you want to know?"

I said that I would.

He deliberated. "It's been almost five years since everything started falling apart, and four since the divorce. I fell apart inside, but it was getting better when Mike died. That was a setback for my mental health. During those first months after Jill left I often thought about packing a suitcase, getting in the truck, and driving off somewhere. You probably know why I didn't."

"My guess would be Robin."

"That's it. He was just out of high school. It was bad enough for his family to break up but he didn't need his old man to crack up too."

"Michael was pretty worried about you," I remembered.

"Yeah," he sighed, "when I could get past thinking about myself I saw there were quite a few people who cared. The weird thing was, people you thought would be there for you weren't, and some others you never would have expected were trying to help. I'm not talking about you and Mike, now," he added hastily, "and Rose drove me batty she called so often to see how I was. But I know she meant well."

Rose was George's sister. We had met once. I liked her.

I knew what George was talking about and told him so. Being newly widowed had been an eye opening experience, too, but I didn't want to get into that. I told George what David White had shared with me about his brother.

"So here you have a guy who is a widower for over a year and suddenly takes off. He's been gone now for over six months."

George was methodically wiping his hands with his napkin as I finished my story.

"It could be," he said cautiously, "that what you have here is one of those people who stops for a hitchhiker or something, is taken deep into the forest somewhere, murdered, and never heard from again. Years later somebody accidentally stumbles over the body. I know that's not what his family wants to hear," he added hastily, "but you know it happens. His brother must have thought of this."

"And the person or people who did it got him to write two notes first before bumping him off so no one would start looking for him right away?"

"Oh, yeah," my breakfast partner grinned ruefully. "I forgot that part." He brightened immediately. "But the last note was in April. It could have happened after that."

I allowed this was true.

"But you don't really buy it," George said, and sighed. "No, I guess I don't either, not a grown man with plenty of brains allowing himself to get into a situation like that. Still, maybe he did mean to be back by the end of June. Something just held him up a little."

"That seems more plausible," I concurred. "From what I do know my guess is Douglas White planned to go away for up to six months. Maybe he had some sort of a delayed reaction in his grieving process, or maybe after a year of trying to carry on he just couldn't deal with the life he had known for so long with his wife. He wanted a break. He didn't have anyone left at home he needed to be strong for like you did."

"It is interesting to me," George commented, "that the police officer brother came to you for your take on it. I'd say that's a big compliment."

"You do, do you? Maybe. Maybe he was just desperate."

"Huh." George grunted his disagreement. He added, "does he know you're talking to me about it?"

"No," I admitted, "but he made no stipulations. I certainly would not broadcast his private business all over town. You know how to keep a confidence."

George assured me this was so.

"After the detective gets back to you," he said, "let me know. I'd like to hear how this turns out."

Chapter Four

It was Friday afternoon before David White got back to me. I worked my twelve-hour shifts Wednesday and Thursday nights, both of them busy. Between the two nights I had three deliveries myself, one an emergency cesarean, and there were four others. On a unit that averaged three deliveries a day this boom kept the entire staff running. Friday afternoon I dragged myself out of bed about one-thirty in order to have a portion of the day for living. When I got to the kitchen there were two messages on my answering machine.

The first one was from Barbara Teal, my employer at my moonlighting job. This job was strictly for fun.

"Sally, Barb here. Could you possibly work for me again this weekend? I could use you Sunday afternoon. Gina bowed out, the brat. Why do I let family work for me, anyhow? Call me ASAP, okay?"

I considered her request. Gina was her oldest daughter and had a high absentee rate. Since Barb had added a small soda fountain to her gift shop business this year she needed two people in the store. Being a soda jerk for three or four hours sounded appealing. I had nothing else planned that couldn't wait. I called her back and left a return message saying I would be there at one.

The second message was from David White.

"Sally, call me as soon as you get up. I bet you're sleeping. You were with friends of ours when they had their son last night.

You made a good impression. Call me at the station."

Before doing that I poured myself some orange juice. He was out and I would have to wait for him to call me again, so I took my juice into the bathroom and started putting myself together.

We finally made contact late in the afternoon.

"Sorry about the phone tag," he apologized. "Something always comes up around here."

I assured him it was no problem. I was glad my tax dollars were not being spent to keep a police detective twiddling his thumbs.

"There's been no word from your brother," I answered the question he expected me to ask.

"None," he confirmed grimly. "My dad called me yesterday. He's getting upset. We're a pretty close-knit family. Dad doesn't think Doug would walk out like this never to get in touch again. He's never been that callous, never; he knows how it would hurt our folks."

"What are you going to do?"

"I've been back in touch with the police up there. I've given them a description of his car and we've had an APB put out throughout the country. Other than that there's not much I can do. If he hasn't turned up in a few more weeks, I'll take leave so at least I can visit my parents and make them feel like I'm trying. They think because I'm a cop I should work some magic here."

I told him I was very sorry and wished there was something I could do.

"Do you mean that?" he asked quietly, intensely.

For a fleeting second I had a strong sensation of standing on the edge of a cliff faced with the choice of jumping off or turning back. Oh well. I jumped.

"Yes, of course I do or I wouldn't have said so. Is there?"

With deliberation he asked, "How would you like an all expense paid working vacation?"

"What?"

"After Dad called last night I had a long conversation with Marty and a shorter one with my other brother, Phil. They thought I needed funds to go home and offered to pay for everything. Not that I couldn't use their help if I did, I'm the poorest of the lot. But that's not the problem, as you know. Then I had this

30

brainstorm and told them a little about you. I told them I might be able to persuade you to go up there and nose around for a few days, and that you'd be able to figure out as much as I could."

"All this confidence makes me nervous," I replied. "You think that just because of what happened last year?"

"I do," he said firmly. "Besides," he added, probably not meaning to spoil it, "what other options are there? Everyone is busy. If they had any knowledge of what to do Jan or one of my brothers would do it, but they don't."

"You think I could?"

"I'm willing to give you the chance. If you can get away you can go up there and follow whatever leads you get, carte blanche."

"Well, this is certainly the most intriguing offer I've had in a long time. How long do I get to think about this?"

There was a short laugh on the other end of the line. "I'm in no position to bargain. If you're willing to go the sooner the better. The only stipulation is," his voice took a firmer tone, "if you start digging up anything questionable you have to promise to go to the authorities right away. We don't want to put you in any danger. You have to back off if this turns out to be sticky."

"You don't think it will, though."

"If I did, I'd be packing my bag right now and the department would have to take it or fire me. Don't tell anyone I said that. But I think there's a logical explanation. I want to know what it is, where he is, and why."

Even though we agreed to talk about it again Saturday morning, I was already hooked when I hung up the phone.

Through the late afternoon and evening of that same day I did routine things. I had something to eat, took a leisurely walk, put a load of laundry through the washer and dryer, checked my e-mail and answered a few. But the entire time my mind was on the amazing offer David White had put on my plate. With an hour of daylight left I took a pad and pen with me, got comfortable in a patio chair outside, and started making a list of what I needed to do before it was feasible to leave town. It had been a warm day and the breeze coming up as the sun was setting was very welcome. I eyed my petunias and marigolds. They need to be watered before bed.

After about ten minutes of making considerable progress with the list I heard the doorbell ring. I was too curious to let it go and reluctantly left my chair and went through the house to answer the front door.

"Anne Carey!" I gushed, reaching out to her.

Beaming, she opened her arms for a hug. Her little dog was with her. As we embraced, Yippy ran in excited circles around us both, her leash becoming a dangerous weapon, threatening to seriously trip us up. Anne's scolding did nothing to stop it, so I quickly bent down and pulled the leash loose enough for both of us to step out of it. Carefully I assisted Anne, thinking a broken hip in her future was to be avoided at all costs. She was thinking along the same lines.

"I've been more than halfway across the country and back without getting a scratch," she glared at her pet. "No wonder I didn't take you along."

Yippy cocked a delicate ear and settled down. She had been with Anne for almost six years and knew her position was secure, but perhaps she didn't want to be sent back to the vet where she had been boarding.

As we got comfortable in my living room, Anne's dog secured on a long leash on the front entrance rail, we asked each other the inevitable questions. She had gotten home earlier in the afternoon. The trip was wonderful and the California coastline gorgeous. Yes she was tired, and these long vacations might be a thing of the past.

"I can't wait to have a night's sleep in my own bed," she admitted, " and right now the idea of going any where for longer than an overnight sounds overwhelming."

"You might change your mind in a month or two," I smiled at her. "All you need is a little time to rest up."

"Maybe," she allowed, "but I don't bounce back like I used to."

She did look tired but that was to be expected. Her faded blue eyes had dark circles under them. With my prompting she leaned back in the chair she favored in my sitting room and allowed me to serve her iced tea. With some more encouragement she went into greater detail about her visits to family and friends. Almost an hour went by before she insisted on hearing what I had been doing while she was away.

I glanced outside at the now darkening summer sky.

"It will take a little time to tell. You're tired. How about breakfast together in the morning, say about nine thirty?"

She looked at me speculatively. "Sally, what have you been up to?"

I grinned at her. "Looks like we might have another adventure in our future. What do you say?"

Her mouth dropped open. "Not another death!"

I assured her there was no reason to think there had been another untimely demise quite yet. Still it was another twenty minutes before she left because I had to tell her enough to satisfy a little of her curiosity. I stood on the top step of my entryway and watched the elderly lady and the dog until they were out of my sight, which meant they were almost home themselves. Closing and locking the front door, I laughed a little out loud. Weary she might be, but my geriatric friend had perked up like a wilted flower in a summer rain when she caught another adventure in the works. She would be ready in the morning when I stopped by for her, no doubt about it.

****

"Does George know about this?" Anne asked less than fourteen hours later, first swallowing a large bite of a strawberry muffin. Ten hours of sleeping in her own bed had done wonders. The dark smudges under her eyes were almost gone. Wearing a pale blue cotton blouse and a pair of khaki colored pants, the inevitable bobby pins holding salt and pepper gray hair out of her eyes, she looked like her old self again.

"He knows almost as much as you do. I talked to him last night. The only thing David White had to add this morning were a few details about his hometown, plus the addresses of his sister and his parents. Once I clear my schedule at the hospital, which I hope to do on Monday, I'll let him and both you and George know when I plan to leave."

And my children I thought, plus probably my mother in Arizona. There was no way I could be gone for a week or more without some explanation to them.

"What do you think?" I asked my companion. "You know as much as I do now. What do you think happened to Douglas White?"

"Oh, I think it could by any number of things," Anne looked thoughtful and took a sip of her tea. "It is not so unusual for people to disappear. When it is someone you are fond of and think you know, as Detective White thinks he knows his brother, you can't fathom their being selfish enough to just walk away and never return."

"I'm surprised to hear you say that. Are you speaking from personal experience?"

"No, not really," she allowed. "No one I have known well has done it. But I do know of a few cases by fairly close association. Listening to your story has brought them back to my memory. One was a former student, and two others well known to people I know."

"Go on," I urged, picking up my own cup but my eyes not leaving her face, "tell me what happened to them. Do you know?"

"I know what happened to two of these three. My former student was in her thirties – yes, it was a woman – when she disappeared. One day she didn't come to pick up her children from school. This happened, let's see, yes, in nineteen sixty-eight. I had an aunt living in the same town who sent me the newspaper clipping because the article stated where Molly grew up. Ten years later she resurfaced in Savannah, Georgia. The explanation was she had been suffering from severe depression. Not a very good explanation if you ask me. Be that as it may, she was alive and there had not been any foul play."

"I'm sure there's more of a story here," I interjected, "but let's move on to disappearing artist number two."

"That would be the father of a family I knew slightly during my teaching years in Iowa. They owned a restaurant and bowling alley, so almost everyone in town knew who they were. They made arrangements for the paternal grandfather to come live with them after his wife died. It seemed to be working out fine, but one day he bought a ticket for a train going to Los Angeles and left without telling anyone. It was a small town so it got a lot of attention and I heard the story several times over."

She stopped for another sip of tea and another bite of the

muffin. I waited expectantly, munching my own toast.

"His relatives thought he had gone senile. He hadn't offered any warning or explanation so of course they worried. I think it was about six months before they found him. He was staying with an old friend and working part time in a hardware store. When he was asked why he left without telling anybody, he said his friend had written asking him to come and he hadn't wanted anybody to try to stop him. He said he meant to write he just never gotten around to it!"

"Some women I know would say that sounds just like a man," I commented dryly.

"Yes," Anne agreed. "I have noticed when it comes to certain facets of life the male species doesn't think there is as much to get upset about."

"That's only two of the three," I moved her along. "What's the story on the person who didn't reappear?"

Her face grew grave. "A sad story. It's the sort of thing you read about in a detective magazine. It seems to me many disappearances are of troubled young people, especially young girls, and they often come to violence by someone who picks them up on the road or in the big city. But this is another male and a very unlikely person to disappear, or so it was thought at first."

"How do you know about him?"

"He was in the Army with my nephew, Bradley. They were fairly good friends, they had been in Vietnam together. When he disappeared Bradley heard from the mother of the young man. She contacted Bradley on the slim chance he might have heard from her son. It was thought perhaps his military experience there affected him adversely, as it did many young men."

Anne stopped her story telling momentarily as the waitress came by with the coffee pot and left our bill. I scooped it up, she protested, and we argued amiably back and forth for a moment. I won. We both knew she would not forget and the next time we ate together she would make sure she got the ticket first.

"He was married," Anne took up her story. "His wife went to spend a weekend visiting relatives and took their little boy with her. Bradley's friend, his name was Jim I think, didn't go because he had to work some hours on Saturday. When he didn't show up at work his foreman thought he had gone with his family, so it

35

was two days before anyone realized he was missing."

"That gave him a two day head start," I noted, "unless he never really went anywhere and there was foul play."

"As time went by a lot of Jim's family and friends did think there had been foul play. It came out in time Jim's wife had been seeing someone else. A year after he disappeared she had their marriage dissolved, and a few weeks later she married the man she had been having an affair with while Jim was around."

"But nothing was ever proven," I guessed.

"Nothing. No one ever heard a word from Jim again, but long investigations never turned up any solid evidence he had been murdered, either. The people who knew him well never accepted the idea he just walked out. They said there would have been some indication, and he would not leave his little boy without a word."

"You know a lot about this," I was fascinated. "How long ago did this happen?"

"Oh, let's see," she considered. "It's been over twenty years!" She shook her head in wonder. "I hadn't realized it's been so long. Bradley got really taken up with it for a while, you see. He wasn't married himself; Bradley didn't marry until he was almost thirty-five. Anyway, I digress. The point is, whenever I spoke with my sister I would ask her how he was, Bradley that is, and she would tell me how preoccupied he was with the disappearance of his friend. Sometimes I would talk to him myself. Eventually he had to let it drop."

"What did he think happened?"

"Oh he agreed with those who believed Jim was killed," Anne was matter of fact. "He said there was plenty of circumstantial evidence to support it, but no body was ever found."

"How sad." I shook my head, and leaned back in my chair. "I certainly hope my trip up north doesn't turn out so tragically. George theorized Douglas White might have been the victim of a roadside crime. You make a case for foul play closer to home. From what I know, I think the most plausible explanation is his two kids doing Douglas in so they can have their inheritance. I hope that didn't happen."

"I hope not either, dear," Anne said sincerely. "It's just a hunch, you know, but I don't think this will be like that."

Over the next few days Anne's comment about the people closest to the person who disappeared not being objective enough to realize what really might have happened stuck with me. It made a lot of sense. On the other hand if you truly knew someone as I had known my husband, you wouldn't have a doubt about some conclusions. When Michael didn't come home one night I knew he was badly hurt or dead. The odds of his deciding to live another life somewhere were nil. He had been a part of my own soul, and I knew him as well as any human being could know another. Did David White know his brother that well? Or was he in denial?

Chapter Five

Sunday morning I attended the eleven o'clock service at a small church two blocks from my home. The pastor liked some of the old fashioned hymns and so did I. It was a pleasure to sing them with his fifty enthusiastic other attendees, about ten over sixty-five and about ten under ten. I had plenty of time to get home, change my clothes, munch an apple, and show up promptly at my friend Barbara's gift shop. This was my third year as a seasonal part time employee. I enjoyed the change from my health care profession. It was usually fun to deal with the customers, watch the scene in the pretty downtown area of our small town from the windows and, when there was time, chat with my friend.

This day there was no time for idle chatter. It was another warm, humid, summer day. A great many tourists and several of the locals stopped in to order an ice cream soda, sundae, or cone. Several times Barbara had to desert her post at the gift counter to give me a hand and the time flew by. When Barbara turned the front door sign to the "closed" position I sank onto a stool in relief.

"My right arm is killing me!" I complained. "I'm in poor shape to dish out ice cream for hours at a time."

She grinned. "You did great. You can rest up all week. You don't have to lift any of the pregnant ladies do you?"

"You might be surprised, but they won't get much help from me for a couple of days. I think I can manage the babies."

I considered telling her about my upcoming trip, but while we cleaned up we discussed the customers and what sold that day besides ice cream instead. Both of us indulged in a cone before putting the dairy bar away.

As we locked up I said, "Barb, I don't think I'll be here to help you next Friday. I've got to go up north for a few days, maybe longer."

She looked stricken, and I said contritely, "I'm sorry, this is something important. If I'm not fired I should be reliable for the rest of the summer."

"Gina and Melinda will have to be more dependable," she replied firmly.

Privately I wouldn't have put any money on Barbara's daughters. They were spoiled. "Maybe your mom would like to help out a little," I suggested. "She seemed to enjoy it last time. Just don't expect her to scoop ice cream."

My friend was too preoccupied with her employee problem to ask me what my trip was about.

I spent the entire day Monday getting permission to take some days off, and getting coverage for the three shifts the staffing office told me I had to take care of myself. I could hear the disapproval in the coordinator's tone. Asking for vacation time at the last minute during peak vacation season was frowned upon. I didn't feel guilty about it because I rarely took my time off between June and September. Finding someone to work for me was no easy task, and it was nine o'clock in the evening, with the return call of a float pool employee, when the last shift was covered. With a whoop of triumph I called the evening supervisor and told her to make the changes. I was now a free woman for over two weeks.

It took another day to inform my family I would be away, cover a few details of leaving my house empty, and pack. I also made one more phone call to David White at his desk to tell him I would be leaving on Wednesday morning. His parents and his sister were expecting me. We had already discussed finances and the arrangements were already made for my flight and a rental car when I was ready to use them.

"Marty is good at this sort of thing," David said. "He travels quite a bit."

All I had left to do was call the airline and tell them to schedule my flight for the next afternoon. They had an open-ended ticket for me in their system, and gave me a seat assignment on a commuter from Indianapolis to Milwaukee. As for expense money, I offered to keep a running tally of my expenses and use my own credit card for later reimbursement.

I got a surprise when I called Everett and Judy, who I saved for last and called late Tuesday afternoon. I talked to Judy, as Ev was predictably out on his job site. Since they knew nothing about the disappearance of David White's brother it took a few minutes to explain everything.

"Another adventure, Sally?" Judy chuckled. It was a pleasure to hear the upbeat tone of her voice. Only now did I realize that had been missing since her hospitalization. "Are you leaving from Indianapolis?"

It was a fair question. Louisville was closer for me but the flight from Indianapolis was more convenient. My plan was to take the chance and leave my little car in the long-term parking lot, but Judy wouldn't hear of it. She insisted I make the detour to their house and let her take me to the airport.

"This will take most of your day," I said, "Are you sure you want to, and on such short notice?"

She certainly did.

As any of my family and friends know, I am pathetic when I have to get up early in the morning. Whenever someone points out that twice a week I am up at dawn anyway, I tell them it is one thing to be up at five in the morning and an entirely different matter to get up at that time. This Wednesday I didn't have to get up until about six but that was only slightly easier. Six weeks earlier when Everett summoned me to the hospital, an adrenalin rush had gotten me going. Not so this morning, but sometimes one has to swallow the bitter pill and do what has to be done. The detour to my son's home plus driving time to the airport would take more than five hours. My flight was leaving about two in the afternoon so there was no time to waste.

Knowing my brain would not be fully functional before nine, I packed everything the night before. I was on the road in thirty minutes with a stop for coffee and a donut to go.

I am a punctual person and Judy is not, but she was waiting

for me when I arrived. Judy's long red hair was swept back in a low ponytail, and she looked casual and pretty in Khaki shorts and a lime green blouse. Joel had a grin on his scrubbed, clean face, and his backpack was clutched in his right hand. Looking at the two of them as I put my car into park I thought, "These are two of the people I love the most in this world."

"Hey Grandma!" Joel hollered.

"Hey yourself! Are you ready to take a little trip?"

"I am if I get to see some airplanes," he declared.

"Okay, let's go." And after a bathroom break we did.

At that time airport security was not so tight. Judy and Joel accompanied me to my terminal. I was starved, they were hungry, and there was time for us to rectify that situation. We took our sandwiches to a table in front of the huge windows overlooking the tarmac, which pleased my Grandson no end. He munched and watched the planes taxi back and forth, which gave me a chance to chat some more with Judy. Our conversation on the drive had been very one sided because Judy wanted more details about my mission.

"You are looking just wonderful," I complimented her.

She smiled self-consciously but looked pleased. "I'm finally getting some sleep."

"You hadn't been?" I asked, concerned. "Why not?"

"Getting my hormones balanced for one thing," she replied ruefully. "I've been back to the doctor twice. Since I still have my ovaries they weren't sure if I would need to take anything. I think we're finally getting it right." She paused to take a bite of her turkey club and to wipe some mayonnaise from Joel's mouth. Then she admitted, "but that wasn't the only reason."

"Care to share?"

She smiled again. "I was hoping I'd get a chance to talk to you." She lowered her head, rubbed her forehead, then raised it again and looked at me.

"Has Ev said anything to you?"

"Nothing I would regard as personal. Of course I've thought about you, wondered how you are, emotionally as well as physically."

She considered her words. "This hasn't been hard on just me. Ev has to put up with me."

Joel interrupted for a moment to excitedly point out what he considered to be an exceptionally fine aircraft. He turned back to the window and Judy continued.

"We both wanted this baby so much. After the fuss died down and I was home a few days the depression set in."

"I was afraid of that."

She gave me a sad little smile.

"We were certainly warned. That helped a little, knowing it's normal. But the worst of it was Ev being so brave about it all. I could be mean, unreasonable, moody, and he just took it. That made me feel even more terrible."

Her normally low toned voice was down another decibel so her son could not hear what she said. Oblivious to the serious discussion we were having, Joel again piped in. We both acknowledged with interest the baggage cart rolling by below and he proceeded with his observations. I glanced at my watch. We had about fifteen more minutes before boarding.

"It wasn't hard all the time, don't think that. But there has been a lot of tension and frustration."

"You look so happy today," I said. "Are you a good actress or has something changed?"

She sighed hopefully. "I think we're through the worst. Sunday everything sort of came to a head."

"Go on."

"It started when we dropped Joel off at Gran's. Ev suggested we let him play there while we did some serious grocery shopping and maybe we could get a hamburger after, just the two of us. I said okay but when we got there I found out Lacey's pregnant." She eyed me to see if I remembered who Lacey was.

"One of your first cousins," I ventured.

"Right. It wasn't that she was having a baby; I never expected the family to stop having them because I'm not having anymore. But she's over three months along! Everyone was keeping it from me."

Her voice had gotten a little louder. She toned it down before Joel noticed.

"So I was bummed to begin with, not a nice way to start spending a little time alone with Ev. But while we were shopping, I met a girl I knew from high school and haven't seen in ages."

42

Judy smiled sadly. "She had her newborn with her, a little girl. She has red hair. I got through it somehow, trying to say all the right things. We were almost finished with the shopping so I got through that, too. But when we got to the truck I started crying."

Judy paused for a second. I looked at her expectantly. "Well the thing is, after a minute I looked at Ev and he was crying too."

Judy's eyes were tearing up a bit as she replayed the moment.

"No doubt some of what was said or happened is very personal," I said gently, "but that was a turning point?"

"We sat out there in that parking lot for awhile, I don't know how long. Neither one of us cared if anyone saw us or noticed. We got a lot of feelings out. Ev really needed to do that. I guess I thought he was so scared of losing me he wasn't grieving about the baby like I was. That wasn't true."

Totally oblivious to the drama enfolding around him Joel interrupted again. "My bottom is tired. I need to get up. I'm not hungry anymore, either." The last remark was for his mother, as he had eaten just over half of his sandwich.

"Okay, mister," she allowed. "But no sweets for now. You need to drink some more of your milk, then you can get down."

In compliance Joel picked up his milk carton and sipped.

I reached over and ruffled his hair but my words were for Judy. "You're getting through this. I thought you would but it's a relief to hear you tell me."

"I wanted you to know," Judy said earnestly. I leaned over impulsively and squeezed her hand. Did she know how much it meant to me, hearing her say that?

Joel set down his milk carton with a definite thud. As Judy gathered our trash to discard, I scooped him up and tickled his neck. As he giggled I remarked, "Since you have been so nice to me today you can use my car while I'm gone."

"Grandma!" he squealed delightedly. "You know I can't drive!"

"Oh that's right," I acknowledged. "We'll have to let your Mom do it. Come on. I've got a plane to catch."

Because of Judy's confidence I got on my flight in a very positive frame of mind, almost light hearted, you might say. Their situation had concerned me more than I wanted to admit. It was a huge relief to know my son and his wife were facing and dealing

43

with the biggest crisis of their marriage to date.

I turned my thoughts to the issue at hand. Time to focus, Sally, I thought, if you don't want to let David White's family down and don't want to make a fool of yourself.

The shuttle flight was not very long and it went without mishap. About four in the afternoon I was standing in front of the desk at the car rental agency where a lanky young man informed me brightly I had been upgraded to a minivan.

"I don't want a minivan," I replied politely. "I'm not used to driving something so large and I won't be comfortable."

"That's all we have, ma'am," he said, just a little bit less brightly.

"I had a reservation," I was still very polite. "There is supposed to be a compact car here for me."

We faced each other at an impasse. He reached down and pushed a button on an intercom. "Hey Gerry! Has that Beretta come in yet?"

"Yeah," Gerry's voice came through clearly from the garage, "But it's not cleaned up."

The agent looked at me and said drolly, "Will that do?"

"A Beretta would be fine, thank you."

"Get it washed, Gerry. There's a lady waiting."

I haven't survived this long alone by being a wimp.

Doing nothing all day long can be exhausting, plus I wanted to call David and Douglas' parents before it got very late. Some of the older people I know are in bed by nine. I stopped at a motor inn between Fond du Lac and Oshkosh well before dark and dialed the number as soon as I got into my room.

Mr. White senior answered on the third ring. His "hello" had a little quaver to it, giving away his age.

"How do you do, Mr. White," I said warmly. "This is Sally Nimitz calling. I hope your son David has told you about me."

There was a brief hesitation but then, "Oh, Mrs. Nimitz! Yes! We're expecting you! Cora, it's Mrs. Nimitz, that lady David told us was coming. Where are you?"

I told him and he relayed the information on to Cora.

"But that's not very far from here." I could hear his wife's voice in the background, and he repeated what she said. "You should come along and stay here with us tonight. No need to spend money on a hotel."

It wouldn't be tactful to say it was not my money I was spending. "That is very kind of you both. But I have already checked in here and think it would be better to come the rest of the way tomorrow. Are you free to see me tomorrow?"

They certainly were. It took a bit of doing to get directions to their home. The Whites were not in agreement as to the best way for me to get there, and they had some discussion about it while I was waiting on the line. Their son David had told me how to get to their little town, but not the street and house number. It was amazing the different routes possible in a town of a few thousand people. Eventually I had a pretty clear idea how to find Adler Street, and knew I would be okay from there. I asked if eleven o'clock would be a good time and they assured me it would.

"She must stay for lunch," I heard Mrs. White say, and her husband obediently repeated the directive.

I grimaced because my lifestyle doesn't make lunch a regular occasion for me, and it was my least favorite meal. Oh well. In the interests of an investigation I had eaten at lunchtime before.

****

It would have been no problem to be at the White's home long before eleven, but first I wanted to find the house Douglas had lived in before he disappeared. I knew it was only blocks away from where his parents lived. The quest was complicated by the weather; it had been raining heavily all morning. Being in new territory that slowed me down, but I found the place about ten-thirty, and sat in the driveway looking at the last house Douglas and his wife Ingrid lived in together.

Mr. White senior, or someone, was still mowing the lawn and trimming the shrubs. If you were a casual observer you wouldn't notice the small signs of neglect. If you were observant you would. There was weeding that needed to be done and pots on the front porch without the flowers that would normally bloom in mid summer. It was a very appealing house, probably three bedrooms, with well-proportioned windows and a nice layout. The siding looked expensive and the dark color of the roofing complimented it.

Out of the corner of my eye I saw someone walking toward my vehicle. I turned slightly to my left. A beefy middle-aged man with thinning gray hair was slowly approaching. He looked rather ludicrous under a pale blue umbrella. The rain had slowed to a steady drizzle. I turned down my window and called out a greeting.

He did not bother to return it but came directly to the point. "Are you interested in buying this house?"

"Well, no," I admitted. "But why would you think so? There's no for sale sign here."

"No," he agreed, "but no one has lived here in months. When I saw you sitting here that was the only thing I could think of." He added, "I've never seen you before. Sorry."

"Oh, it's all right," I reassured him. This could be a source of information, after all. "I happen to be a friend of the family of the owner. I don't live around here." I extended a hand out of the window. "My name is Sally Nimitz. I'm from Indiana, and Mr. White's younger brother is a friend of mine."

He obligingly took my hand and shook it. "Lou Gretske. My wife Nancy and I live over there." He pointed to the house well to our left. Due to the generous size of the lots and a large weeping willow tree it was partially hidden.

"Do you know the owner?" I asked politely, casually.

He shrugged. "Just to say hello to. We've lived here for about six years but they moved in much later, and she passed away after that." He eyed me speculatively from under the umbrella. "I would guess you know that."

"Yes, and I know your neighbor hasn't been around all year. His brother told me."

Mr. Gretske lowered the umbrella. "He wouldn't happen to know where he is, would he?"

"No, he doesn't," I admitted. "Do you have any idea where he might be?"

"Me?" he looked surprised. "No, I wouldn't know. I just wish he would come back and live here or sell it to someone who wants to live in it."

Smothering a small smile I guessed, "Afraid the place will be neglected and make the neighborhood look bad?"

"Something like that," was the grudging reply.

"Well," I said lightly, "at least you don't have a problem with noise, children, or wild parties."

Mr. Gretske seemed nice but he didn't have much of a sense of humor.

"That's true," he replied seriously, "but it won't be long and the place will show its not well taken care of. Not," he added hastily, apparently not wanting to give any offense, "that we don't appreciate having the lawn mowed and the greenery trimmed. Some old man has been coming to do that."

"I think that would be the owner's father." I saw no reason not to inform him.

"Oh." Mr. Gretske didn't have anything else to say. He gave me a polite goodbye and walked away, not seeming to care that someone who knew Douglas White's brother decided to stop by and sit in the driveway.

It was pointless to hang around any longer but I wanted to see the inside of the house. The senior Whites probably had a key, and hopefully they would allow me to do that.

Chapter Six

I went on to keep my luncheon date with Mr. and Mrs. White. Their home was older, larger, and had a number of huge trees gracing the front yard. It was the house grandchildren would love to visit for their dose of chocolate chip cookies and holiday turkey dinners. There should be roses in the living room wallpaper, and the smell of fresh home baked bread coming from the kitchen.

I left my car parked on the street and approached the front of the house. The faintly discernible aroma from the kitchen was nice, but not fresh yeast bread, and I would soon find out the living room was painted a very light shade of pink with a dark green border, no roses. But the front porch was huge and the screen door creaked just like the one I remembered at my own grandmother's house, as Mr. White senior opened it for me. He was tall, slightly stooped, and thin. He held out a veined hand for me to shake.

"You must be Mrs. Nimitz," he said as he did so.

"I am, sir. It is very kind of you and your wife to have me."

He gestured me in as his wife appeared from the kitchen. She was shorter than her husband, and plump. I initiated the greeting this time.

"Mrs. White, I'm Sally, and it is so good of you both to invite me into your home." I held out my hand for her and she took it.

"I love these big old houses," I added sincerely, "and you

have a gem here."

The mister gave me a bashful chuckle. "I like keeping it up now that I'm retired, but I guess it will get too big for us someday."

His spouse opened her mouth to say something then closed it. Aha, this was delicate territory. Perhaps the missus already thought it was getting too big for them, or to the contrary, she might not intend to ever move no matter what the challenges.

My host proceeded to ask me if I would like a tour, and Mrs. White opened her mouth again to say lunch would be about twenty minutes so there was time. She went back to the kitchen, and I followed Mr. White as he happily led the way, starting in the living room.

We ate in the kitchen with a view through a large bay window of the back yard. I was informed this was Cora White's pride and joy. She even mowed it on the rider lawnmower. There was plenty of grass, plus shrubs, delicate impatience blooming in the shade, and several varieties of daisies blooming in the sunshine. Under the maple trees were lawn chairs, two wrought iron tables, even a hammock. It was all very restful. Mr. White, whose first name turned out to be Porter, or Port, as his wife called him, admitted he liked to take an afternoon nap in the hammock when the weather allowed it.

I had braced myself for eating a lunch cooked by a woman who used to cook for five children. In my experience some women never got used to cutting down on portions and were always happy to find victims to eat all the food. It was a pleasant surprise to be served homemade chicken vegetable soup with crackers and multigrain bread.

"I hope you like soup," Cora said as she ladled some into my bowl. "Port and I don't eat like we used to, we don't need to." She gave her hips a little pat after she handed my bowl back.

Very honestly I assured her the soup smelled and looked delicious, and it was a relief not to be expected to eat a fried chicken dinner for the noon meal. They both grinned and told a couple of stories about how hard it had been to keep up with feeding four growing boys and one girl with an appetite just as healthy.

"I hardly even bake now," Cora confessed, "except when the

grandkids come visit. They have to have their home made cookies and lemon meringue pie!"

The conversation stayed light and easy as we ate. The dishes were cleared away and I was offered coffee in the sitting room. I said coffee was welcome but it was very pleasant in the kitchen, there was no need to move. After the coffee was poured we began to talk about what was on all of our minds, their missing oldest son.

"It must seem rather odd to you," I ventured, "my coming up here to look into this situation."

Porter White shook his head in denial. "David explained it pretty well," he said. "We were both relieved to think something would be done." He glanced at his wife. Her expression did not contradict him.

"Are you worried?"

"We were," he admitted, "and we still are but maybe not as much." He saw the puzzled look on my face and added quickly, "we heard from him again."

The Whites had not sent this letter on to David as they had the others, already knowing I was coming up to see them. They gladly produced it for me and I realized with a twinge of regret I hadn't asked to see the other two.

"We haven't even told David about this one," Cora White confessed, as she went to a drawer in the kitchen and pulled it out. "We talked about it and we still know something is wrong. There didn't seem to be any point in bothering David. He said to confide in you, as we would him. He said we could trust you."

"A tall order," I observed, scrutinizing them both. "Both for you and for me. I'm honored. We just met. Do you think you can do that?"

Since my arrival they had not had the opportunity to compare notes on their individual impressions of me, but living together for over half a century must give a couple a special sense of communication.

"Oh, we think so," Porter said mildly. Cora took her seat and handed the letter, in its envelope, across the table to me.

This was not a letter but a brief note, scrawled on a piece of plain unlined paper and folded into a small standard white envelope. Like the other two, this one was also post marked from

Chicago. The handwriting was large and untidy but quite legible.

"Dear folks," it began, "I suppose you've been wondering what's happened to me. Sorry to be so mysterious. I planned to be back before this but got delayed. Tell David I'm sorry I missed his birthday. I shouldn't be gone too much longer. Take care, hope you're well. Love, Doug."

They both watched me as I read it through twice. I volunteered my opinion they might want to let everyone know they had gotten another note to alleviate some anxiety. The personal remark about the birthday surely verified he had voluntarily written it.

I added, "From what David told me, the others were about like this one, not very detailed, just saying he was alive and not to worry. Is that true?"

They both agreed that the other two notes were similar but even shorter, and they were sure the handwriting was Douglas'.

"But why all the mystery?" Cora asked anxiously. "We just don't understand this."

There was no answer to Cora's question, not yet, and any ideas I had must have crossed their minds already, both the reassuring and the not so reassuring.

"This could change everything," I opined. "You're sure your son Douglas wrote this note and it was sent recently. Perhaps my being here is not necessary."

There was another quick exchange of looks between Cora and Porter. Porter spoke up.

"For my part, and Corie agrees with me, I'm still worried. If Doug comes home in the next few days while you're around trying to figure this out, fine. If he doesn't, someone will at least be working to clear this up. Otherwise there's more time wasted."

"I do agree," Cora said stoutly. "This has gone on long enough." Her face changed as a sudden thought occurred to her. "You are still willing to see what you can find out, aren't you, Mrs. Nimitz?"

Her question was considered. "I am if you'll call me Sally."

"Sally it is, and you must do the same; Porter and Cora."

"How about if we take this right from the beginning?" I suggested. "I would like to hear much more about Douglas, especially since his wife died. Do you have anything else you need to be doing?"

"Nothing this important," Port said firmly. "Cora, make sure there's plenty of coffee brewed. I'll call Ray and tell him I won't be over for awhile."

Ray was a crony of Porter's who wanted some help in a landscaping project. If he was disappointed to be put on hold no one said so. While Porter phoned him I produced a pen and pad of paper from my shoulder bag. The Whites seemed eager to talk. They were relieved to be doing something with their anxiety, even if it was giving their son's history and their own impressions to a virtual stranger.

We talked for almost two hours, my hosts doing most of it, of course. With the second pot of coffee Cora produced some molasses cookies leftover from a ladies Bible study, which contradicted her claim she baked only for grandchildren. They were delicious; I polished off two.

Cora and Porter's narrative of Douglas and Ingrid's marriage and her illness corroborated everything David said. Theirs had been a happy union, marred only by their disappointment in their two children, and for the last year of their marriage by Ingrid's health. The senior Whites were also in agreement about these particular grandchildren.

"They were cute when they were little," Port said morosely, "but things changed when they got to high school."

"I've noticed they're always mentioned together," I commented. "Have they always been close? They aren't twins?"

"Not twins, but they got along ever since they started getting into trouble, it seems like," Port continued, while his wife just looked unhappy. "Like two peas in a bad pod. They always covered for each other."

Cora produced a photograph of two very good-looking blondes, taken when they were in their late teens. They looked enough alike to be twins but there was twenty-one months difference in their ages. She explained the picture was taken several years earlier at a family get together before the siblings moved to California. Even without knowing the history my impression would have been these two were troublesome. It showed in their posturing and bored facial expressions. I heard a little more about the shenanigans of Douglas and Ingrid's

52

offspring, but it seemed to have little bearing on what I was interested in. Their grandparents knew they had been given a sum of money when they moved out west with the stipulation they could ask for no more. However, two airline tickets had been sent for them to return home and say goodbye to their mother and they had come, even staying for the funeral.

"They both look older, harder," Cora commented quietly, "but they behaved themselves pretty well. They each have someone and went back the day after the funeral. You could tell they couldn't wait to leave."

"It was easier for Doug and Ingrid after they left home," Porter contributed. "At least they didn't have to know it when they were doing wrong. Doug stayed busy with his business and Ingrid was promoted at the bank to a loan officer. They had about five more years while Ingrid was in good health I'd say, wouldn't you, Cora? They took a couple of nice trips, too."

Cora concurred. Douglas and Ingrid White had a normal, healthy lifestyle. They enjoyed their professions, hobbies, extended family and friends.

Ingrid's breast cancer was discovered on a routine physical examination thirteen months prior to her death. Treatment had gone well at first and everyone was optimistic. But after a five-month remission, metastasis was discovered to the liver and Ingrid's health deteriorated steadily after that.

"She was a brave woman," Cora said with pride, "and if she felt sorry for herself we never saw it. Doug stopped everything else the last two months and took care of her himself."

I asked how they thought Douglas had coped after his wife died. They both thought their son's grieving process was totally normal. Being of an age to suffer losses themselves, and seeing many others go through it, they had expected the withdrawal and depression.

"We did what we could," Porter told me, "but losing someone close to you like that, well, getting over it is something you have to get through. It takes time."

I agreed. Little did my host and hostess know I understood all too well. "Did you think your son was getting through it?"

They thought so. From their standpoint, Douglas' behavior seemed totally appropriate to what he had suffered and lost. He would come for dinner or to visit if they asked him and put up an appearance of normalcy, but they weren't fooled. He was lonely and quite miserable. They understood. When he sold his successful business to his younger brother they urged him to make sure this was what he wanted.

"But it was last July before he decided to sell and we knew Marty hadn't pressured him." Porter supplied this information. "He said his heart wasn't in it anymore, but Marty asked him to stay on for a few more months as an advisor and he did that."

When I inquired if Douglas had shown any behavior they were not comfortable with, they had to give it some thought.

"We didn't see a lot of him sometimes," Porter said slowly. "There would be two or three weeks that went by we didn't see him even though he has that house close by. We didn't expect him to be here all the time; he's a grown man. But this is a small town and we would have heard if there was anything funny going on." He gave me a wry smile. "People can't wait to tell you if they notice anything."

"He was a man who lost his wife," Cora summed it up. "Not only that, a wife he really cared about. He was hurting and trying to get by. By last fall he seemed to be getting better. He seemed more interested in things. If he had taken off like this a year ago I wouldn't have been surprised, but now I don't know. It just don't seem right." Her brow was furrowed in her perplexity, and she shook her head.

"Okay." I leaned back in my chair and stretched a little. "Let's move on to when he sold his other house and decided to go away. Tell me what you know about that."

The Whites organized their facts. They told me the country house Douglas and Ingrid bought when their children were small had been put on the market in the spring after Ingrid's death, but with no big push to sell it. A serious buyer had come along in October and escrow closed in early December.

Douglas' parents had no clue their son was planning a long absence until he told them about it on Christmas Eve.

"Everyone but David and Deborah were here Christmas Eve," Cora explained. "Douglas came late. He would get restless at the family get-to-gathers after Ingrid wasn't with him and wouldn't stay as long, but he usually came. That night he stayed around and seemed to enjoy himself. He brought presents for everyone and horsed around with the children. Janice's youngest even got him to arm wrestle."

Port grinned in reminiscence. "Life of the party," he agreed.

"Well," Cora continued, "Doug told everyone he would help me clean up. Our son Paul and his family were staying here with us and my daughter-in-law gave him an argument, but he won out. She went up to bed and while we were doing the dishes, he told us."

"Do you remember exactly what he said?" I asked, encouraging them to go on.

"We've thought back on it often enough," Porter said ruefully. "I remember Doug saying, 'Mom, Dad, I'm going out of town for awhile.' Then we asked him where, and he said he really wasn't sure, he just thought he could use a little space. He said he was going to spend some time traveling around and doing some serious thinking about the rest of his life."

Cora said, "I remember it pretty much the same. We asked some more questions but Doug didn't say much more about it. We wished him well and told him to stay in touch. Four days later he came by and asked us to do a few things, like mow the lawn. He gave us an envelope with cash in case we needed to pay someone or if anything unexpected came up."

The couple also remembered asking Douglas if David was aware of his plans. They were surprised when he said no, only Janice and Marty knew. He asked his parents to let David and Paul know he would be out of touch for at least several weeks. Both Porter and Cora had thought this a little odd at the time but didn't say so.

"David told me the post office was holding his mail for six months," I went on. "Have you or has anyone picked it up? What about his utility bills at the house? My understanding is everything was taken care of through June but not after that."

Porter had picked up the accumulated mail just the week before when they got a call from the post office saying they could not hold onto it past the time agreed upon. Arrangements were made for the mail delivery to be continued again, and Porter or Cora checked the mailbox about once a week. They produced a shopping bag full of their son's mail.

"We went through it and threw out all the advertisements and old fliers or there would be twice this much. You're welcome to look through the rest."

"Did you?"

"Not really," Cora admitted. "We looked at the outside of the envelopes in case anything looked important enough to need attention." She smiled a little self-consciously. "It's hard to look through someone else's mail. It doesn't seem right."

Looking through Douglas White's mail wouldn't bother me at all, but I kept that to myself, too. Porter offered it all for my inspection before I had to ask permission, and I hoped my response was a nice balance, willing but not nosey.

"I called the electric company and the town utility company two weeks ago and asked them not to turn off his power and water," Porter said. "It's summer now so it's no problem, except it would be expensive to have it all turned on again. We're going to get the bills for that but we don't need to use the cash he left because I have access to one of his checking accounts. We haven't needed it before, but we'll use it for this."

That gave me an idea. I fished through the pile of mail and found three monthly bank statements.

"I think it would be good to see if he's withdrawn any sums of money. Do you agree it would be a good idea to check?"

They agreed.

The statements I pulled were for February, March, and May. A quick perusal showed no large sums withdrawn, but there was a minus balance of three thousand dollars from March to May. We found the April statement and there was the withdrawal. The money had been transferred into another account of some sort, with only account numbers listed on the statement. Douglas White still had a healthy balance left in his checking account. There were statements indicating Douglas also had a savings account at the bank, and an account at a savings and loan with separate investments. With his parents' help we opened all of the bank statements from January through May and looked for any interesting expenditures or withdrawals. There were no more withdrawals, at least not through May. Brother David knew about the money removed from the account; he had mentioned it. How did he know that?

That brought me to another point.

"I think it would be a good idea to look through Douglas' house," I ventured. "We might find some more information there to help us. One of you should be with me, of course."

Cora and Porter thought it was a reasonable request. Porter got up again and disappeared, returning a moment later with a set of keys.

"I think there's enough time to see the inside of the house before going on to Deaver and talking to Janice yet today. Is that practical?"

My host and hostess said it was. Port drew up some directions to tell me how to get to their daughter's home.

"Sally, you are welcome to come back here tonight and stay with us," Cora offered generously. "We have plenty of room, as you can see, and," she hesitated a little, "she might offer but I don't think you'll want to stay with Janice and Mike."

I looked at her in mild surprise but she didn't elaborate.

"I'd like to get there in time to have a chat before the dinner hour, but if I'm not there before five o'clock I'll call and arrange to come by later." David had supplied his sister's phone number with the other information he gave me prior to my departure for Wisconsin.

I used my tentative schedule as an excuse not to come back for the night. It would be criminal to hurt the feelings of these wonderful people, but privately I wanted to be alone after seeing Janice to put together thoughts and impressions. I would find a place to stay somewhere near Deaver I said, and would not dream of abusing Janice's hospitality even if she offered.

"Let's plan for me to come back sometime tomorrow to meet again. If something keeps me away, I promise to phone you."

They seemed mollified. Porter gave Cora a peck on the cheek as we got up to leave. I liked him even better. After I expressed sincere thanks to this lady for her meal and coffee, she asked if there was anything else that she could do to help.

There was.

"Would you make a list of your son's close friends, with a way to get in touch with them? By the way," I added casually, "It hasn't come up but would that include any lady friends?"

Chapter Seven

Not one time since I was approached about Douglas had anyone brought up the subject of female companionship. It seemed like an obvious question to me, but the Whites weren't expecting it.

"I know Douglas and his wife were very devoted to each other," I felt compelled to explain, "but many widowers who have been happily married find life so lonely they start dating right away. David never mentioned it and neither have you, but I had to ask."

"Shoot, you're absolutely right," Porter said, a little over the top with his hearty reply. He had been caught off balance. "I had an uncle who was just like that, married less than a year after my aunt died, and they'd been together almost forty years." He gave me a quizzical grin. "Funny I haven't thought much about Douglas having a girlfriend." He looked at Cora. "You've never said anything. Have you?"

"Of course I have," she answered tartly. "He's still a young man. But he never said so, and if there is or was a girlfriend he kept that a secret, too."

"Andy Weller would know," Porter contributed, looking at his wife with certainty.

"If anyone would know Andy would," Cora agreed. "He'll be on your list."

The shopping bag full of mail was still sitting on the chair by the table. I asked if they were comfortable with my taking it to look through at my leisure.

"If you aren't," I said, "I'll look more carefully through it all when I come back."

"Let her take it," Cora said impulsively to her husband. "I don't see why not."

Porter hesitated just a moment and who could blame him. "Okay," he agreed and added candidly, "David trusts you and you sure seem all right."

"You two worry me, trusting me so blindly," I said, only half in jest. "You could call David and give him a description to make sure I'm the lady he sent out here."

They both thought this was funny and laughed. They wanted to know who else could I be, and they had a point.

****

The rain had stopped completely while the Whites and I were coffee clutching, but it was still partly cloudy and the air was humid and heavy, the way it can be in the north in the summer time. Someone had set the main thermostat in Douglas Whites' house to eighty degrees, but the thermostat read five degrees warmer yet, which was pretty oppressive for me. Douglas' father went to the windows without comment and opened several while I took an initial look around. Although it was about the same temperature outside there was a strong breeze and it helped.

Looking at houses interests me. I love seeing different building and interior decorating styles, color schemes and room layouts. It could be compared to someone quite content with their compact car always admiring the Mercedes and the Porsches. My guess was due to Ingrid White's illness and her relatively short stay in this residence, she had not had the time or inclination to give it some of the final touches a house like this deserved. It was a lovely place, with airy, spacious rooms, stained hardwood beams across the living room ceiling, and many extra touches a master builder would offer to those who could afford it. I paused to admire stained glass trim around the mirror in the front hall. But the whole effect was of a high-class hotel suite. There were few photos, just basic pieces of furniture in most of the rooms –

albeit high quality furniture – and the walls were quite bare of ornamentation. As we walked slowly through the house I ventured to ask Porter if it had always looked like this.

He stroked his chin and looked around contemplatively. Pretty much, he thought. He had not spent a great deal of time in the house while Ingrid was ill, or since.

"Cora's been over here a couple of times this year," he volunteered. "She gave the place a good cleaning this spring. You might ask her." He grinned sheepishly. "She notices things like that better than me."

He looked rather uncertain about what to do with himself and settled for casually following me around. After a sweeping assessment of the entire house, I suggested we start in the kitchen for a more thorough inspection. The bathrooms, spare bedrooms, and living room showed little promise.

The quality of the house was not diminished in the kitchen. "When I had a growing family I would have killed for a kitchen like this," I confided to Porter. "This is domestic heaven. What beautiful cupboards, and look at these countertops!"

To my surprise he blushed. "I did the cabinets in the whole house," he admitted quietly.

After pouring a little more well-deserved praise upon him, Porter told me he had been a master finish carpenter before his retirement, his specialty cabinetry .He had done all the work in his own home as well. Again I complimented him. My personal taste ran more toward the beautiful pine used for Douglas and Ingrid's home, but all of the workmanship had been superb and I said so. It was my own fault that Porter started enthusiastically telling me about his craft and we got sidetracked. It would have been rude to interrupt.

Fortunately Mr. White came up short on his own volition and said lamely, "But you didn't come here to hear about making cupboards. Guess we'd better get back to what we came for."

"Right. Let's take a peek in the drawers."

The kitchen drawers had nothing in them of interest to us. Some of them had very little in them at all. We went into the dining area and opened the drawers of the hutch. There was the expected place ware, china, and some nice water and wine glasses, but no paperwork.

We moved into the den, a room I had higher hopes for. There were two bookcases and a large desk in here. It was obvious this room had seen more use. Under the thin layer of dust that had accumulated since Cora's cleaning there were several masculine objects of a personal nature. I thought my late husband would have admired the small bronze sculpture of a hunter and his dog.

There were no papers lying on top of the blotter on the desk or in front of the silent computer. I glanced at my guide as I opened the desk drawers. None of them were locked, but the file cabinet adjacent to the large desk was.

"If Doug doesn't get back here pretty soon," Porter commented, looking at the file cabinet, "guess I'll try to find a key and take a look to see what's in there."

"If the police get involved, I imagine they'll want to look at everything."

Porter looked troubled at this. "I sure hope it won't come to that."

"Because of your last word from him it probably won't, at least for awhile longer." I made an attempt to be reassuring. "If you and Cora weren't still worried I'd head home myself."

Porter's response to that was to open another drawer. We found appointment books for several months of the previous year, some photographs, a few letters, and the paraphernalia one would expect in an office setting. Several pens and note pads were still in their wrappers.

I took the time to take a closer look at the date calendars and appointment books and made some notes of my own. Douglas' father looked through the letters and said there was nothing to indicate where his son had gone. In fact, nothing was said about his departure at all. Two of them were several years old, personal letters from Ingrid when she had been away without him, and we didn't read these.

In the bedroom I found what piqued my curiosity the most. Now I did feel a little intrusive as I opened the wardrobe door and went into the spacious walk in closet. I had wondered if Ingrid's personal things would be cleared away. They were, for the most part. In one corner there were a few items of clothing in garment bags and out of the bottom of one peeked an expensive woman's coat. I didn't open the zippers to look at any of these things. What had already claimed my attention was the left side of the closet, where Douglas' things were kept. Toward the back there were neatly hung shirts and slacks for all seasons. In the front were shorter racks, the bottom one covered with jeans and one above with shirts and sports jackets. It was all very neat and orderly. Several pairs of shoes and one pair of western boots sat on the carpet below the clothing. On the right side and in the front hung four well-worn flannel shirts.

"Mr. White," I called. He was rather unenthusiastically opening a couple of bureau drawers and turned to me as he heard my voice. "Does your closet look this well organized?"

He obligingly walked over to peer in and I stood to one side as he took a look.

"Afraid not," he admitted. "My wife is the tidy one, I'm not."

"Do you know if Douglas was this neat about his personal habits as a rule?"

He did the stroke of his chin move again.

"Not when he was a kid he wasn't," he remembered. "He was pretty organized about his business, but his desk was cluttered. Ingrid mentioned more than once how he could locate a piece of paper on his desk in five seconds flat no matter how confusing it looked to anybody else." He added as an after thought. "His vehicle didn't look this good, either."

"His closet looks like he had someone professionally come in here to organize and to clean. Could your wife have done this?"

"I doubt it," was his opinion. "To her mind it would be prying. She would have opened the door long enough to vacuum."

"Hmm." I looked at the racks of clothing again. Because most of Ingrid's clothing was gone, most of the right side of the closet was empty.

"Could I ask you one more question?" I continued, taking it for granted that I could. "Would you be able to notice how much he took with him? Do you remember any favorite shirt he had, for example, that's missing?" I added, "Let's see what seems to be gone from the dresser. That might make it easier."

We both returned to the bureau drawers. We did not rummage through them, but only opened each one and looked in. Everything was as organized as the closet was. There was a drawer for his skivvies, one for socks and one for tees. A smaller drawer had belts, and another swimwear and three pairs of shorts. There was enough room in each of the underwear drawers to conclude a few pairs were missing.

"Perhaps he went south," I observed. "There aren't many pairs of shorts here."

"I haven't seen him wear shorts in years," Porter replied.

"So, back to my question. Did your son have a lot of clothes, or did he leave with very little?"

Porter White hesitated and considered this for a long moment, no chin stroking this time.

"I think we should ask Cora," he answered finally, which was no surprise. He obviously considered his wife more observant than he was, even if he did remember Douglas didn't usually wear shorts.

Now my companion offered a thought. "There should be luggage missing. Let's check the garage. There's a storage area in there."

"Built by you?" I guessed with a smile.

He nodded. "Doug is good at a lot of things but carpentry is not one of them."

The garage was large enough to easily hold two vehicles, even with the storage area of flaked wood enclosing the left hand corner. The storage enclosure had a door that could have been secured, but it wasn't. When Porter opened it I saw the only part of the property that could even remotely be called cluttered. The space was almost full and some of the items had been hastily stacked. But there was no trash and it wasn't hard to spot the luggage. There were four pieces of a dark red, good quality, which must have belonged to Ingrid. There were three pieces of a plainer more masculine style, also expensive, and a duffle bag. I looked at Porter, not having to verbalize what I wanted to know.

He sighed and shook his head. "Looks like the one suitcase is missing and I know he had at least another duffle bag. That's all I can be sure about."

We closed the door. Looking around the empty garage I had another thought.

"Your son had only one vehicle?" I questioned. "Did he sell his wife's?"

"He sold Ingrid's car," this time Porter knew the answers.

"He took his Toyota Camry and left his jeep with Andy."

"His friend Andy Weller," I clarified. That was the case. It would be crucial to have a talk with Andy.

I wanted to take a closer look in the bedroom. My companion left me on my own this time and wandered back into the kitchen. During my marriage, the dresser had been for my things and the bureau had been for my husband's. This proved to be the case with Douglas and Ingrid. As with the closet, most of her clothing had been taken away, and several drawers in the large oak stained dresser had nothing in them. The two top drawers held some more photographs, a few pieces of costume jewelry and two watches. The only item sitting on the top was a casual framed snapshot of the couple themselves. I picked it up and looked at it closely. It would be a good idea to know what the man looked like I was trying to find.

Looking happy and posing obligingly for the picture taken was a thin, handsome brunette with a wide, beautiful smile. As I looked closely I guessed this picture had been taken during Ingrid's remission from her disease. The hair could well be a very nicely done wig and Ingrid looked a bit too thin. My gaze moved to the man beside her, his hand around her shoulder, squeezing her to him in a possessive and loving gesture. Douglas was tall and broad shouldered. In a police lineup I would have picked him out as David's older brother; there was a strong family resemblance, although Douglas was blonder.

Lastly I turned to the bureau, skipping the clothing this time, but opening the top drawer again. There had been no indication anywhere else in the house that Douglas smoked, but there were two books of matches in the top drawer. I pulled them out to take a closer look. They each had only two matches missing. Both said Griff's Place in gold lettering on the black match covers. With no more than a slight hesitation I dropped one of them into my purse. Sifting through the rest of the odds and ends I found nothing else to interest me.

"Your son seems to have traveled lightly when he left," I remarked to Porter as I walked back into the kitchen. "I don't supposed you noticed that when he came to say goodbye that day after Christmas?"

"No," he admitted. "Not until today. I guess we thought he

had all his luggage in the trunk of his car." Porter was getting himself a drink of water out of the refrigerator dispenser and he offered one to me. I accepted.

We leaned over the counter, drinking from the glasses he had taken from the cupboard.

"Any ideas?" I asked him.

"Not a darn one," he declared, "But I'm starting to get mad. He better have a good explanation for this unless he's hurt or something. This is crazy. I never saw until here with you today that it almost looks like he cleaned up the place to leave it for good."

"I noticed that too," I admitted. "Certainly he planned to be away a long time and yet it looks like he took very little with him."

"What are you going to do next?" Porter queried.

"First I'm going to go see your daughter, as planned. And I had better get moving. The afternoon is wearing on." He was hoping for more so I added, "When I come back tomorrow I want to talk to Andy Weller. Tonight I'll spend some time looking closely at all of that mail."

Porter seemed cheered by the thought of action, never mind if it was mine. We put our glasses upside down on a towel pulled from a drawer next to the sink and left the house.

Chapter Eight

Porter closed the windows and locked up as I got into my vehicle and pulled away. We waved to each other. I wondered if the neighbor Gretzke had noticed our presence. Judging by his behavior in the morning not too much went on close to home without his noticing.

The clouds were parting and the late afternoon sun made an appearance as I drove northwest. The car air conditioning was very welcome. The countryside was of a familiar but also pleasant variety and made for a scenic drive. My mind wandered back and forth, sifting through all of the information accumulated since showing up for lunch with Douglas' parents.

The directions to Janice's home were clear enough, but it was over an hour's drive and it would be cutting it close to make it before the five o'clock goal set as the latest time it was polite to show up. That was still taking the chance Janice's family did not eat their dinner at an early hour. I drove through the town they lived in, which didn't take very long, and to their street on the outskirts of the other side, taking a left turn. The sheet of paper with my instructions on them was open on the passenger seat and I glanced at it again for a street number.

As it turned out the house I was looking for was the last one, almost a mile further down the street. It was called a street, Sunflower Lane, but driving along it looked more like a country road. I passed only four residences en route and there were actually some horses grazing in a pasture between two of them. Janice and her family were isolated from their neighbors by almost a quarter of a mile and a dense cropping of trees. Across from their property was a field of ripening corn.

Of course I knew this had to be the right address as there was nowhere else to go. Sure enough, the mailbox was plainly marked The Markhams, 315 Sunflower Lane. As soon as I got past the mini forest and approached the house I couldn't help but laugh. I had to smother it turning into the driveway because Janice herself was out in the front yard.

It was hard, though. The place could not have been more of a contrast from Cora and Porter's home. Later I wondered if that was the whole idea. Maybe Janice was in a life long state of some type of rebellion against her upbringing. The front yard had no less than three old vehicles parked on what could not be called the lawn. Two more were visible behind the house. There was a large porch to this house, too, as I could just discern because of the railings. The entire space was full of junk. Well, it looked like junk to me; someone more kind might have called at least some of the stuff antiques. I don't pretend to have a good eye for it. As I turned off the ignition and the lady of the house approached, so did three barking dogs.

I will admit they were obedient. A few firm words from their mistress and they retreated to sit in the shade under a rusting green pickup truck. That was reassuring. I opened my car door.

Janice was about three inches taller than I am, putting her at close to five foot nine. She had inherited the height gene from her father but not his lean physique. There was a warm smile on her tanned, lined face, and she held out a hand. Without hesitation I extended my own.

"I know you're Mrs. Nimitz," she announced gaily. "Mother called to tell me to look for you. Any trouble finding us? Let's not stand out here in the yard. Come on in."

She left no room for argument, turning around and marching toward the front door, taking it for granted I was right behind her. I was, too. Those three German Shepherds might not stay friendly without Janice around. Wearing sandals, I carefully avoided the weeds, two empty motor oil containers, several doggie bones, and one rusty trailer hitch. Having successfully maneuvered the front yard it was time to tackle the porch. Janice had sailed through the debris to the entryway without problem, but she had done this countless times. It took me a few more seconds to walk around an old washing machine and dryer, squeeze past a rocker without tripping over it, and avoid knocking down a huge horse harness hanging precariously from a large nail on the side of the door jam.

"Kind of a mess, isn't it?" chuckled Janice, but again mercifully not waiting for a response. "We just never seem to get around to cleaning up this stuff. We usually use the back door but the goat is back there today and she's a little persnickety about strangers." We were both inside now, in a hallway of sorts, and she led the way toward the back of the house. "Mike!" she bellowed. "We have company!"

I could hear a late afternoon game show on a television set in a room off to the left. Out of that room and over the volume of the TV a voice yelled back, "Who is it?"

Janice told him. Mike yelled a hello to me and what else could I do? I hollered a loud hello back. Apparently that was considered sufficient. I never saw the man. During my visit he never left his program.

When I was urged to have something to drink a canned root beer seemed a safe choice. The kitchen fell into the same category as the yard. The counter tops were heaped full of canned goods and groceries of all sorts. The sink was piled high with dirty dishes on one side and clean ones on the other. I took the seat offered to me at the kitchen table and with another cheerful apology Janice pushed aside a stack of magazines. There were two pots boiling vigorously on the stove. My hostess turned the burners down under both of them before opening her refrigerator and pulling two sodas out of the huge amount of food crammed into it. A bottle of mustard fell to the floor; thankfully it was plastic. Janice crammed it back onto the shelf and quickly shut the door. It was really hard not to giggle.

Before handing the can to me Janice wiped off the top with a fairly clean towel. The frosty beverage hit the spot and I said so. Janice gave me another amiable grin as she opened her own and took a swallow. She cleared another chair to sit on and we got down to business.

"You want to know what Doug told me before he left, don't

you?" she said. Janice's tone and her words may have been blunt but didn't sound offensive.

"That's about it," I admitted. "Although any impressions you might have would be welcome, too."

She shrugged. "I have no problem with it but there isn't much to say."

I eyed her. Was she as totally uncomplicated as she looked and acted? She gazed back at me guilelessly, brushing her graying hair out of her eyes and swinging one long leg over the other. It was a disaster for such a large woman to wear a baggy pair of cut off blue jeans, but my guess was she could have cared less.

"You aren't worried about him, are you?" I decided to be as straightforward as she was.

"No, I'm not," she declared, but another grin softened the response.

"Well, if your instincts are correct you must think I'm wasting my time."

"You might be," she allowed, "but that's your business, yours and David's. Besides, I might be wrong, I'm willing to admit that."

"Can you explain why you're not anxious like they are?" I asked, then added for clarification, "your brothers and your folks."

"It's sort of hard to explain," she replied slowly. "More of a feeling than anything else." She unfolded her legs and leaned lazily back in the chair, putting her soda can down on the table and rubbing both of her thighs. "Doug came here before Christmas just to tell me he was going away for awhile, probably a few months. He sat right there where you are and said, 'Jan, this is under wraps. No one knows yet but you. I need some space, and I need some time. The country house is almost out of escrow and I plan to be gone by the first of the year.' And that was about it. He said he didn't want any of the family to worry about him, or insist on knowing where he was going. He was telling me because I'm the one who lives closest to Mom and Dad, and maybe because he knew I was the least likely to insist on a lot of details."

"It doesn't sound like your parents asked too many questions, either," I commented.

"No," she admitted, "they didn't. But he couldn't have

known that. I'm pretty sure that's why he waited until the last minute to let them know. They didn't have much time to worry about it."

Douglas and David's sister was right; she didn't have much to help me out.

"Do you have any suspicions about where he would have gone?" I persisted. "Do you know anyone he would have confided in?"

"Maybe Andy Weller," she replied.

Ah, Andy Weller again. I definitely wanted to talk to that man.

"Doug got along with Mike, my husband, okay, but they aren't bosom buddies." She got up and stirred whatever was in one of the pots. A faint aroma of pasta sauce wafted through the warm air.

"You have children, don't you Mrs. Markham?" I asked conversationally.

"Three," she beamed, "and three grandchildren. My youngest was like David, rather a late edition and he's still at home. The other two are grown and gone. And you?"

I answered her and asked another question. "Did I hear your youngest son – it is a son, isn't it? – and Douglas get along real well?"

"They do," she said without hesitation. "And Neil has been wondering about his uncle, too, especially lately. I'm sure he doesn't know where he is, though." But to continue her cordiality Janice called for Neil, using the same decibel level she had used to tell her husband they had company.

Rather than yell back and ask what she wanted, a lanky teenager presently appeared and leaned against the refrigerator, giving his mother a questioning look. I was introduced and Neil obligingly said, "hi."

"Neil," Janice explained, "your Uncle David has asked this lady to come up here and try and figure out what happened to Uncle Doug. She wants to know if you have anything you could tell her to help."

The expressionless but not unintelligent face turned to look from his mom to me.

"Anything at all," I encouraged, "anything he might have

said to you at your grandparents at Christmas, for example."

Neil shrugged. "I asked him about it, asked him where he was going. He said he wasn't sure."

The boy rubbed the back of his neck as he thought back to the family Christmas party at his grandparent's house.

"I kidded with him, I remember, told him it must be nice to be able to take off when you want to." He looked directly at me now and added, "he said something like, 'it's not exactly what you might think.' Then I asked him what he meant and he just shook his head. He said maybe next time he left town he'd take me with him and we'd go hunting next fall."

"He did?" his mother looked interested. "You never mentioned that."

In typical adolescent fashion Neil replied she hadn't asked him.

"Are you worried about your uncle?" I asked Neil now.

"I don't know," was the slow reply. "Sure thought he'd be back long before this."

"Did he say he'd send you a card or anything?" I prodded some more.

He had not and there had been none. I told them about the latest note Cora and Porter had gotten. They were both glad to hear it.

"I have considered dropping this, since it looks like your brother is alive and kicking," I spoke to Janice. "But your parents aren't sure they want me to just yet so I'll call David tonight and talk to him before I make a final decision."

There didn't seem to be anymore to say. I got up to leave. Janice did invite me to stay and join them for dinner, but she was not insistent when I declined. I would have asked one of them to walk me past the dogs again but it wasn't necessary. Janice escorted me all the way to the door of my vehicle, and cordial to the last, like her father had, she waved to me as I left.

****

I found a decent hotel and a decent supper before calling David White. Because of the hour I called his home number first. His wife answered, but he was there.

71

"Am I interrupting anything important?" I asked politely after he said hello.

"A good ball game. But I can keep an eye on it while we talk. How's it going?"

"The case isn't solved, yet," I admitted drolly, "but since I just got here I hope you aren't too disappointed."

He chuckled and asked me if I had connected with his parents. I told him, trying not to be too wordy, about my visit with the senior Whites, Janice and Neil, and also the visit to his brother's house. He was very interested to hear Douglas had sent another note. Having the foresight to copy the message, I quoted it verbatim.

"So, my question is, if your brother is okay and coming back soon, maybe I should stop snooping around and go back to Hanley. After all, I'm spending your family's money."

"Well I agree with Dad," he said. "It's still darn odd."

There was no argument from me about that. I waited while he considered.

"You said the letter came five days ago?" the voice at the other end of the line spoke. I said that was correct. "How about this? Go ahead and see Andy Weller tomorrow as you planned and then see what you think. Doug said he'd be back soon and he hasn't made it yet. I'll call Marty and Phil and see what they want to do."

"Your folks gave me the mail piling up at the post office to sort through," I told him. "Is that all right with you?"

"If Doug doesn't want people poking into his private affairs he had better communicate better," David said sourly. If he was relieved to hear there was a strong indication his older brother was alive and well, he was also frustrated by all of the secrecy.

I took that as a yes and told him I would call again the following night.

"One more thing," I suddenly remembered, "how did you know your brother had withdrawn money from his bank account since he left? Do you know what month that was?"

The answer was simple. Douglas did most of his business with a federal bank that had branches in Indiana. David had pulled in a favor from a local bank manager, who accessed Douglas' checking account. I wondered if that was legal without

72

some sort of court process - probably not. David told me to keep that fact to myself. That was how he found out about the large withdrawal in April.

Before hanging up he commented, "I guess you survived a visit to my sister's house today."

When he heard Janice's home was where I had been just prior to our conversation he laughed. Janice and her husband's domestic lifestyle might be a bit of a family joke.

My room had a desk but the bed was much bigger. I picked up the shopping bag and dumped the contents out on the bed. With a tall glass of ice water nearby and a pot of decaf coffee brewing near the sink, I started to sort through the months of mail.

The job wasn't completed when I gave up three hours later, bleary eyed and too tired to pay close attention anymore. There was still a small stack left in the pile put aside as interesting. My method was to go through everything a first time and discard what was obviously of no use to me. That was roughly half of it. I didn't want to throw anything away, so I put it back in the shopping bag. Looking through Douglas White's mail was one thing but tossing it was another. Next I went through the 'keep' stack more slowly and weeded out several other envelopes as not worth very much attention. Some of it was work related, from colleagues who at that time did not know the business had been turned over to brother Marty.

That left about a third of the shopping bag contents to go through more closely, which included the rest of the bank and credit card statements. There was nothing from the children in California.

Before I cleared off the bed and went into the bathroom to brush my teeth and wash my face, a few facts had stirred my interest, mainly financial. First, there was a credit card statement with a zero balance as of the first of the year. There had been a large amount due in early December and it had been paid in full before the posting of the January statement. The bank statement for December, the first one in the bag of mail, listed a withdrawal of two thousand dollars in cash. The next time any amount of money was withdrawn was April, which I already knew, and there was another for an even larger amount in June, which was the most current. In April and June the money had been transferred into the same account; the numbers were identical, but the account wasn't named. It was also of interest to me that Douglas White had cancelled his home computer service provider until further notice.

There was no doubt about it. Not only had the elusive Mr. White made plans to be away for several months, he had carefully arranged to cover his tracks. Did he have a destination in mind?

Chapter Nine

Since I took the time in the morning after breakfast to finish examining the mail, I got a late start back to again visit the senior Whites. On the drive my mind whirled. Douglas' absence was decidedly mysterious and I was intrigued. But was it any of my business, even with the request and blessing of the rest of the White family? If nothing had happened to Douglas and he was due home any time, what was I doing involved in this situation? I envisioned a scenario; I drove into Porter and Cora's driveway where Douglas' car was parked. They would introduce us and I would sheepishly return the shopping bag of mail. Douglas would give a perfectly good explanation of where he had been, and I would go home feeling foolish.

On the outskirts of town I parked my vehicle in the empty parking lot of a country church and took a walk. It was still humid but cooler today. For almost an hour I walked up and down the residential streets of the peaceful town and eventually wandered about half a mile down a road much like the one Janice Markham lived on, where two new homes were being built. I turned around when a canine started barking and I could see the animal wasn't confined. There was no way of knowing how territorial the dog was and I didn't want to find out. I had gone far enough anyway, and my conclusions were still stymied. After guzzling water from the bottle on the passenger seat I went back to see Porter and Cora again.

It was almost one o'clock and lunch was over, but as I said before, I usually don't eat lunch. My intention had been to call ahead which had not happened, but I had no doubt someone would be there for me and someone was. Before I took the keys out of the ignition Porter was outside to greet me. There was no Toyota or any other vehicle that didn't belong to the Porters parked nearby. Cora was home too, and twenty-four hours after our first encounter we were again sitting at the kitchen table. There was another pot of freshly brewed coffee on the counter but no cookies this time. After Cora poured and served she sat down and I had the floor.

"I gather Douglas didn't come home last night," I said. They verified this was true, as far as they knew.

I told them about calling their son David the night before, and about telling him word for word what the last note from his older brother had said.

"He's not sure what to do and neither am I. Since you've had another night to think about it, what do you want to do?"

They both wanted to know what my impressions were so far and what I had learned, if anything, from the mail.

"It won't take me too long to tell you that," I said flatly. "First, your son knew he was going to be away a long time, probably several months. Mr. Porter, you saw that yesterday as clearly as I did, and what I saw looking through the mail only verifies it. Second, he didn't take very much with him when he left, and third, he didn't want anyone to know where he was going or what he was going to be doing. Those are my conclusions so far."

When Porter returned home from his son's house the day before, he shared our observations with Cora and asked her if in her infrequent visits to dust, she noticed the same things. Cora had been able to supply a little information. During Ingrid's last months an elderly local lady had been hired to do the housework, coming in two mornings a week. Porter had forgotten all about this. After talking to Porter, Cora took it upon herself to call this lady and asked her if she had done a final cleaning when Douglas closed up the house. She had. Before his departure Douglas asked her to come back one more time to thoroughly clean and do whatever laundry there was. When she locked up the house she brought the keys to Andy Weller. Because she put the laundry away, the lady had also noticed her employer didn't take much with him.

"Mina thought it was a little odd," related Cora, "so she remembers it now. All I noticed was that most of Ingrid's things were gone. Doug took care of that himself."

Neither of my companions at the table knew what else to say, so no one said anything for a long minute. I sipped my coffee and looked idly out of the window into the back yard. My attention was drawn back to Cora when she pulled a folded piece of notebook paper out of her pocket.

"I have the list you asked for," she explained, and handed it over.

There were ten people on the list, with their names, telephone numbers, and for several, also addresses. The one I especially wanted to see, Andy Weller, was at the top. Cora leaned over the table to point out who each of these people were, and I pulled a pen out of my purse to make some notations next to each name as needed.

Andy was a machinist and welder who owned his own shop. The number on the slip was his business phone. There was no physical address written for Andy so Porter obligingly looked it up. I inquired into Andy's private life. He was divorced, had two grown children and, they thought, lived alone. He and Douglas had known each other since high school.

Next came Bob and Dena Janascik, long time friends with Douglas and Ingrid. Ingrid and Dena had worked at the bank together. This phone number was for their home address. I wrote down the name of the bank, too.

Paul and Anita Farmer were long time neighbors near the house Douglas had sold. They were in their eighties and Paul was frail, but Douglas and Ingrid had loved them like family. Porter's opinion was they were worth a visit.

That gave me another thought. "Are any of these people Ingrid's relatives?" I asked. "No one has mentioned her family."

Porter and Cora gave each other one of those glances. Cora answered my question.

"Ingrid came from Minnesota," she explained. "She met Douglas when he went out there on a fishing trip with some friends. When she married him and moved out here she didn't go back very much. She told us she didn't get along well with her family. I know her father drank heavily. A sister came to see her every few years and Ingrid did go back when her mother died. When Ingrid was so sick the same sister came and stayed for a couple of weeks, and she came back again with a brother for the funeral. There was a big arrangement of flowers at the funeral home from 'the beloved family of Ingrid Svenson White' but even Douglas, except for the sister, Helen, hardly knew them."

That answered my question. No one from Ingrid's family in Minnesota would be on this list.

Number four was a cousin and his wife; Porter's younger brother's son. They lived near Oshkosh and no one had seen them in months. But they too had been close to both Ingrid and Douglas at one time. The cousin and Douglas had been school chums and hunting buddies.

Number five was the name of the man who had been Douglas' business partner for several years, Todd Denzel. He sold out his interest in the business about 4 years earlier but Cora thought they were still friends, so she put his name down.

Numbers six and seven were Douglas' brother, Martin and his wife, Karen, who lived in Michigan. They were included because of the frequent contacts the brothers had due to business concerns.

"And not much gets by Karen," Cora said. "She might have noticed things that would help you."

That made perfect sense to me. I nodded my approval. I asked if they thought I should talk to the other brother, Philip, too; he wasn't on the list. They said no. Philip lived in Minneapolis and his busy life was centered there. They doubted very much he had any access to Douglas' more private thoughts or activities, and Philip would have already shared anything obvious.

That brought us down to numbers eight and nine, written on the same line just as the married couples had been, but these were two single ladies. I read the names Marian Rhodes and Lillian Tillman. There was one phone number and the name, Do Drop In Café, printed on the second line. I looked up for an explanation.

"We thought of them last night," Porter told me. "These two old gals have been running the diner downtown for twenty years.

Everybody knows 'em. I know for a fact Doug got in there four or five days a week for a meal or a cup of coffee." He grinned. "There isn't much that goes on around here they don't know."

"They sound very worth my time. I think I'll eat at the Do Drop In tonight. Are they open for dinner?"

They were, except Mondays and Tuesdays.

The very last name was Pastor Richard Weymouth. I read it out loud and looked up for my explanation. It was Cora's turn again.

"He's the minister at the Cherryville Living Faith church. That's about fifteen miles west of here."

I asked if that was the church Douglas and Ingrid had attended.

"No, there's a Lutheran church near here where they were members most of their married life. But the minister they knew for years retired, and neither one cared too much for the one who replaced him. By the time Ingrid's life was ending they hadn't gone to church there for several months. Douglas told me they never asked the new minister to come by and he never did. Ingrid's friend, Dena, asked Pastor Weymouth to visit Ingrid when it was clear her life was ending. Both Ingrid and Doug really liked him. He officiated at the funeral, too."

"And it's possible Douglas went to see him for support after Ingrid died?"

"He never said so," Porter allowed, "but he might have."

"Yes, he might." Again I approved. "This is a very comprehensive list. If I can't find out something from contacting these people it's hard to imagine how else we can learn anything."

"It was harder to put that together than I thought it would be," Cora admitted. "I know this spring David called and talked to Andy, Todd Denzel and the Farmers, but maybe they would be able to help you just the same."

I told her if my mother put a list like that together for me she probably couldn't have come up with five contacts. "She lives in Arizona," I said conversationally, "and doesn't know that much about my private life, now that I think about it. It helps that you still live in the same surroundings as your oldest son."

I didn't deem it appropriate to add that I didn't encourage my mother to delve into my personal life.

The day was slipping by and I wanted to make at least a couple of contacts in what was left of the afternoon. The Whites understood. Their intention was to ask me to have my evening meal with them, but of course I couldn't do that and show up at the café, too. This would be mixing business with dinner. Before I slipped away, Cora again broached the subject of my staying at their home and her husband backed her up. With the common sense and frugality of their generation they thought it was ridiculous for me to stay at a motel when they had three empty bedrooms. It was harder for me to refuse this time.

"It is a wonderful invitation," I said very truthfully. "This is a great house."

"Please don't give us the 'I don't want to put you out' speech," Cora warned me. "You wouldn't be. We'd like to have you."

"Okay, but on one condition, no, two. I'll stay tonight and tomorrow night if necessary, but I can't promise to be here at mealtime. And you must not wait up for me."

They agreed. I brought my suitcases in and let Porter carry them upstairs to a guest room overlooking the backyard.

****

David White could not complain I was wasting time on his family's payroll, I thought self-righteously four hours later, sliding into a booth at the cafe run by the two ladies on Cora's list. Opening the sheet of paper with the list of names and smoothing it out on the table, I covered it with my book and accepted a menu.

The waitress was not Ms. Rhodes or Ms. Tillman. She looked about eighteen. But the lady seated on a stool behind the cash register held more promise, she had definitely seen her sixtieth birthday come and go. I eyed her over the top of my menu, watching her banter with an older couple as they paid for their meal.

The waitress carried a tray of food past me to a booth occupied by a family of four. The cheeseburgers looked and smelled too wonderful. My mouth watered. I was going to cave tonight, no chef salad for me. I also changed my evening beverage habit and had lemonade to drink instead of a glass of milk. After placing my order and while sipping the refreshing lemonade, I pulled the list out from under my book, took a note pad and pen from my purse, and contemplated my notes and the two visits I had made after leaving Cora and Porter.

One stop at a local gas station and five miles of driving had taken me to Andy Weller's machinery shop. It was an impressive place both for size and noise. Four men, including Andy, were hard at work. It was the place to bring your heavier equipment to work on. There was a small office on the side of the huge garage where another man was answering the phone and posting grimy pieces of paper on a pegboard behind him. I expected to see a pin up calendar somewhere and was not disappointed. This one was put out by a motor oil company and featured a redhead in a black bikini. It was two years old. The up-to-date calendar was a large desk type with with block spaces, sitting under the telephone and adding machine. There were coffee stains and grease marks on it in various places.

When the employee behind the counter walked into the shop and told one of the men working he had a visitor, I found out which one was Andy. He glanced at me, murmured something to the messenger, and disappeared behind a huge tire.

"It will be about ten minutes, ma'am," I was told politely.

I thanked the man and sat down on a dingy straight-backed chair to wait. No expense was being wasted on visitor comforts here. There was a coffee station but the coffee looked and smelled hours old. This was a man's territory, no doubt about it.

It was fifteen minutes before Andy approached me. After introducing myself, he suggested we go to his office where the noise level wouldn't be so high. It would have been but he shut the door, which meant we could speak to each other in a normal tone of voice. I won't say the man's behavior had been friendly but until now it was courteous. It came as a complete surprise when after motioning for me to sit down in the chair in front of his desk he said bluntly, "Why should I tell you anything about Doug White?"

I looked directly into a set of light blue eyes and weighed my words. "I thought you might be wondering what happened to him. And I thought you might want to help his family to find out."

He was a stocky man with a full head of graying curly brown hair. He shifted his weight in the chair, leaned back, and twiddled his thumbs across his abdomen as he assessed me.

"No offense, ma'am," he said, in a tone that strongly suggested he didn't care whether he offended me or not, "but I don't know you."

"No," I had to agree, "but I have plenty of credentials to identify me as the person Douglas' brother, a law enforcement officer, asked to come up here to look into the situation."

"I haven't seen much of David since he was a kid," Andy wasn't impressed. "If he's so worried maybe he should come up here himself."

"If he could get away he would," I rejoined levelly, "and if his brother doesn't turn up soon I promise you he will. It won't be too much longer before local, state, and possibly federal cops will be involved. The man has been gone almost seven months, Mr. Weller, and all his family has to prove he didn't drop off the edge of the earth are three very skimpy, impersonal, little notes."

He looked directly at me, his gaze no friendlier than before. "If the cops come around I'll cooperate."

"Meaning, you'll tell them what you know about Douglas White's whereabouts but you won't tell me," I translated, returning his look, my tone steely.

"Something like that," he admitted.

"All right." I got up from my chair. "I'm sorry to have wasted your valuable time, Mr. Weller." I turned to leave, but couldn't resist. I turned around and gave him a small smile and said sociably, "you've told me more than you know."

I was rewarded. The mask on his face slipped a little bit; I had disturbed him.

My first unfriendly encounter didn't bother me too much. It would have been childish of me to think everyone would welcome my enquiries. Was it possible someone knew where Douglas was, but wasn't willing to come across enough to reassure at least the older folks that the man was all right? Something about Andy's attitude and response made me suspect he knew more than anyone else about this affair. Did he know where his friend was? Or, perhaps he had known where Douglas went initially, but now....

I hoped Dena Janascik, Ingrid's long time friend and co-worker at the bank, would take a different attitude.

She did. A teller pointed her out to me; a well turned out fifty something blonde in a well-tailored suit. She smiled and rose from her desk, extending a hand with beautifully manicured nails and blood red nail polish for me to shake. Her professional attire made me aware of my own casual dress and the hair I hadn't combed before entering the building.

"I haven't come for the reason you might suppose," I confessed, taking a chair after she asked how she could help me. "I don't need any advice today on investments, Mrs. Janascik. I came on a more personal matter."

As I launched into my explanation, the wary expression on her face eased and she leaned forward slightly to listen.

"How amazing," she said when I stopped talking. She looked at me the way I may have looked at David White when he initially told me about his brother's disappearance. "Doug's just driven off into the sunset?"

"You lead me to believe you and your husband haven't seen much of him since his wife died."

She verified it. "We invited him to dinner a time or two after Ingrid's death and he came once, but that was long ago. He declined the next invitation. I know it hurt, being there without her. Bob coaxed him out for a game of golf one weekend and called him a couple of times after that. But," her tone was regretful, "it wasn't the same. If we ran into him somewhere it was friendly and we always said we'd get together, but he never encouraged it and we seldom see him anymore."

I pulled the book of matches out of my purse and handed it over to her, asking if she knew of Griff's Place. She picked it up, read it, and considered. No, she didn't.

"You would know if it was somewhere near here?" I guessed.

Dena said emphatically there was no Griff's Place in the county. She had lived locally her entire adult life, and both privately and professionally had contacts in all of the local towns. She didn't ask me where I found the matches and I didn't tell her they came out of a dresser drawer in Douglas White's bedroom.

I did ask her if she thought Ingrid's husband was dealing with his grief.

Dena sighed. She glanced about the bank's reception area, saw there was no one waiting for her services, and asked me if I'd like a coffee or tea. I declined, and she leaned back in her chair to talk.

"I don't think most men wear their grief on their shoulders," she ventured. "Have you noticed that?"

I agreed that was generally true, but had there been more subtle signs?

"What I think," she said cautiously, "is that Douglas could have been in a bad way but not many people would have noticed. I think he was good at hiding his feelings from people."

"Do you miss Ingrid?" I asked impulsively.

"Very much," was the quiet reply. Dena gave me a sad little smile. "She was a wonderful lady. I still think about her almost every day."

Switching gears again I said casually, "People say Douglas White and Andy Weller are close friends."

"Oh they are," Dena agreed without hesitation. "I know they were spending time together. It seemed pretty natural, they've known each other all their lives and both ended up businessmen. They even played high school football together and stood up for each other's weddings. Andy's marriage didn't last," she grimaced. "Well, to be specific, neither of his marriages lasted. He's been alone, let me think, at least three years. You would expect them to hang out together now that they're both single. You should talk to him."

"Oh, I tried," I said candidly. I was about to go on, but late afternoon customers had started to arrive, and there was a young couple that wanted Dena's services.

"Can you wait?" she asked me.

I said that I could, and did so. Fifteen minutes passed, then twenty, as Dena helped the young couple, then an elderly lady. I used the restroom, took a cup of coffee, which was tolerable, and read the bank's brochure on investments. My mind is not inclined toward understanding financial jargon, so I gave that up and scanned a real estate paper instead. A teller came from behind the counter with a set of keys and locked the front doors so no one else could enter. My watch said five o'clock. As all of the employees finished up their work and Dena's last customer left,

84

she got up and walked over to where I waited.

"I'm allowed to stay until six," she informed me pleasantly. "We all have to leave by then." She sat down in the chair next to mine, crossed her legs, and looked at me expectantly. I was being invited to continue my interview. Dena prompted, "You were telling me about Andy Weller."

"I was about to tell you how little Andy Weller told me," I said wryly. "He did not welcome my intrusion."

"Really?" she raised an eyebrow. "That's interesting, isn't it?"

"Maybe," I allowed. "Or maybe he's the type of guy who doesn't welcome strange women coming into his shop and asking about his friends."

"That might be understandable under normal circumstances," Dena expressed her opinion, "but this is a little different." As she considered it her puzzlement grew. "I've never known Andy to be hard to get along with, in business or socially. You can guess he may not be a good judge of women but I don't think he has a dislike for them." She added generously, "I don't see how he could consider you a threat."

"His attitude makes me wonder if he was in Douglas White's confidence," I admitted. "And if he knows, at the very least, what Douglas' destination was when he left here."

Dena thought about it. "If that's true," she opined, "it's about time he told somebody, don't you think so? Douglas' parents, at least."

"I guess that would depend on where Douglas went," I answered.

Dena Janascik and I conversed a little longer. She asked my permission to tell her husband about our meeting, which was nice of her. She was assured all in-put was welcome, but I did request that she and husband Bob keep the discussion between themselves.

"I know this is a small town and I'm not trying to be super secretive, but for as long as possible I'd like whatever conversations I have with people not to be gossip in the supermarket."

Dena understood and agreed. I showed her the list given to me by Douglas' parents and asked her if she knew anyone else she thought it would be worth my while to talk to. With regret, Dena said no. Her close friendship had been with Ingrid White. She did not know Douglas so well. I told her she could leave a message for me with Porter and Cora if she thought of anything else. We parted on good terms.

The possibility of my quarry just showing up was always at the back of my mind. It had been tempting to ask Dena if I could use the phone at her desk to call my host and hostess before going to the café. I didn't because it would have held her up. You have to realize fifteen years ago the average person did not carry a mobile phone. Finding a convenience store with a phone booth that worked, which was located far enough from street traffic so you could hear the person you're talking to, discouraged me. It was easier to drive to Porter and Cora's home and see for myself. That worked out fine and it wasn't necessary to stop. There was no Toyota Camry parked in the drive. Porter was outside trimming bushes in the front yard and did not notice me driving by. I was sure Porter would not be casually doing chores if his long lost son had shown up, so my question was answered. It was now Friday evening, six days since The Whites had gotten a short message telling them Douglas would be home soon. I wondered what his idea of "soon" was.

****

On my way back to the Do Drop In, I considered what my approach to one of the owners of the café would be if the opportunity came up. The plan of action settled upon was never implemented.

Just as the cute young waitress was setting my aromatic cheeseburger in front of me, who should walk into the restaurant but Andy Weller. My back was to the entrance, but the entire front of the café was windows, and he parked an ugly brown pickup truck in an empty parking space right in front of me. I couldn't help but see him. Since I was partially hidden behind curtains, it was doubtful he noticed me before entering. He called out a friendly hello to the lady at the cash register, calling her Marian, and strolled past me, still in his work clothes, to the restrooms at the other end of the dining room. It was possible he hadn't spotted me yet, but a minute later, when he retraced his steps to find a table or booth of his own, he would have been blind not to see me. Casually I munched and read my book. It would be more honest to say I munched and pretended to read my book, ignoring him. He ignored me too and sat with his back to me in one of the two empty booths. That meant we could both eat our meal without facing each other, but it still put me in an awkward position.

How could I talk to Marian Rhodes with Andy listening? I could just imagine him walking up to us and advising her not to tell me anything. Whatever he did or didn't do, it was no good with Andy watching, trying to find out information about his best friend.

So I gave it up for the time being but didn't let it spoil my meal. I thoroughly enjoyed the cheeseburger, half of my French fries, and a pint of lemonade before getting up to leave.

Chapter Ten

The senior Whites weren't home when I returned. They had gone to visit friends, they explained in a note scotch taped to the front door, and "please make yourself at home." The front door wasn't locked, a good thing since I didn't have a key.

There was still over an hour before dark. I postponed phone calls, changed my shoes, and went for a walk. There was a nice breeze blowing, little traffic on the residential streets, and plenty of people enjoying themselves outdoors. I patted a friendly dog, said hello to three young urchins trying to sell lemonade [I had no money with me, or I would have bought some, even if I was overloaded with lemonade already], and three times greeted local residents sitting outside in their front yards.

When I returned Porter and Cora had gotten there ahead of me and Cora was talking on the telephone to her grandson, David's eldest. I got a glass of water from the kitchen and found myself a comfortable chair before she handed the phone to me. David White had initiated the call to find out if his older brother had finally appeared. Since he had not and there had been no more little white envelopes in the mailbox, I was asked to continue on, and I agreed to do so.

"Would you give Dad the phone? Courtney wants to talk to her grumpy Port."

"Your husband goes by 'Grumpy Port?'" I couldn't help but ask Cora incredulously. "He seems like the least grumpy person I ever met."

Cora chuckled. "Courtney started calling him that when she was only two. She heard her brothers call him Grampy Port, and that's how it sounded to her, I guess. Since Port is so easy going it struck everybody as pretty funny and the name stuck. The grandchildren all call him that now."

The two of us chatted for a little while. It was very pleasant to sit in their comfortable, attractive home and relax. Finally I said good night and mounted the stairs to my room. There was a phone next to my bed and I had permission to use it. Actually I also had permission to raid the refrigerator, make coffee, get extra towels or linens out of the closet in the hallway, and turn down the thermostat, just to name a few of the options offered. It would be hard going back to a motel after this.

There were two people I wanted to talk to before going to bed, my friends Anne Carey and George Thomas. My children could wait until the weekend, which was when they usually heard from me. It was likely I wouldn't be home yet on Sunday.

Anne and George were both at home. Since Anne was older and might go to bed earlier so she was first. Just hearing her chirpy little "hello dear" made me smile. Anne had become very dear to me the previous year when we had gotten to know each other well upon the death of our mutual friend, Amelia Marsh.

"Let me run the facts by your orderly school teacher mind," I begged. "It would be a big help to hear your opinion."

Given the expected go ahead, I plunged into all the information given to me since my arrival the day before, beginning with Mr. Gretske, Douglas' neighbor, and going through the chats with all the family members, Andy Weller's reception, what Dena Janascik had to say, the cash withdrawals and transfers from Douglas' accounts, and finally my report back to David White.

"What do you make of it, Sally?" she asked, with her habit of often answering a question by making you think your own opinion is more important. It was a quality she had developed to become a successful educator administrator.

I told her. She gasped. "You don't think!" But of course it was just a reaction and there was no need of saying that's just what I did think. Did she?

"It is one very good explanation," she thought. "There must be ways you can find out for sure."

"Certainly. But going to the man who asked me to do this is not one of them, at least not yet."

"Oh, no," she agreed fervently. "You must be sure. And if you are right...."

"If I am right," I said firmly, "I want to find out the why and several other particulars before I even consider telling the family."

"Another possibility comes to my mind," Anne said slowly. "Suppose Mr. White found out he was ill, very ill, as his wife had been. I wonder if he was the type of person who wanted to face that alone rather than have everyone know. After all, he had just gone through so much with his wife. Perhaps he didn't want to put his family through that."

"Very interesting," I responded approvingly. "Maybe the treatment called for kept him away longer than he expected. I don't see how the poor communication fits into that. How hard would it be to send a postcard at least every month? In my scenario he may have had to arrange for someone else to be the messenger. Whoever it was, they all had a Chicago postmark."

Miss Carey admitted that was one hole in her theory. She asked me what I was going to do next, and I told her most of the people on my list of names still had to be contacted. She wanted to know more about the list so we went through it together.

"I have some cousins up there in that part of Wisconsin," Anne informed me conversationally. "I haven't seen them in years."

"Well, maybe you should consider a visit sometime; when you aren't all tired out from traveling to California."

"I'm about recovered," was the bright reply. Then, "Have you talked to your friend, George?"

This was my chance to end our chat. "So you think my conclusion is a plausible one," I prompted.

"Yes," was the reluctant response at the other end of the line. "How are you going to verify it?"

I told her how I hoped to accomplish that, and she signed off after exacting a promise to get back in touch as soon as there were any new developments.

George didn't answer so I had to leave a message on his answering machine, which I hated because my hosts were going to bed and it was possible the phone ringing would wake them up.

"I'll try again every fifteen minutes until we connect," I promised into the recording.

It was twelve minutes when I tried again and he answered on the second ring. He apologized, which wasn't necessary.

"I was out in the garage. What's up?"

"I am being treated royally by Detective White's parents," I said glibly. "Anything I desire, it's mine. They might be offended if I steal the family silver, but otherwise...."

"You must have charm I haven't seen too often," was the droll reply. "Just kidding. Any leads on that guy?"

The door to my room was closed, but if Porter or Cora were in the hall could they hear me? I lowered my voice a little more.

"George," I said soberly. "I wonder if Douglas White went to jail."

"You what?" he asked after a three second pause.

I repeated it. He asked what gave me that idea, so I explained how Douglas had covered his tracks so no one would have a clue as to where he was going.

"Where would a guy be that he didn't want anyone close to him to know about, especially his youngest brother, a guy who looks up to him and also happens to be in law enforcement? Why has there been so little communication and all of that so, well, generic."

"But you're still convinced this guy is still alive?" George asked, the surprise still in his voice.

I told him about the latest note.

"And if you think it was a fake," I added quickly, "the parents are both sure it's his handwriting. Not only that, this time he mentions missing David's birthday."

"I take it there was no postmark from the state pen."

"Of course not," I said with exaggerated exasperation. "That's one of the things about this situation. All three mailings were from Chicago, impossible for an average person to trace. I think that was deliberate; Douglas arranging ahead of time for those cards to be mailed."

Before George could say anything else I added, "If my guess

is right, I wonder where Douglas was incarcerated. It could be Illinois or Michigan rather than Wisconsin. I'm almost positive if he did get into trouble it wasn't near home, but no one has mentioned him going away for any extended period of time before he left after Christmas. That doesn't leave out Wisconsin, of course."

George had a question. "If it was in any of those states, especially Indiana, wouldn't his brother know?"

That seemed like a reasonable conclusion if David White looked in that direction, but I told George it was almost a certainty it never occurred to David his brother might be in prison, and certainly not in Indiana. I also told George about my interview with Andy Weller.

"He knows." George said positively. "I'd bet a paycheck on it."

"It would certainly save a lot of trouble if I could wring it out of him," I grumbled.

We both may have been trying to think of ways to do that because there was a longer pause between us. George broke the silence first.

"Accepting your explanation for the moment, you wouldn't have any ideas as to how this law abiding, normal person got himself jail time would you?"

I had to admit that was a problem. "But it's plausible," I insisted. "Some people don't act like they normally do when they've had a great loss. You know that as well as anybody. What keeps coming to my mind is the idea he may have done some heavy drinking. A lot of unpleasant things can happen if you get into the habit of getting drunk."

George summarized. "The suspicion you have so far is, Douglas White goes off by himself where no one knows him and drowns his sorrow by drinking a lot. While on one of his binges he gets himself into some serious trouble. Does that about cover it?"

"Pretty well."

"You do see there are some other problems with this," my friend said, always the realist. "If I remember right, you told me before you left there is now an APB out for this guy's car, plus, the younger brother has already made inquiries with the local

92

cops out there. Wouldn't that have already blown his cover? In this day and age you put somebody's name into a computer, push a few buttons, and you should get an answer."

George's rational mind irritated me a little, but he was right. "What you're saying is true," I granted. "But this man has been a respected member of this community his entire life and a successful business man, too. He has many friends, and I'm wondering if some of those friends aren't with the police department. Isn't it possible they're helping to keep his secret?"

George allowed it was possible but he was obviously skeptical. He also thought maybe if Douglas White didn't want to be found he should have that luxury, at least for a little while longer.

"I'm not going to run to anybody with my theories," I promised. "Believe me. I don't want to cause these people any more heartache. But what about this, George? If someone is sentenced to a term in prison, unless they cause a lot of trouble they don't lengthen their sentence, do they? Just say I'm right. If I am it looks like the term must have been for six months. If anything, Douglas expected to be released a little early. Where has he been for the past three weeks? Why didn't he come home? The note to his parents said he was delayed unexpectedly. It also said he'd be home soon, but they got the note almost a week ago. And," I added before George could slip a word in, "someone, probably our man, withdrew money from his banking accounts twice. He couldn't have done it from prison, going with the theory that's where he was."

"You're not expecting me to answer these questions are you?"

"Not really. But you could be helpful. Remember what you said a minute ago about pushing computer buttons and coming up with answers?"

My conversation with George went on a little longer. I asked him if there was any way he could find out if Douglas White was on a list anywhere as being sentenced to a state prison. George said he would consider it. Next I asked him if he could do a search of businesses in Wisconsin and look for a Griff's Place, perhaps a sports bar, outside of Waupaca County but within driving distance.

"I'm guessing this place must be at least forty miles away from here." Dena Janascik surely would have recognized the name of any bar or lounge located closer than that.

I felt a little guilty asking George to spend so much of his time helping me and told him there was no rush, by the weekend would be fine. He pointed out it was already late Friday night. We parted on that note.

After hanging up the phone, I collected a few things and tiptoed down the hall to the guest bathroom. While soaking in the bathtub I thought about my conversations with Porter and Cora, their daughter Janice and her son, Dena Janascik, and Andy Weller. I thought about the three times Douglas had sent word to his family, and went on in my mind to my talks with my friends Anne Carey and George Thomas. Was George right? Should I leave this whole thing alone? It was hard to think dispassionately. The White family wanted me to keep looking, or most of them did. Janice didn't seem to have any strong opinion on the matter. There was no question what Douglas' friend Andy wanted. He would have been very happy to see the last of me. Was my curiosity too strong for me to back out or was it a hunch somewhere in my psyche that made me reluctant to back down? The bath water was getting cold by the time I climbed out and finished my preparations for bed.

Slapping the pillow around to make it comfortable, I decided to go back to the café in the morning for breakfast. That would be my starting point. I now knew what Andy Weller was driving for a vehicle and if he were there I wouldn't stop. Even if he did eat his breakfast at the Do Drop In, if his shop was open on Saturday morning he should be long gone before my arrival.

Chapter Eleven

With my mind in such a tizzy it took awhile to shut it down and fall asleep. Before that happened, I put Pastor Richard Weymouth on the mental list as my second attempt for contact on Saturday. He was worth a try. It would be rude to call before nine, so that would wait until after breakfast.

The Whites were as good as their word. Neither one tried to coax me to eat with them or even to sit down for a cup of coffee. Descending the stairs, their voices could be heard from the kitchen and I called out a good morning as I sailed out the front door. They both returned the sentiment but neither one of them followed me.

Andy wasn't at the café but the place was packed. There was one empty table left but I felt uncomfortable taking it for only one so I took a stool at the counter. That turned out to be a blessing in disguise; Lillian Tillman was servicing the counter. While ordering coffee and a light breakfast, I tried to figure out how I could start a conversation with her. It seemed to me there would be quite a reaction if I just called out, "I'm in town to try to find out what happened to Douglas White. What can you tell me about him?" It was likely some of the other people at the counter knew Douglas, too, but the response might not be favorable.

"Lill", as everyone was addressing her, was seventy if she was a day. Her hair was dyed auburn, her eyebrows plucked thin, and her wrinkled face carefully made up. It did nothing to erase the years but she probably didn't know that, and it was a good guess no one who knew her would spill the beans. By the affectionate banter that was going around she knew a great many people and was well liked.

Being squeezed between two other customers at the counter, I left my notes in my handbag and pulled a paperback out instead for morning reading. The eggs were scrambled nicely and the bread was toasted just right. There was homemade raspberry jam, too. The food compensated for the stool, which was not very comfortable.

It was my book that gave me the introduction I needed.

"What are you reading, dear?" Lill asked me as she poured a refill into my coffee cup.

I showed her the book, a Ngaio Marsh mystery with Inspector Allyn.

"Ooh," she cooed, looking at the title. "I like some of her stuff. I don't think I've read that one."

We were off. With four or five interruptions we had a running dialogue going about the British authors of the mid twentieth century. When she got called back to the cash register or another customer, I patiently sipped my coffee and waited for her to return. When the morning breakfast crowd thinned out briefly she produced a pad and pencil to write down some of the book titles and authors I recommended. Eventually she gave me the break I was hoping for.

"I haven't seen you before," she stated. "Are you a new resident or just visiting?"

"I'll answer that with another question if you don't mind," I said politely. "Do you know the Whites, Porter and Cora, a retired couple who live here?"

"Oh sure," she replied congenially. "Not well, mind you, but I guess I know everybody around here. Their son, Douglas, now, he was a regular customer here."

"Was?" I prodded.

The lady shook her head a little and shrugged. "He took off, I guess. It's been several months now since he came by last. He's a widower you know, lost his wife to cancer winter before last."

Another interruption. It was several minutes before Lill wandered back to my end of the counter, and now there was no one seated on either side of me. The break had apparently given her pause to consider my curiosity and she was curious about me, too.

"What's your connection to the Whites?" she tried to sound casual about it.

"This will sound odd. The reason I'm in town is because Douglas hasn't come back. Do you know Douglas' younger brother, David?"

She remembered him and she did know he was a police officer in Indiana.

"He asked me to come here," I told her frankly. "We got to know each other pretty well last fall during a murder investigation in Hanley, where we live. He's worried about his brother and asked me to come here and let him know what I could find out. Douglas was not supposed to be gone this long, but the family isn't sure if they should be worried." As an after thought, with the idea it would give me more credibility I added, "I'm staying with their parents right now."

She looked at me in amazement. "Do you mean to say nobody knows where he is?"

Her voice was an alto and low pitched. I glanced around. No one seemed to be listening to us.

"If anyone does they're not sharing," I said.

Lill stared at me as she processed what I was saying. "I had no idea," she finally managed. "Douglas White disappeared?"

"I was wondering if you and your partner, Miss Rhodes, could help me," I continued earnestly. "Douglas' father knew he came in here quite often. Perhaps you noticed something, or he told you something that could help."

"Why sure, honey. I don't see how but we'd be glad to do what we can." The elderly lady glanced at the ever-demanding cash register. "Can you wait just a minute?"

It was after nine-thirty. I had waited a good many minutes already and a few more wouldn't matter.

But here was another plan that didn't go according to plan. I had it in mind to ask Lillian if she and her partner could meet with me in the middle of the afternoon when business would be slow. While waiting for Lillian to come back someone sat down on the stool to my left. It was Andy Weller.

97

****

There was no way I could ignore him this time. It was obvious he had taken the seat next to me on purpose. I decided to take the lead.

"Oh it's you, Mr. Weller," I greeted cheerfully. "How are you?"

He casually picked up a menu and gave me a sidelong glance. "Mrs. Nimitz, isn't it?" he queried innocently.

I admitted it and boldly continued, "but you knew that when you sat here. Do you want to talk to me about anything?"

"What you mean is, have I changed my mind and decided to discuss Doug with you," he countered.

We sat there, sizing each other up.

"Can I buy you a cup of coffee?" Andy asked.

"I've already had two but yes, I can sip a third," I accepted.

Andy put in an order with Lill, who now stood in front of us, for two coffees and one Danish. He asked her to bring it over to a booth at the back of the restaurant. She didn't bother to hide her disappointment.

"You're going to have a pow-wow about Doug White," she accused. "This lady was just inviting me to have a part in that."

"Yeah, I figured," Mr. Weller said. "But how about you let us talk a little first?"

She reluctantly agreed. There wasn't much she could do about it. I told her I still wanted to meet with her and Marian as well, which pacified her a little. Andy Weller led the way to a booth just vacated in the back of the restaurant.

He waited to say any more until Lill personally delivered his Danish and the coffee pot, filling both of our cups. He winked at her and she glared at him but it was just for show. She wasn't really that miffed.

Wasting no time on preliminaries Andy asked, "How much do you know?"

There was no point in beating around the bush. If this man was going to tell me anything the best way to get it was to be candid.

"The facts, or what I've concluded from them?"

"Both," he responded.

"All right." And I did. As he munched his pastry and sipped, he heard it all. When I stopped he said nothing. I raised my lukewarm java to take a couple of sips and waited, keeping my eyes on his face.

He glanced around the diner, then met my gaze and finally spoke.

"Who have you told about this?"

"Two close friends back home, both of whom know how to keep a confidence. I needed their input." I couldn't resist adding, "Which I might not have done if you had talked to me yesterday."

He grimaced. "You think I should have come right out and told a total stranger secrets one of my best friends trusted me with?"

He had a point. "But you could have asked me for some time to verify who I was and why."

"You took me by surprise," he defended himself. "The last I expected was a broad, excuse me, lady, walking into my shop the way you did yesterday."

Again, there was validity to what he was saying. "What about now? Are you going to talk to me now?"

He leaned forward and put his elbows on the table, heaving a sigh as he did so. "It's probably you or the cops," he said. "I'm not quite ready for the cops yet."

Lill must have given up on us. It was another waitress who stood by our table and offered to refill our cups. After she left I waited for Andy to continue.

"You've hit it pretty head on. Doug did go out of town to do his drinking in private, and he got into some trouble."

We stayed in that booth long enough for Lill to charge us with loitering but she kindly didn't. For a long time Andy did the talking. He began his narrative by saying it would be hard for people to understand what Doug had been going through, but I quickly set him straight.

"I do understand." I said firmly. "My husband died in a crazy accident over two years ago. We were as close as everyone tells me Douglas and Ingrid were."

So he backed up and conceded that maybe I did but a lot of people didn't. As it turned out, it was Andy Douglas had finally gone to with his despair. He had been a widower several weeks when he sought Andy out.

"Divorce isn't so different from death," Andy stated quietly. "Maybe in some ways it could be worse. Doug had all of his good memories."

Andy Weller did not digress into his own tragic marital history. As he narrated, I disciplined myself to listen and save my questions until he finished. He might not take kindly to interruptions.

Condensed and with a bit of my own assumptions added, Douglas' private life by three months after his wife died took on a certain format. He was functioning pretty well during the day, putting his mind to his work. It was the hours in the evening that were agony for him. He no longer had an invalid wife who needed him; in fact, he had no one who needed him. He became depressed. Old friends and church were just reminders of what he had lost. He became painfully aware of his estrangement from his children, he didn't want to bother his family, and he didn't want their pity. A few weeks after the funeral, he started patronizing a local sports bar for the casual company of people he didn't know very well. He would have a few beers and watch a ball game on television before going home to bed. The problem here, said Andy, was the women.

"I can speak from experience," Andy said emphatically. "Women can be very aggressive when they find an eligible guy. Here was one just ripe for the picking." Andy added a mild expletive, which he did not feel the need to apologize for and I asked for none. He followed it by saying Douglas White was not only a pretty good looking single guy, but had some financial means, too.

"So," I surmised, "Douglas was the object of unwanted attention by single women coming in looking for male companionship."

"Putting it mildly," Andy agreed. "Doug didn't know how to handle it. He tried to be nice about it, make it obvious he wasn't interested, but that didn't work. At least," he amended, "it didn't work for a couple of the women. One even called him at home and that did it. He stopped going."

I didn't mean to show off but I interjected my conclusion. "Instead he started going somewhere farther away, more private.

Maybe somewhere like Griff's Place?"

"Yeah," Andy admitted, giving me a wary look. "Quick, aren't you?"

I pulled the book of matches out of my purse. "Your friend covered his tracks pretty well, but he left a couple of these around at home. Where is this place? Is this where he got into trouble? Were you with him?"

My companion put up a hand to stop the flow. "Whoa."

I apologized. "Sorry. Of course I want to know."

"Yeah, well, I guess I've gone too far to stop now." He relaxed a little. "I haven't talked to anybody about this since Doug left. I guess it's time."

Andy Weller had not been with Douglas the fateful night he had gotten into his fix, and it had not happened at Griff's Place. The event had occurred in early June and Douglas had been alone. Andy freely admitted he went with Douglas sometimes, at first to make sure he didn't drive if over imbibing, then just to keep him company. Griff's had been a frequent hangout but not the only one. When it was too crowded he had a couple of other places he would go. When I asked how often Douglas White went out of town like this Andy shrugged: maybe once or twice a week. Griff's Place was fifty miles north, about a fifty-minute drive.

"No women hang out there?" I asked idly.

"Well, some do, but they're complete strangers so it made it much easier for either one of us to tell 'em to get lost," Andy explained.

I was told Griff's was a successful establishment, often frequented by vacationers, hunters, and fisherman. Doug was able to have his company but maintain privacy. Andy moved on to tell me what me knew about the night his friend got into trouble.

The disaster happened on a weekend night, a Saturday in early June. Douglas White had started at Griff's but it was very crowded, and about nine o'clock he went to a smaller bar further north.

"He told me he was sipping his third beer about two hours later and the place was getting full so he decided to shove off. When he tried to move toward the door he had to push his way through a crowd and that's when it happened." Andy paused here to take a sip of his coffee. It felt like we had to stop for a commercial break.

"A couple of the guys he rubbed shoulders with while he was trying to leave took offense and said he was shoving them on purpose. They were getting drunk, looking for a fight, and Doug was there." The disgust in my narrator's voice was thick. "I guess the details don't matter too much. One of them was a little guy with a big filthy mouth. He finally made a comment that set something off in Doug and he let loose and nailed him."

In real life a bar room brawl may not be like a John Wayne movie, I thought.

"It didn't turn into a free for all but there were a few more fists that hit home. As it turned out, these guys weren't exactly popular and a couple of others in there took up with Doug. They shoved the trouble makers out the door but the first one, the one that started it, fell down and didn't get up."

"Oh no," I whispered as an idea crept into my mind, "You don't mean…"

"Yeah," Andy said bluntly. "He died on the way to the hospital. It turned out he had some kind of a brain tumor or something that nobody knew about. The blow he took to the head started him hemorrhaging. A guy like that must have been in fights before, but poor Doug had to be the one to give him the punch that did him in."

My nurse's training told me the problem could have been a silent aneurysm but I didn't go verbalize that, as it hardly mattered now.

Andy Weller seemed to be waiting for me to say something. I didn't disappoint him.

"How in the world," I said in a low tone, "did this get kept quiet?"

The explanation made perfect sense. The victim had been taken to the nearest emergency room in a small town that had no trauma center, but only a doctor who had pronounced him dead on arrival. No one who had been at the fight could believe that one blow could have killed the man, and said so to the sheriff's deputies who arrived at the scene. When a coroner had given his report, all the statements had been taken, and the dust had settled, Douglas White was summoned to the sheriff's office and questioned. What had looked like a simple disorderly conduct charge was now turning into manslaughter. The dead man's family was screaming for Douglas White's blood. They were the only ones doing so but it was a large family and amounted to a significant noise. Within days the local sheriff, the district attorney, and Douglas' attorney, were working together to sort things out. Also involved was the local police chief, who Douglas knew as a casual friend.

"So," I spelled it out, "this has been kept from the White family intentionally. David has made inquiries with law enforcement here and hasn't learned anything."

Andy admitted it. I had been right, guessing Douglas had some influence locally. Only the sheriff had been someone he didn't know, and the sheriff was willing to go along with whatever the district attorney wanted. The dead man's relatives were known to be troublemakers. Some of them had prison records. They might get justice but they wouldn't get much sympathy. Because of the small number of crimes of this magnitude in the county and the important people involved who had the clout to cut through red tape, the whole process was expedited into just a few months.

"Don't think they tried to get Doug off scot free," said Andy a bit defensively. "Doug felt awful and he was willing to do what he had to. He just didn't want his family to know about it, which meant nobody else around here could know, either."

"There's no local newspaper that got a hold of this?" I asked. Living in a small town myself I knew how difficult it was to keep secrets.

Andy shook his head. "I guess not. The guys at the bar must have done some talking among themselves but they didn't want any trouble either, and don't forget some of them had gotten into the fight. The owner sure wasn't spreading it around. Doug had to appear in court in Green Bay twice and that's certainly public record, but it never got out locally. If the dead guy's family wanted press they didn't get it."

"So you're the only one in this town, outside of a lawyer and a few people in law enforcement, who knows this happened," I summarized.

"That's it, until now. And you can leave out the lawyer, he doesn't live here either." Andy ran his hands through his hair and leaned back in his seat with a grimace. "What are you going to do?"

"Before I answer that can I ask a couple more questions?"

He nodded glumly.

I took my hands from around my coffee cup and leaned onto the table. We had both become oblivious to our surroundings, but the diner was emptier now and no one was in the next booth. Lill must have decided we had drunk enough coffee and no one came back to offer us more. She was right about that.

I sorted through and clarified everything Andy had just told me. "This sad affair takes place last June. After investigation Douglas White gets a few months in jail for third degree manslaughter. The whole thing is hushed up. He is sentenced to a short term in prison, beginning in January, and should be out now. Is that right?"

That was simplifying matters but it was all correct. The sentencing had been in November. It was a coincidence that the country house Douglas had up for sale closed in December. It was Andy's understanding that Douglas had been ordered to report on January 15th, for one hundred and sixty days in the state penitentiary.

Chapter Twelve

There was one other matter I needed to know about but we both felt we had over stayed our time at the Do Drop In. On the way out I stopped to thank Lill profusely for her hospitality, and asked if we could see each other in the middle of the afternoon. She was more than willing and said Marion would also be there, so I knew she had been on the telephone and talked to her partner. It was debatable if it was necessary to talk to both of them, but I decided to leave that door open and stay on good terms with Lillian.

Andy had parked his truck down the street at a service station where his oil was being changed. Apparently the services offered at his business did not include personal vehicle maintenance. I walked with him so we could finish our talk.

"There's one side to all of this you haven't talked about at all. How did Douglas deal with all of this on a personal level? I mean, another tragedy in his life, more troubles." I said this remembering what the senior Whites had told me. Their eldest son had been in good spirits at Christmas time, about six months after the accidental death, and just before he had to begin serving his time.

"I've thought about that quite a bit," Andy said, hands in his pants pockets, his shoulders hunched forward. He didn't look at me but looked straight ahead. "I would say, to put it plainly, that Doug decided he wanted to live after all."

Before we parted company Andy Weller asked me again what I intended to do with what I now knew. All I was sure about at that moment was what was not going to happen. On that side, on the top of the unwritten list, was a certainty the senior Whites should not be told as yet, at least not by me. Since Douglas' best friend was emphatically opposed to telling them himself, it was going to stay a secret for a while longer, because the second not to do thing on the list was to tell younger brother David.

Mr. Weller was openly relieved. Our conference must have reassured him about trusting me. He could, but like he said, he didn't know me very well.

There was a huge piece of farm machinery that needed to be ready by Monday and Andy said he had to get back to it. I thanked him for his time and his confidence and promised to keep him informed of developments.

"There is still the little matter of where your friend has been keeping himself," I pointed out. "He still should be back by now."

Andy agreed.

I walked slowly back to my car, deep in thought. I got in, turned the windows up, the air conditioning on low, and thought some more. What now? Before anything else maybe it would be best to call George back. Since the theory was now a known fact, George should be spared the time and effort trying to find out if Douglas had gone to prison. Should I go back to my hosts' home and call him from there? That idea made me uncomfortable.

I went to the convenience store and bought a phone card. The weather was nice and this time I stood outside at the phone booth and made my call. George wasn't at home. I left a message telling him not to pursue the line of inquiry we had talked about the night before, but to wait to hear from me for an explanation. That was the best I could do.

It was going on eleven o'clock. It wouldn't hurt to go on with my plans. I had Pastor Richard Weymouth's phone number and four hundred and fifty minutes left on my phone card. Pastor Weymouth's wife answered. She was friendly but sounded a trifle preoccupied. After introducing myself and apologizing for disturbing her I tried to make it brief. Was there any chance her husband had a few minutes to spare for me? It was about Douglas White.

"Douglas White?" She had to pause and consider whom I was talking about. "Oh, the man who lost his wife to cancer some months ago. I don't think Rick has seen him in a long time."

I told her no one else had either and that was the problem. Of course she wasn't told about the morning's revelations, but simply that Mr. White's family was trying to locate him and I was acting on their behalf. Would it be possible to have a little of her husband's time?

She considered it. "He isn't home at the moment but he's supposed to be back later for lunch. If this is important, I know he doesn't have anything pressing until later this afternoon. Could you stop by here at the house?"

I could and I would. We agreed upon one o'clock. With sincere thanks and a promise my questions wouldn't take too long, we were both hanging up when I remembered I needed directions. Fortunately she heard me urgently calling her name before putting the receiver down, and obliged.

It would be a thirty-minute drive to the Weymouth home. The church they pastored was in Cherryville and their residence ten miles further on. I say "they" deliberately. There is no such thing as a minister who is married leading the church without his wife's assistance. At least I have never seen it. At the very least she has to put up with all of the people who make demands on his time, like me.

Making that trip and getting back to meet the ladies from the diner would take most of my afternoon, but I still had the rest of the morning. It couldn't be helped. I simply had to go back to the home of my hosts and see if Douglas had finally come back. If he had it was time for me to pack up and vacate the guest room. Of course you know he hadn't.

Making more phone calls away from the house turned out not to be necessary. Porter was gone when I drove up and Cora was leaving. She was backing her sedan out of the garage and turned her window down to speak to me.

"Just make yourself at home, Sally," she said brightly. As if she hadn't told me to do that numerous times already. "I'm meeting a friend for lunch and running some errands, and Port isn't due home until suppertime."

She backed carefully out of the drive and drove slowly down

the street. Watching her, I hoped Cora limited her driving to familiar and sparsely traveled places. She made Anne Carey's driving look skillful.

I helped myself to a large glass of ice water and tried to call George again. There was still no answer and there was no point in leaving another message. It would be nice to call my son and to talk to Joel, but apparently everyone had things to do for the weekend. There was no one home at Everett's house either.

I sat down in a comfortable chair in the living room and pulled out the list of names Cora and Porter had given me. I also studied the dates on a small pocket calendar I kept in my purse. While I was listening to Andy Weller talk no written notes were made, so now was a good time to catch up. There was plenty of time before I needed to leave for my appointment with Pastor Weymouth.

Was there any point in contacting the other names on the list, with the exception of brother Marty? Andy and the Janasciks had been covered, and by the end of the day so would the ladies at the café and the man who ministered to Ingrid when she was dying. What could possibly be learned from the others? Among all of my contacts so far, Andy Weller was the only one Douglas had shared the depth of his grief and loneliness with. It was not too likely he had let his old business partner or very elderly former neighbors in on his personal feelings. My only hope could be they had noticed something by chance, and the focus of my inquiry was different now. The mystery was, where had the elusive Douglas White taken himself off to after he left prison? The last note to his parents indicated he was out there somewhere.

The remark Cora made about her daughter-in-law Karen was the reason Marty and Karen White was still included in my 'get up with' list. If she was as observant as Cora claimed, a call to Michigan was a must and there was no reason to put it off. I dialed the number listed next to their name.

The effort was not a total washout. A teenage daughter answered. She turned down the music blaring in the background so we could hear each other, and cheerfully told me her parents were both out somewhere. When I asked if there was a better time to talk to them she was vague about the whole day, but thought they would both be home on Sunday afternoon. Could I call then?

Certainly. I gave her my name, knowing both Marty and Karen White should recognize it since they were in part paying for my services.

The Weymouth home was in the country. Coming down a long gravel driveway to their front entrance, four people sitting down to lunch were clearly visible through a large picture window. I was reluctant to interrupt the meal, but it was silly to sit in the car since they could see me as well as I could see them.

The pastor was opening the door before I reached it. He was still chewing. I apologized for interrupting and offered to wait while he finished, but he assured me, quite convincingly, he was almost through anyway. He introduced me to his wife, Valerie, to a son, and a son's friend. After the appropriate pleasantries were exchanged he led the way to his office, explaining he had a larger office at the church, but there was a Saturday cleaning being carried on by the high school youth group. This one looked like a converted closet. At least there was a window.

Asking about his work, I found out Pastor Weymouth's congregation consisted of about fifty families, which was not enough to support a full time minister. Both he and Mrs. Weymouth held down part time jobs. He chatted for a few minutes about the parish and I listened politely. As an after thought he also offered me something to drink, which I declined.

In turn he listened intently as I explained my reason for showing up on his doorstep on such short notice. Scratching his sunburned, balding head, he expressed total bewilderment.

"I keep pretty busy, Mrs. Nimitz," Mr. Weymouth admitted, "and I haven't kept up with Douglas the way I should have. I liked Douglas and Ingrid and was happy they called upon me when they needed comfort. I hoped after Ingrid died Douglas would keep in touch, continue to worship with us, and maybe come to our prayer group sometimes. When he didn't I called him and we spoke once, maybe twice. He was very pleasant and told me he was fine, which I doubted, and he was included in my prayers for a while. But I don't know what's become of him."

Instinctively I could understand why Douglas and Ingrid would reach out to this man. There was honesty and candor in his words. He had fine lines of fatigue and early aging around his eyes and etched into his forehead, but there was a patience and kindliness about his persona that quickly put me at ease. Being a minister or leading a church, if you will, did not mean one has these qualities. From personal experience I knew some who did not.

There seemed little hope of finding out anything here that could help me and there was no point in dragging out the interview. Douglas may have liked and respected Mr. Weymouth, but he was not comfortable enough with him to lay out his grief.

"I'll put Doug back on my prayer list," the pastor commented while showing me out.

****

Now what? On the leisurely drive back the way I had come, my stomach was growling. Breakfast was long gone. Cherryville had a grocery and I bought a large apple, peanuts, and a carton of cold milk. I remembered a rest area along the road on the other side of town, found it, and enjoyed my snack there. Because the talk with the good minister hadn't taken very long there was time to spare. I noticed a walking path while seated at the picnic table, locked up my vehicle and sauntered down it, smelling the grass and appreciating the lush, pretty countryside. The truth would be a part of me was doing that. There is no need to spell out what the rest of my mind was involved in.

To be honest I felt a little foolish. What else could I do? Where else was there to look? This guy had covered his tracks very well. He wanted his solitude both before and after incarceration. As George clearly stated, maybe we should all leave him to it. But for the umpteenth time there was a nagging feeling of unrest in the back of my mind. If Douglas was in trouble there was no one to know it or to help him out. The longer it took to find him the worse it could be. Rats, rats, rats. Instead of enjoying the fact my conclusions about Douglas were correct and verified as such, I was frustrated and uneasy.

Because of my footwear, sandals, my pace was leisurely down the trail and back, roughly two miles. As I unlocked the car again and climbed in, only two courses of action came to mind. The first was to go ahead and have that visit with the owners of the Do Drop In. Now I needed to hustle to make our appointment.

Marian looked like the younger of the two by roughly eight or ten years. Her hair was gray but her skin was smoother and her hands not quite as veined. As Lill introduced us the look on Marian's face gave me the impression she was skeptical. Curiosity could have been her motivation for agreeing to this tete-a-tete. If she remembered me eating my meal in the diner the evening before she never said so. Marian the practical one, Lillian the romantic, I mused silently.

Lill greeted me warmly, and led me behind the counter and through to their private office off the kitchen. Marian was waiting for us there The room was as large as my bedroom at home and besides the serviceable desk, cabinets, and computer, also had a nook under a small window looking out into the yard behind the restaurant. There were two comfortable armchairs here, a round glass table, and freshly picked roses in a small vase in the middle of it. The parking lot that accommodated the staff and the customers who couldn't find parking on the street was off to the right. In front of the window was a small fenced off area with roses growing up a trellis, two maple trees crowding the fence, and a small patch of grass that needed mowing but somehow looked just right as it was.

"How charming," I complimented.

"We like having a little space to relax," Lillian said. "We spend so much time here, you know. When people want to see us we can't always visit with them at home, but we can come back here when we have some free time. Sometimes we sit outdoors," and she pointed out of the window at a small heavy white wrought iron table and two chairs sitting under the tree. She added, warming to her subject, "Of course we often aren't both here at the same time, which has been one of the advantages of partnership. But still, six days a week, fifteen hours a day, plus payroll, venders, ordering and deliveries, makes it a full time job here for both of us."

"That is amazing," I said with a bit of awe. "I hope you don't mind my saying so but you ladies are amazing, having this kind of a commitment to your business at an age when many people just want to retire."

During this discourse Lillian had ushered me to one of the armchairs and taken the other one herself, because Marian had already taken a folding chair from behind the door and seated herself to my left. There was room enough around the table for three or four to sit comfortably.

"That would be nice," Marian said shortly. "We'd both work less hours if we could find someone who knows how to work hard, and we could trust to be here when we're not knowing they won't steal from us." She had emphasized the "and."

"That has been a problem," Lillian admitted sadly. "We've tried to find someone over the past few years. Eunice was good but she moved, and there was Perry, but he had to take that manager's job in Green Bay, the pay was too good to pass up."

"But this isn't what you came for, Mrs. Nimitz," this from Marian. "Lillian told me what you told her this morning. How do you think we can help you?"

I admitted I wasn't sure, it was grasping at straws. In the time lapse between breakfast and coming back I had considered how to tell these ladies the truth without giving away Douglas' secret.

"Much of what Andy Weller told me this morning is confidential," I began. "I can't help that. It just is, because of the circumstances and in consideration of his family. But the fact is, Douglas White went away right after Christmas; that's about seven months ago. As of this minute no one that I know of, including Andy and the White family, knows where he is. If you think it's odd that I've been asked to help figure this out, so do I. I'm here as a favor to Douglas' younger brother David. Douglas' father, knew he came in here often. Of course it's a long shot, but perhaps he chatted with one of you and said something that might help me."

They listened to my little speech and looked at each other.

"He did come in here a lot," Lill confirmed. "We've been talking about this since I met you this morning. I think he came in for breakfast the most but Marian saw him quite often, too."

Marian nodded. "On an average, once or twice a week. If he was alone he usually sat at the counter and made small talk. That was what it was, just conversation about little things. I haven't been able to remember anything important."

"Neither of you remembers him telling you he was going anywhere?" I persisted.

They both considered. Lill answered. "Somehow," she said

slowly, "I knew he was going to be away. It didn't surprise me not to see him for a while. It was only, maybe March, I finally asked Andy what had happened to Douglas."

"Oh? What did he say?" I asked idly.

Lill shrugged. "Nothing really, something about wanting to get away for a few months. I never thought much about it after that. A few weeks ago his folks were in here for breakfast. I asked them how he was and they said they thought he was probably fine. They seemed a little funny about it, but I was busy and forgot about the whole thing."

I turned to Marian. There was a look on her face that kept my eyes focused on her.

"Anything," I urged, "anything at all."

"Last fall," she said slowly, "it was last fall just before hunting season. It was a weeknight, quiet, with only a few customers. Douglas came in and sat at the counter for supper. He was alone, which he often was, although sometimes Andy would eat with him."

It was a lousy time for an interruption, but there were two loud raps at the door and a perky middle-aged female face peered in without waiting for a response.

"The pies are cool enough," she announced cheerfully.

"Oh, good," Lill beamed, seemingly oblivious to the poor timing. "How about a piece, Mrs. Nimitz? Our treat of course. We have lemon meringue or cherry, both fresh."

I accepted, and the door closed again.

"Go on," I urged Marian.

"I feel like a fool," she said curtly. "This just came back to me and it's probably nothing."

"Could be," I agreed, "but tell us anyway. What harm can it do?"

"We were talking about taking vacations, and about how so many men enjoy hunting, something like that. I guess I asked if he was going this year and he said no, maybe next. Then he asked me something kind of funny. He said something like, 'Marian, with your busy life here have you ever considered going on a retreat somewhere? You know, get away from it all, somewhere nice and quiet where you can just think and get your priorities straight?' I laughed it off and said the only place I had ever been like that was the time I went with my sister to a cabin in the Upper Peninsula without my husband. We had three days of blissful peace and quiet, and I remembered it all even if it was twenty-five years ago."

Lillian swung her gaze from her partner to me, a hopeful look on her honest face. "How about that?" she asked eagerly. "He could have done that, gone someplace like one of those church retreats."

"For seven months?" Marian said skeptically? "Isn't that a bit extreme?"

Lillian's countenance fell slightly.

"It's an idea," I said cautiously, since I knew it wouldn't have been a seven-month retreat. The ladies would never consider a prison term a retreat. "I don't suppose he gave you any idea of what he had in mind?"

Marian was sure he had not. There was another loud rap on the door and Marian was called out into the restaurant. A moment later our pie was delivered, along with two mugs of coffee. Lill assured me it was decaf, and freshly made.

The two of us visited for a while longer with nothing else of consequence coming up in our conversation. Lill mentioned people she remembered Douglas White sometimes meeting for breakfast, other than Andy Weller, and that before Ingrid died she and Douglas would occasionally come for breakfast, sometimes with another couple. I complimented the cherry pie and made my departure, getting away only after I promised to come back again if possible and let them know what had become of Douglas. Lill, optimist that she was, thought I would find out. She brashly offered me a breakfast on the house if I came back with good news.

"She was a nice lady, Mrs. White," said Lillian. "I used to see her at the bank, too. She would want her husband to go on and have a life now that she's gone."

114

Chapter Thirteen

Still discouraged, I drove back to Porter and Cora's. There had to be a way to find more pieces and put this puzzle together. My only option was to look more carefully at the pieces I had. I also wanted to try and get in touch with one of my children again, probably Everett. Janelle would not consider it odd if she didn't hear from me for several days longer. On the outside chance she was looking for me, she would call her brother when I wasn't to be found.

But there was a big surprise in store for me. Driving up to the front of Porter and Cora's home, another vehicle was parked there already, and it did not belong to their oldest son. It was a white extended cab pickup truck and I knew very well who the owner was. George Thomas was sitting on the front porch, and he hadn't come alone. Beaming at me and waving gaily was Anne Carey.

To say I was surprised would be a gross understatement. I was flabbergasted. George and Anne, Porter and Cora, were all sitting on the porch having a great old time.

Not being able to come up with anything original on such short notice I squeaked, "What are you doing here?"

They had driven up from southern Indiana in about nine hours, leaving bright and early in the morning and arriving only twenty or thirty minutes before I came back. Enroute they had come up with a good excuse for their appearance.

As I walked up and climbed the few steps to the porch, Porter pulled up another chair for me. His wife poured me a glass of something cold, which looked like raspberry tea. In answer to my question Anne picked up the ball. She chirped cheerfully about how wonderful George had volunteered to drive her up to see her cousins, since he had a long weekend, wasn't that nice of him, and since they were driving right by where they knew I was staying they couldn't resist dropping in. A nice clerk at the convenience store in town told them where the Porters lived and really, it was just too tempting to see how I was getting on.

I thought it was a bit thin and glanced covertly at my host and hostess. Their faces revealed nothing except good humor.

For half an hour it was Cora and Anne chatting about relatives who knew relatives, and Porter and George talking about the reliability of pickup trucks and how to keep the lawn free of crab grass. It was a regular love fest. I sipped the tea I didn't need and smiled dutifully when it seemed called for. No one seemed to notice that although George and Anne were supposed to have stopped to visit with me they were visiting with everybody but.

Finally George said they had imposed long enough and apologized again for dropping in unannounced. If he was going to deposit his passenger on her relatives' doorstep before dark it was time to go on.

"Oh really," Miss Carey twittered, "George is so right. We must go."

It took a little longer for Porter and Cora to say how nice it had been to meet them, and please, come back again when you can stay longer. I walked them to their truck, looking for an opportunity to find out what was going on.

"We're staying at a nice place right off highway thirty-nine," George said in a low voice. "Take the main road out of town, north about five miles and you'll be able to pick up the highway there. It's another fifteen minutes; you can't miss it." He proceeded to give me the name of their hotel and a room number as he assisted Anne into the passenger side. Climbing into his own seat he added, "We'll order supper in as soon as you can make it."

I suppressed my questions and watched the two James Bond wannabes drive off.

****

Cora and Porter's retirement lifestyle included a busy social life. An hour later they were off to a potluck church picnic. They generously invited me to come along, but expressed appropriate regrets when I begged off. They weren't too surprised and continued to honor our pact by not pushing their invitations.

"Nice friends you have there," was Porter's comment about the surprise afternoon guests.

I gave the expected feedback.

"I'll be out again for a while this evening," I changed the subject. "I don't expect to be too late and I should be back here to stay for the night."

"We'll leave the front door open if we go to bed," Cora said. "Just lock it behind you when you come in."

"Crime not a big problem here?" I asked with a smile.

"Not when you have geriatric neighbors with insomnia," Cora replied with a smile of her own. "No one comes and goes on this street without being noticed."

I thought I should keep that in mind.

We rendezvoused in George's hotel room. His was the larger of the two, almost a suite, with a couch and small desk in addition to the usual amenities. They both looked at me sheepishly. It may have had something to do with the look on my face.

"Okay you two, spill the beans," I ordered. "I want to know what you're doing here and don't tell me you just decided last night to come up here and visit distant relatives."

"First cousins, dear," Anne said serenely. "But of course you are right. We came to see you."

"Here I am," I pointed out.

There was a loud rap on the door.

"So is our food," George added with a grin. "Italian. Hope that's okay."

Since they hadn't waited for me to turn up before ordering, I knew they must be ravenous. I let them eat something before starting with an explanation. Anne had gotten in touch with George right after my calls to each of them the night before. They had agreed if it turned out my theory was correct and Douglas was in prison, they weren't too comfortable with me trying to go on without help. Within the hour George knew my guess about prison time was correct and they made last minute plans to join me.

"Just before midnight," George said triumphantly. "I didn't need my computer and don't ask me to divulge my source. He broke confidentiality and doesn't want to get fired."

I eyed them both narrowly. "First of all," I kept my voice pleasant, "I don't see why you think there's any harm that would come to me here. Second, and this is directed at you, George, Miss Carey looks exhausted. You both cut your sleep short last night and you've had a long day of driving. What do you think you can do here in a couple of days?"

Miss Carey came to George's defense. "I'm quite all right, Sally, I napped quite a lot on the drive up. I am tired, but not at all in a bad way. I'll get a good night's sleep tonight. This was my idea, you know. George was totally for it but only after I suggested it."

"We did think you'd be a little happier to see us," said George, a little hurt.

"I was almost speechless. Seeing the two of you at the White's home was the last thing I ever expected. Then I grinned at both of them and relented. "Honestly, it is good to see you. This whole thing has hit a brick wall even though I found out for sure this morning what you also now know, that Douglas has been to prison."

Anne, who had been looking rather anxious since I had come across as miffed, now relaxed and smiled back. "Tell us everything you know, dear. We can just sit here and review everything. You're the one who once said we're a team, you know."

There was no denying it was very therapeutic to go over everything again verbally and without having to make phone calls to do it. After talking it over we all came to complete agreement on two things. First we came to the same conclusion Andy Weller and I had come to earlier that day. It was not yet prudent to tell anyone who didn't already know that Douglas had gone to jail. Anne and George were with me on that point immediately. Second, the three of us all thought that Douglas was alive somewhere.

My companions found the circumstances surrounding the incarceration very interesting. George even admitted if they had known they might not have come. His informant had not had access to any details other than the third degree manslaughter charge.

"But since we're here," he added hastily, "we might as well make ourselves useful."

It wasn't clear how they could do any more than be my sounding board and give feedback on my facts and frustrations.

"My idea was to speak to that older couple you mentioned last night, the Farmers," Anne volunteered. "My cousins can't live very far from where they do and they're not much younger. It seems to me they might know each other and that would give me a chance to visit. If it's true what Mr. Weller says and Douglas White withdrew from almost everyone it's not likely I'll learn anything, but what harm is there in trying?"

I put aside the pasta I had been pushing around my plastic plate and got up to stretch. I went over to sit on the edge of George's king size bed for a change of position. "No one has told me that Douglas White did much traveling after his wife's death, not even a trip to Michigan when he sold his business. If he is staying with someone or secluded somewhere I don't think its Hawaii. If he boarded a plane his car should have been found by now. And remember, he didn't take much with him."

They both thought my reasoning and conclusions were sound. "But you say he has withdrawn a good amount of money from his bank, so that could be wrong." George pointed this out.

I eyed him speculatively. "I thought you would be reminding me of what you told me last night."

"And that is?"

"That we should leave him alone, wherever he is. If he doesn't want to be found that's his affair."

George rubbed his clean-shaven chin. "Maybe we should. There's just something about this.

"Yes there is," I said emphatically. "You feel it too, don't you, Anne?" I turned directly to her.

My elderly friend surprised me by asking a question in return. "Do you remember when I told you about that friend of my nephew, the Vietnam veteran who disappeared and was never found?"

"I certainly do."

"I think," she continued gravely, "it would be better to risk a little embarrassment than to have this man disappear forever."

I looked from her to George, who held my gaze for a second and nodded. "I'm in," he said. "At least until Tuesday. I'm supposed to be back to work Wednesday."

I wondered how he had managed to take another short vacation so soon after the week he had taken off to go fishing. I asked him.

He smiled. "Yesterday morning Vince Steuben's wife sprained her ankle. They've postponed their vacation from next week until next month. I left a message on the office answering machine last night saying I had a little emergency and wouldn't be in until Wednesday. I knew the boss wouldn't care too much being short only one man."

"Only a little white lie," Miss Carey opined virtuously. "This could be a little emergency."

"You told the Porters another little white lie when you said you were going to arrive at your cousins' home this evening," I said blandly. "That's two already."

Anne just smiled serenely.

We sent her off to bed about an hour later. Before that we did came up with a plan. I had already been toying with the idea of visiting Griff's Place and The Dugout, which was the name of the bar where the fight had taken place. I was desperate and didn't know what else to do. George said fine, but he was coming along. We had to find out if they were open on Sunday nights, and I would call Andy Weller's home number to see if he could tell us.

Anne knew very well she would stick out like a sore thumb at a sports bar. She was expected by her cousins to arrive the next morning and would go on as planned, in time to attend morning worship services with them and hopeful the old friends of Douglas and Ingrid's, the Farmers, would be there.

"In a rural area so it's very possible they attend the same church," she said.

Although the access to her own room was from an inside hall, we watched her go down the hallway and unlock her door. As we bid her a final good night, she reminded George they would have to leave at eight-thirty. He nodded and gave her a salute.

I poured myself a fresh glass of water, took a final nibble on a breadstick, and sat down again at the table. Rather than take a seat, George swayed back and forth on the heels of his harness boots, hands in his back pockets, and looked at me.

"Might not be a bad idea to try that guy now. What's his name, Andy?" he remarked casually. "If he's home on a Saturday night."

"Okay." I reached for my purse and found my list from Cora White with all the contact information. It was a local exchange so I didn't need to use my phone card. There was no answer but there was an answering machine with two voice boxes, one for business calls and one for personal calls. I left a message in the personal one, asking him to call me as soon as possible, leaving the phone number to George's hotel room.

"That should make him very curious," I told George. "He knows I'm staying with Douglas' parents and he'll have no idea why I would be calling him from here. There's just one problem; I don't want to stay here half the night. If he's out on the town or partying he may not get back to me for awhile"

"Then he'll get me," George said, and not without relish. "I can explain what's going on."

Privately I thought it would be much better if I paved the way with Andy Weller concerning George and Anne, and when back at the Porters it was my intention to call Andy again from there. Instead of sharing that, George listened to my plans to call Marty and Karen White back on Sunday afternoon, and heard about my decision not to contact Todd Denzil, Douglas White's former partner, or the cousin in Oshkosh.

George listened to it all, and finally sat down again.

"You realize," he said, "if we went to the police they could probably trace the account numbers where the cash withdrawals went. That could tell us a lot."

"Of course it would, and you're right. But first the authorities have to agree he is a missing person. If they do and start a real investigation, it is sure to get out. I can just see the headlines in the local rag now, 'local businessman missing.' Then it wouldn't be too long before they found out exactly where he's been, at least for the first few months after he left home."

"Yeah," George agreed sadly. "One way or another the time in jail can't be hidden forever. It would be a good thing if he was the one to tell it."

Telling the younger brother who looked up to him as he did was going to be a task I did not envy Douglas White, but it would be even worse if he never had the chance.

About nine o'clock, as I was getting ready to leave, Andy Weller returned my call. When it rang George let me pick up the receiver, but Andy's tone was guarded anyway.

Brief and to the point, I told him about my friends showing up and why. Andy recalled my friends being mentioned in our conversation that morning. Maybe that was why he didn't have much to say about it. I went on to tell him our reason for calling; we wanted to know if those two taverns were open on Sunday nights. As the words came out of my mouth, I remembered the matches in my purse and realized I could have called Griff's Place to find out their hours myself. Oh well; that still left The Dugout.

He thought they were open. They might not be in the dead of winter, but during tourist season and hunting season it was unlikely they would be closed. He had never been a customer himself on a Sunday night, but he was pretty confident they would be open, because he happened to know that county had no rules about Sunday closure of businesses that sold liquor. Why did I want to know?

I told him. "I know it might be a waste of time, but I want to ask around up there and see if anyone remembers Douglas or that fight. Now I have someone who can go with me, which might be even better."

There was a pause on the other end of the line. It was a long pause but I knew he was still there so I waited, rolling my eyes at George.

"Would you have any objections if I came along too?" he finally asked.

"Well," I was taken aback and hesitated. "I don't see why not. You want to?"

"Yeah, I do."

"Okay. Would they remember you?"

"They will at Griff's unless they've changed bartenders, although I haven't been up there in weeks. The Dug Out, well, probably not."

I considered if Andy being recognized would be an asset or a liability. Impulsively I asked him if we could meet ahead of time.

"Are you free tomorrow morning?" he asked me in return. "Will you be going to church or anything?"

Patronizing bars had been an infrequent occurrence in my life and never, ever, had I gone to church in the morning and a bar at night. It seemed ludicrous. I asked him to hold on and asked George how long he thought it would take him to deliver Anne and come back. He guessed thirty or forty minutes.

"Do you know somewhere else we can have breakfast around here?" I returned to Andy.

I knew Lillian and Marian closed their diner on Sundays but I didn't want to go there anyway. We needed somewhere with more privacy. Andy did know of another local restaurant and we agreed to meet, the three of us, about nine-thirty. It wasn't far from the motel.

"I hope the third member of our trio won't feel left out," I remarked to George after hanging up.

"No secrets between us," George said piously. "She needs to go on to her family, but we'll keep her informed."

"You'll have to be the one to tell her. I won't see her tomorrow."

George felt he was up to the task. There was a good breakfast served by the hotel in their lobby in the morning and he would escort Anne, explaining to her what had transpired after she had gone to bed. There was no doubt George was also capable of having a little breakfast with Anne and eating again in mid morning.

"George," I said, "I've done most of the talking tonight. Have you shared everything your contact told you about Douglas White's prison time? Did that guy give you dates, the date Douglas arrived to begin his sentence and the day he left?"

In fact he had. Douglas had arrived at the state penitentiary in Waupun, Wisconsin, on January 16th, and left that facility on April 26th.

I was incredulous. "That's about three months ago!"

George agreed with my arithmetic. "But as you told us," he reminded, "he's sent word to his family since then. Well," he amended, "you said one letter in April so that could have been before he left. But that other one is recent."

I sat down again, crossed my legs and thought. There was something going on here, something very fishy.

"You've got an interesting look on your face," George noted after a bit. He had spread his frame out onto the couch. With his legs stretched out and his hands clasped behind his head, he had been watching me.

"If it's the last thing I do," I said brashly, "I'm going to get to the bottom of this. If that guy is alive, or even if he's dead, we are going to get to the bottom of this."

With that pronouncement I got up and left to go back to the Porter White residence.

****

Port and Cora were in bed when I returned to their home. Before going up to the guestroom I pulled out my handy phone card, which still had four hundred minutes on it, and called my children from the phone in the kitchen. Janelle didn't answer, which was no surprise. It was an hour later in Massachusetts, but it was Saturday night. She might be out with Robert, or she might not feel like answering the telephone. My daughter had these moods sometimes. I left a cheery message telling her I was still out of town and would call her again when I got home.

My son and his family were home. Joel was in bed but awake. As children sometimes do he had broken his routine, which was asleep by nine, and heard the phone ring. When he heard my son's "Hey Mom," he hopped out of bed begging to speak with me. His wish was granted with a reminder it was way past the time he was supposed to be asleep, and he must promise to go right back to bed and no further monkey business after we concluded our conversation. He promised.

"Hey there, Gram'ma," he greeted happily. "How are you doing?"

Assured I was doing well but of course missing him, I asked Joel what he had been up to.

That led to a ten-minute dialogue. Joel is not shy over the wire. It was fun to listen to his running explanation of life since we had seen each other on Wednesday. I asked questions at intervals to keep him going. Finally he ran out of steam. He asked when I was taking the airplane back so he could go to the airport again. I told him I wasn't sure about that, he would find out later. Accepting this answer he sent me a noisy smooch over the wire and gave the receiver back to Everett. In the background Judy's maternal clucking could be heard ushering him back to bed.

It would have been impossible not to tell my son something of what had been going on, but in line with my decision not to spread the word about Douglas' incarceration, I told him only about my contacts. He wanted to know what conclusions I had drawn and I said it was still too early to say. The previous year when I had been involved in the death of my neighbor, Everett had given some good input. Although he expressed interest and asked some pertinent questions about my current activities, this time he did not commit himself.

"It's all pretty weird," was all he had to say in summation.

"I'll be back in touch in a couple days," I promised, and asked how Everett's current contracting job was going.

He said a cautious all right and the slight hesitation in his voice was not lost on me, but I decided not to pursue it. Instead I asked how Judy was. Now there was no hesitation; she was doing great.

"She wants you to know she's enjoyed using your car," he added. "We hope you don't mind."

"Of course not. She was supposed to." Everett and Judy's second vehicle was, as the proverbial saying goes, on its last legs.

"She's registered to take a couple of classes again in September," he contributed, "and she's been asked to be relief hostess twice a week at Margo's."

Margo's was a posh restaurant. It was popular for small wedding receptions and other elegant dining. Judy and Everett's wedding reception had been held there.

"Really?" I was interested. "Will she do it?"

"Probably."

I prodded for more details.

Judy was offered about twenty hours a week to relieve the other hostess, who was tired of working every day. Grandma Liz would care for Joel of course, when Everett was unavailable himself. At times like these I wished I lived closer so I could assist in the baby-sitting department. But overall, I had to admit keeping a little distance between us was the wiser course. The way things were now they were happy to see me coming when it was time to visit. My house was also an occasional oasis when Judy needed some space from her side of the family.

Judy was lying down with Joel so he would settle, so I passed on conversing with her this time and ended my chat with Everett on an upbeat note. I was glad my son could see it would do Judy no harm to have a job, especially one where she didn't need to leave Joel in full time day care. He didn't say so, but there was no doubt they could use the extra income.

The weather had been warm and humid all day. I felt gritty and my hair needed washing. Fatigue was setting in. Tonight I took a shower rather than lounging in the tub and shortly after welcomed my guest room bed. I slept like the dead for over seven hours.

Chapter Fourteen

After pressing some clothes and fixing my hair, I impulsively went downstairs to have coffee with the senior Whites, still in my bathrobe but very presentable. They seemed pleased to see me. Porter pulled back a chair for me to sit on as Cora poured and handed me a cup of coffee. I declined the breakfast they offered explaining I had a breakfast commitment. If they were curious as to with whom they both stifled it.

Cora played the hostess for a bit, asking if I was comfortable, needed fresh towels, etc. After being reassured on all points there were a few moments of pleasant silence, the only sound being Cora and Porter munching toast and eating oatmeal. Watching them, I made another spontaneous decision.

"Your hospitality is superb," I announced. "I have enjoyed staying here, but tonight I'm going out of town and I'm not sure when I'll get back. It would be better if I packed my things and took them with me so I can find lodging more locally if it gets late."

They looked at me, then at each other. It was obvious what they were thinking about.

"I do have some ideas," I said cautiously. "Until I know more, I don't want to say anything except I have a strong hunch all of this can be explained and will be, soon."

"That would be nice," Porter said laconically. "I'm getting too old for all of this mysterious stuff."

****

As it turned out, Miss Carey was very reluctant to leave us for her cousins when she found out George and I had a meeting with Andy Weller. But she was expected and George urged her to go ahead with her plans, and to try to make contact with the Farmers, the elderly couple Douglas and Ingrid had known so well. He swore a Boy Scout oath to keep her totally informed as to what we were up to until she could join us on Tuesday morning. Right on schedule Anne was delivered to her destination and George was back at the motel before I showed up.

George and I went to the busy restaurant together. I left my rental car in the motel parking lot and rode with him in his truck. Andy Weller had already claimed a booth; we made our way over where he greeted me with a pleasant hello and held out his hand to George saying simply, "Andy Weller."

George held out his own hand and responded in kind, saving me the need to make any introduction. George waited for me to slide in first, both of us facing Andy. I glanced from one to the other to catch them eyeing each other, their faces impassive as they waited to form impressions.

"I haven't placed my order yet," Andy said politely. "The buffet is good if you're hungry."

I was hungry, but not that hungry. A waitress appeared promptly to take our drink orders and until she returned, I tried to think of something to say in the way of small talk. George saved me the trouble by asking Andy how the local fishing was. Although Andy admitted he didn't like fishing as much as hunting, he was still able to provide enough information to fill the time and let me peruse the menu. When the waitress returned both men ordered the buffet. While they filled their plates I considered whether I should put all three of our meals on my expense account with the Whites. I was still undecided when they returned. Their food looked good, there was just too much of it.

It wasn't difficult to discuss our plans without the whole dining room knowing about it. There was no table to our right and a noisy family of eight, complete with a toddler and two individuals who chattered and talked almost non-stop, occupied

128

the large booth to the left. Their voices did not override our ability to hear each other so it was a good cover.

After my order came Andy wasted no time.

"So you think it's worth your while going back to the scene of the crime," he commented as he smeared jam on his toast.

"I don't know," I admitted. "It's been a long time, but it's all I can think of."

"It's been over a year since the fight," Andy rejoined, "but Doug went back up north a few times after that."

I was surprised and let it show. "You astound me. One would think he wouldn't want to go anywhere near after that mess."

"He didn't go back to the Dug Out," Andy clarified, "but I know he went to Griff's again and a couple of other spots."

My initial reaction was disappointment in Douglas. Hadn't he learned not to look for comfort in all the wrong places?

"Griff's isn't just a bar. It has a grill too, and good food." Andy went on. "I went to court with him the first time and we stopped on the way back to eat. Doug tied one on a time or two right after what happened, but after that he stopped his heavy boozing."

"You're sure about that?" I pressed.

"Sure," Andy was firm. He stopped to eat for a moment, but he wasn't through. "He didn't tell me what changed, but something did. I've always thought it was that punch, but last night I got to thinking it all through again and now I wonder."

"Are you saying you don't think it was the accident itself?" My fork stopped halfway on its journey back to my plate.

"Oh I think that had something to do with it all right," Andy clarified. "But a few weeks after, maybe a year ago, he seemed to stop worrying about the whole thing. It was like night and day. Before that, from the time of Ingrid's death on, there was a tense, wired feeling you got just being around him. All of a sudden that changed. The only worry he had or talked about was keeping the whole thing quiet for a while for the sake of his family."

"Seems to me if a man knows he could lose his freedom that could change the way he looks at things." George weighed in for the first time on the subject.

"That's what I thought too," Andy concurred, "but maybe there was more to it."

After eating we discussed the evening ahead. We decided to meet about seven in George's room and all ride together. I wondered what a middle-aged lady wore when she went bar hopping, but decided it was pointless to ask these two. Andy suggested we all save our supper appetites because eating would give us an excuse for spending time at one of our stops. Without saying so he was implying we wouldn't have to order as much to drink, which implied he wondered if I was used to indulging and should be taking it easy. I doubted he had that concern about George. There seems to be a secret code among men about these things. I knew George drank very little but would have no problem handling a few beers. If my escorts had more to drink than was good for them, I could be the designated driver. No bartender would be surprised if I ordered a soft drink.

"Would it be possible for you to bring Douglas' jeep tonight?" I asked Andy. "Is there room for all of us? I'd be glad to pay for the gas."

I wasn't sure if he thought it was a dumb idea or was offended that I offered to pay for his fuel, but he gave me a rather incredulous look. "We'll all fit but why take the jeep?"

"Did he use it when he took his trips up there?" I returned.

"Yes," he admitted, "sometimes."

"That sort of vehicle stands out. Someone might remember it."

Again Andy's look spoke volumes. It said something like, I've gotten myself started on this thing and what options do I have but to go along with this dizzy dame? Glancing at George I caught the look of amusement on his face before he lowered his head to his coffee cup.

George was left to himself for the rest of the day but he didn't seem to mind too much. I asked him who was watching his pets and he said the neighbors, the same ones who were still counting on a fish fry sometime before the summer ended. He asked me what I was going to be doing, and I told him the only thing I was sure about was contacting Douglas' brother Marty and his wife, maybe mid-afternoon. I also told him I was packing my things and I would bring everything with me when I came back.

"You want me to reserve you a room here?" he offered.

"No," I decided. "I think I'll wait and see what we find out

130

tonight before I decide where to stay."

"That could be late. What if you can't find anything by then?"

I couldn't help it. "Then I could stay in your room," I quipped, flashing him a smile, "and you could sleep in your pick-up bed."

He gave me a look just like the one Andy had given me twenty minutes earlier.

"Just teasing. You have a pullout couch that would be fine for me."

Heading back to the Whites, I passed a small church just beginning their late morning service. I turned around, went back, and slipped into a seat in a rear pew. Since many of the others attending were also dressed in summer casual I did not feel out of place.

It was a very traditional service, right down to the singing of the doxology and the children's mini sermon before they were dismissed for their crafts and lesson in the basement. I sang along with the hymns and during both the prayer time and the sermon prayed my own prayers of requests and thanksgiving. During the benediction I slipped out, smiling my thanks to the usher at the door. He smiled back, not seeming to mind the service gatecrasher. Apparently anyone was welcome if they put a bill in the collection plate and behaved themselves. I had done both.

The only thing open on Sunday morning in the little town where the White's lived was the gas station and convenience store. They could have rolled up the sidewalks, except they were being used by bicycles, tricycles, strollers and owners walking their pets. I mentioned this to Cora when I walked into her kitchen. She smiled.

"A lot of people around here still spend Sunday with their families. Some of the people I know still cook a big Sunday dinner almost every week and their kids show up to eat it."

I remembered that tradition with fond nostalgia. Until I was twelve my family often ate Sunday dinner at my paternal grandparent's house.

"Do you miss that?" I asked Cora, pulling out a chair and making myself at home at her kitchen table.

"Not usually," she admitted. "Once in awhile Janice and her

family will still come for dinner, but that's planned in advance. I'm happy not doing it every week, especially when it's hot. The last time they came we barbequed chicken outside on the grill. That was nice."

As we talked she was making sandwiches, just two of them, so I knew there would be no company for lunch today.

"I don't suppose I could interest you in a sandwich," she said perfunctorily, already expecting me to say no.

"What kind do you have?" I couldn't see into the two small bowls she had on the counter.

"Tuna or chicken salad, rye or sourdough bread, American or Cheddar cheese."

"If you let me set the table I'll take half a chicken salad, no cheese, rye bread."

"Agreed. But we're using paper plates."

"Better and better," I beamed. "Plastic utensils or place ware?"

Since we only needed knives we decided plastic, but we used glassware for our iced tea.

Sitting at the table with Porter and Cora was giving them an opportunity to ask me about my inquiry. They were entitled to ask and if they did I would cope. I couldn't begin to imagine how I would feel if my son had done what Douglas did, just stepping out of life without any explanation. Considering that led me to another thought: I had a mother and she was roughly the same age as these two. How would she feel if this happened to her?

My mother and I love each other but we also irritate each other. She is closer to my sister both emotionally and in proximity. My sister persuaded my mother to move out to Arizona to be nearby after my father died. Although we never said so, I was relieved and clearly so were my brothers. Come to think of it, if either one of my brothers did a Douglas White I was sure my mother would be raising holy cane to find out what was going on. She would personally put posters up in every post office she could find. My sister would never think of doing such a thing so if she disappeared we might as well consider it a homicide. And if yours truly did it, as far as my mater was concerned it was probably a stunt to cause her personal annoyance.

The atmosphere was thick with the desire to ask questions but

Cora and Port held back. They would glance at each other, then glance at me, then down at their plates. Port made a comment about the weather. Cora mentioned one of their grandchildren was having a birthday on Tuesday. I was the one who finally broached the subject.

"I have been talking to Andy Weller," I said carefully. "He told me something rather interesting."

They both perked up and Cora asked what that was before her spouse could swallow his bite fast enough to beat her to it.

"He says that last year, maybe late summer, there was a point where your son suddenly seemed different. He says he's been considering it since I came around to ask questions." I repeated what Andy had told us at breakfast, that a tense, high-strung Douglas had changed to a more serene one.

As I have said before, over fifty years of marriage must do that to a couple. By some silent communication they usually seemed to know what each other is thinking, and if one of them should say something. Cora did vary this routine just a little this time. After she exchanged glances with her husband, she looked at her hands resting on the table and gave the matter some thought. Porter said nothing, knowing she would answer me.

"We were away last summer for over a month. We left in mid-July to visit our son, Paul, then we went on to visit friends in Kansas and Colorado. When we got back I don't think we saw Douglas for almost a week more. I remember that because Janice's family was vacationing in northern Michigan and when he wasn't home I thought he had gone up, too."

But he hadn't?" I prompted.

"No," Cora said slowly, "both of them called us shortly after we got home. Douglas was at his country place, and said he was busy taking care of things there but that he would be over in a few days, which he was."

"So did either one of you notice a big change in him?" I asked, now doing the looking from one to the other.

"I would say," Porter said carefully, "that you could be right. As I think back it could be this was when I thought he was feeling better. You know, not so broken up anymore. This was when he told us he was selling out to Marty. We told you about that."

"Port is right," Cora said decisively. "He was doing better

after those weeks we were away. I guess we expected it would come, eventually, and accepted it. Not that he wasn't quiet and withdrawn sometimes,"she added, "but there was a change for the better."

"How often did you see him after your vacation?"

Cora was probably better at remembering such details. "We usually saw him every week at least for a short visit. If he didn't come by he would call us."

Now Porter just couldn't stand it. "Are you getting anywhere?" He didn't look at Cora first.

"Maybe," I said cautiously. "That's why I have to leave today. I do believe he is alive and will come home. I have no idea when, and there are a lot of missing details."

For the first time in my presence there were tears welling up in Cora's eyes. That was too much for her spouse. He lowered his head and clutched his drink glass. I suspected his eyes weren't dry, either.

I got up and put my disposable plate in the trashcan and my glass in the sink. Doing private snooping should be like nursing. One should maintain a certain level of detachment. That doesn't always work in my chosen profession and it wasn't going to be entirely true now.

Cora found a tissue in her pocket and blew her nose. Porter wiped his on the back of his hand. Cora slapped his wrist and handed him the tissue.

"I called your son Marty's home yesterday," I said as this emotional moment subsided. "I spoke to their daughter who suggested I try again this afternoon. Do you want to talk to them after I do?"

In her normal tone of voice Cora said they would and told me to feel free to use the extension in the sitting room whenever I was ready. The two of them would be in the backyard and I should give them a holler when it was their turn.

Marty and Karen White were at home. Marty answered the phone in a voice that was very similar to his brother David's, so I immediately knew who was on the line. He was very courteous and told me they had been expecting my call.

"How are you getting on, Mrs. Nimitz?" he asked.

"I have made some headway," I admitted, "But I don't want

to say too much yet. I certainly don't know where your brother is at the moment."

"How can Karen and I help you?" He sounded like he wanted to assist in anyway possible. So far I liked all of the White family pretty well.

"Tell me about the last few times you spoke with your brother before he went away," I said briskly. "What did you talk about, what were your impressions about how he was coping, his mental health, things like that. Since he's been away so long you and your wife have probably considered this before."

Marty obliged. He told me he had come to Wisconsin briefly in August to finalize the buying out of his brother's share of the business. He told me - if I did not know this already - they specialized in parts for foreign cars, supplying them to dealers and to private individuals. After the buyout Marty moved all of the business to his base of operations in Grand Rapids. He and Karen had come to Ingrid's funeral, the only other time he had seen his brother within the past two years. Most of their communication was done over the phone or by e-mail.

"My job was primarily in the sales end of the operation," Marty explained to me patiently. "Doug had to educate on what he handled, which included a lot of communication with buyers, but we didn't need to see each other to do that."

"Didn't your brother have another partner at one time?"

"Todd Denzil, yes," Marty concurred. "Let's see, it's over four years ago now. Todd was tired of all the hours and wanted to take a job offer he had gotten that would give him a regular lifestyle. That's when Doug brought me on. I agreed to do it if I could stay in Grand Rapids and we opened an office here at that time."

"How much of a staff did Douglas keep here?" I was asking questions as they came to me, not at all sure where I was going.

"Until we consolidated everything, I think five or six," Marty said after brief consideration. "I had to hire more people last summer of course, and two of Doug's staff moved here to join us."

"When it comes to business," I pressed, "it sounds like your brother was able to keep his mind on things even after he lost his wife. Is that true?"

"Yes," Marty said, "I would agree with that. Work can be tonic you know."

I did know, but that was beside the point. "Were you surprised when he wanted to sell?"

Marty had been surprised. He had resisted at first, questioning the wisdom of his brother's decision. For himself he was excited about the prospect and, although they had never talked about it, Douglas seemed to know Marty would be willing to buy. It was for Douglas' sake, Marty told me, that he hesitated.

"Doug is a good businessman and he likes anything with a motor in it. He always enjoyed what he did. I wasn't expecting him to let it go."

I asked if Douglas had given him any explanation.

"He said he needed to start over," Marty said simply. "That's about all he would say about it. 'I think it's time to move on, Marty, and start over,' was what he said whenever I asked. When I asked him what he planned to do he would say he hadn't decided yet. That's all I could get out of him."

"Are you concerned about this long absence of his?"

"Yes," he replied slowly, "I'm beginning to be. That's why I agreed with David to have you look into it."

"How about your wife?"

There was a soft chuckle on the other end of the line. "She's been wondering about him for longer than I have. It's her maternal instinct. We have four children, Mrs. Nimitz, but they're growing up."

I asked Marty if he thought his brother was doing better emotionally by August when the business transaction took place. His impression was, yes.

"Is there anything else, anything at all, you think might help?" I pressed.

Regretfully he couldn't. Karen was waiting her turn to speak with me. Marty wished me well.

Karen had that the kind of clear singsong voice that makes a woman sound eternally young. I grinned when I heard it. A friend of mine has a voice like that and she always complains she is never taken seriously over the phone because everyone thinks they are talking to an adolescent. When she orders pizza the person on the other end of the line wants to speak to her mother.

"I am the mother!" my friend has said more than once, outraged. Hearing her voice made me really curious about what Karen White looked like. I would ask Cora.

Karen started right in, not waiting for me to ask questions.

"I am so glad someone is finally doing something about this," she informed me tersely. "Doug has been away far too long."

"The notes he sent haven't reassured you then," I suggested.

"Pooh!" she scoffed. "Little notes that didn't say anything over all this time. Douglas didn't like to travel without Ingrid and here he goes off like some old hippie traveling the countryside or something? It never made sense."

My ears perked up. "No one has said that. Douglas didn't like traveling?"

"Not without Ingrid," she repeated. "He had to take business trips once in awhile when she couldn't go with him and he always hated it. When they traveled together that was different."

"It could be different now," I offered, "having been alone for over a year as he has."

Karen wasn't buying it. "That's what Marty says," she sniffed. "But I suggested it once, maybe three months after the funeral. Wisconsin is dreary in March anyway, almost as bad as it is here, and I told Doug he should go somewhere warm and cheerful for a couple of weeks. He knows people all over who would be glad to have him so he wouldn't have to stay in hotels by himself. He told me it would be too depressing. Of course he meant too depressing to go without Ingrid."

Privately I thought a few more months and circumstances could have changed her brother-in-law's mind, but I didn't offer that to Karen.

"What else?" I urged. "What else worries you about this?"

The clear little soprano voice faltered and then went on in a tone filled with concern. "This isn't like him. Douglas was always such a gentleman. He never would do anything deliberately to hurt the people who care for him. How could he worry his family like this, especially Porter and Cora? He and David were always close and even David doesn't have a clue?"

I wanted one more opinion from this forthright lady.

"Mrs. White, do you think it's possible he went to visit his children in California? Do you think it's worth my time to contact them?"

She emphatically said no on both counts.

Chapter Fifteen

While Cora and Porter took turns catching up on the news with their second son and his family, I went upstairs. Since it was likely one of the things they would talk about would include me it seemed prudent to remove myself from the scene.

I wandered aimlessly about the guestroom and over to the window to look outdoors. It wouldn't take me long to pack and there was plenty of time before I needed to be at the hotel to meet George and Andy. My window overlooked the backyard and beyond. There was a change in the weather coming and a cool afternoon breeze was whipping up, pushing in some clouds. The trees rustled, giving a little competition to the chirping of the many resident birds. Not in the best frame of mind to appreciate the peaceful scene I turned away, pulled the list of contacts out of my bag, and sat down to scrutinize it. The list was already tattered from being looked at so often. Then something hit me. I scrambled for my notebook and looked at what I had written down while going through Douglas White's mail.

The information had been germinating in the back of my mind but now it came to the forefront. The day I had been to Douglas and Ingrid's home there had been no paperwork lying about in the office. Everything must have been locked away in the file cabinet. All I had access to were seven months of banking and credit card statements. From these records I knew a large sum of cash had been withdrawn in December, and before July there had been two transfers of cash from a checking account to a credit card account. In May a credit card transaction had moved the April amount to another unknown account. The July statement hadn't come through as yet; it was too soon, so I didn't know if the June transfer of funds had gone the same way. Unless someone else was using his credit card, Douglas was shuffling his money around. The questions were not only where and why, but what had he done with a large amount of cash when he was going to prison?

I could think of only one thing to do before meeting George and Andy Weller. It was Sunday afternoon but police stations never close. I slipped out of the house and back to the convenience store. One of the counter attendants told me the sheriff's department had the greater jurisdiction in this little town, and the other one happened to know their headquarters was in Waupaca. They had a phone book in reasonably good condition, and under the addresses for county services I found the physical address. Since the employees were so helpful, I put some gas in my car and bought a bottle of water.

It was a good twenty-minute drive but not hard to find the building. I had been told by the chattier of the two clerks at the convenience store the county was large and there were hundreds of miles to cover in its jurisdiction. That was all right since it seemed to me more likely I would find someone who would be available to talk to me.

As expected the place was essentially deserted. As hoped there was an officer at the front desk to attend to anyone who had nothing better to do than show up on a Sunday afternoon.

"I know it's the weekend," I apologized when the middle-aged man in uniform asked if he could help me. His badge identified him as a deputy. His wide girth hinted of long hours spent behind a desk or in a cruiser instead of being physically active. "But I wondered if there is anyone who could speak to me about a missing person report that was filed here."

There was a computer at hand. Politely he asked me who that missing person might be and I told him. It was almost a given he would pull up the file, scrutinize it, and then ask me what my interest was. Sure enough. I had my script ready for this part.

"I'm a friend of the family," I said, which was loosely true,

"If you can't tell me how the investigation is going, could I speak to the officer on duty today? I might have some information he or she could use."

We eyed each other. I had combed my hair, freshened my makeup, and looked completely respectable in my slacks, blouse and sandals.

"Normally," the deputy said, "there isn't a detective here on the weekend, just someone on call. As it happens one of our men is here writing up a report. I'll ask if he'll see you."

That almost didn't happen. When the deputy, whose name on his badge said Drier, made the call, there was a bit of a discussion. I couldn't hear it because I was asked to take a seat and a see through panel was pulled shut in front of the desk before the call took place. Finally the conversation between the two of them ended and Drier opened the panel.

"Could you come back tomorrow? We don't usually interview people for ongoing investigations on Sunday unless it's an emergency."

I got up and went back to the window. "What is the name of your detective?" I asked sweetly.

"Detective Vrieze, ma'am."

I leaned over a little, but not so much as to prevent the deputy from shutting the window if he felt the need. I didn't want to appear hostile. "Deputy Drier, please tell Detective Vrieze I was sent up here by Douglas White's brother, David, who is himself a law enforcement detective. Tell him also if you will, that I know where Douglas White was from mid-January until mid-April of this year."

He wavered for a few seconds as he tried to decide whether to do as I asked or tell me to leave. I kept my gaze on his face with what was supposed to be an earnest but non-threatening look. He decided it was worth another call to Detective Vrieze. This time the window stayed open and I stayed put.

He relayed the information as I had given it to him. After a ten second pause he said, "right," and hung up. "He'll be with you in a few minutes, ma'am. If you could take a seat?"

I thanked him and complied. The deputy realized he had not asked for my name having referred to me as "a lady," or "ma'am," and rectified that omission as I settled into a brown vinyl chair. There was no one else about and for the next ten minutes it was silent in the lobby except for the phone ringing twice. I hoped it wouldn't be a long wait. It was mid-afternoon and I didn't want to be late for my appointment with George and Andy Weller. If the detective was miffed by my persistence or just plain busy he might let me wait awhile.

But exactly twelve minutes after I sat down and just as I was considering which of the outdated magazines to look at, a door opened to the inner sanctum located behind the lobby desk and my name was called.

"Mrs. Nimitz?"

The man standing there holding the door open and looking in my direction was also in uniform. He was taller and younger than the deputy, perhaps forty.

I stood up and walked toward him. He motioned for me to precede him and directed me down a quiet hallway to an open door on the right, the only door open. I heard voices farther down the hall.

Detective Vrieze indicated I should take one of the two chairs in front of his desk, sat down, and asked how he could help me.

He had a computer on his desk which was facing away from me but which I suspected had information on Douglas White pulled up on the screen. There was a manila envelope sitting open on the desk, but too far away for me to see what was written on it. The desk was large. The only other things on it were a large white coffee cup full of pens and pencils, another coffee cup that proclaimed the detective as one of the world's best dads, and a large pad of blank legal paper. Either the detective was finished writing his report or he had temporarily cleared his other paperwork away.

"Detective," I began, "I live in the same community as Douglas White's brother, David. As I told your deputy and as you probably already know, he is a law enforcement officer in Indiana. As you also may know if you were looking at the file, David White made inquiries this spring about his brother after the family had not heard from him in several months. Last month he made an official request for a statewide lookout for his vehicle."

I stopped and gave the man across the desk an expectant look. He responded by answering, "I am aware of all this."

I chose my words carefully. "Since coming up here, I've learned the sheriff's department knows about the situation that came about in Douglas White's life last year, and where he was when his brother began inquiries. The situation may have taken place outside of your jurisdiction, but you have record of it. You didn't give that information to Douglas White's brother, David."

The man looked across his desk at me, his face an expressionless mask. "And what specific information do you have on this matter, Mrs. Nimitz?" he asked politely.

I chose not to give him my source. "Apparently someone with authority gave instructions that Douglas White's location for over three months was to be kept confidential unless there was authorized approval to release it. Douglas' brother made some phone calls unofficially so it wasn't necessary to tell him where his brother had been."

There was no response. I went on. "In June when David made an official and personal request for the sheriff's department, or any law enforcement agency for that matter, to begin to consider his brother a missing person, you didn't tell him then either. Of course it wouldn't have occurred to him that you knew; I'm referring to the department you represent, of course. And by the time official inquiry was made he had been released from prison and you had no knowledge of his whereabouts. Now he really is missing."

Detective Vrieze did not confirm or deny one word of what I said. He leaned back in his chair and drummed his fingers lightly on the desk.

"Mrs. Nimitz," he said carefully, "if what you say is true anyone can verify if Mr. White was in detention. It is not privileged information. If the department did not volunteer that information there can be several reasons for it. As far as his brother's request, I can say you are correct. David White has officially informed us his brother has not been heard from except for two brief letters to his parents, for over six months. Douglas White is a well-known and respected member of a local community and this matter is receiving attention. The state police have also been notified."

"I know you don't have to tell me and probably won't," I returned, "but I wonder how much longer this man has to be a missing person until you fill his family in on what you know."

He gave me a quizzical look. "You could tell them," he offered, still deadpan.

"I could, but right now I have my own reasons to wait."

He leaned forward, rested his arms on his desk next to the computer and said, "Just how can I help you?" He almost managed to keep the exasperation out of his voice.

"I don't think you can help me," I said candidly. "I have no official status and could be anyone walking in here. But I wanted to let you know that Douglas White probably really is a missing person. I have one small shred of evidence he is alive somewhere but no one I've talked to knows where that is."

"It's a big country, Mrs. Nimitz," Detective Vrieze reminded me. "He could be almost anywhere."

"That's true enough. But I am almost certain he hasn't gone that far. My reasons are pretty vague so I won't bore you with them. I know you will record my visit and what I've said. If the sheriff's department or anyone else is seriously keeping an eye out for Douglas White, you might want to know this one thing; eight days ago Douglas White's parents heard from Douglas a third time. It said very little but was specific enough to convince them he wrote it. The envelope had a Chicago postmark just like the other two."

This time there was some interest registering on the detective's face. "If Mr. White has been heard from again," he said, "he can hardly be considered a missing person. He isn't considered one yet. His brother told us there has been no concrete information from his brother in over six months and asked us to be on the lookout for his vehicle."

"I wondered if there was a difference," I said dryly, as I came to my feet. "You're a busy man and I won't take anymore of your time. It seemed expedient to touch bases with someone here."

The sheriff's officer also stood up. "Mrs. Nimitz, if you come across anything concerning Mr. White that should receive the attention of law enforcement, I hope you know better than to conceal it or try to handle it yourself."

"Douglas' brother, David, has already cautioned me," I assured him. "He trusted my judgment and I don't want to disappoint him."

144

Detective Vrieze didn't look like he had that confidence in me but said nothing, merely escorting me back out to the waiting area and wishing me a good day.

****

You would have thought I was going to Siberia or at the very least back to Indiana. Maybe they thought I would fall into the same abyss their oldest son seemed to have found. Both Cora and Porter had very solemn faces as Porter carried my two pieces of luggage downstairs and out to my car. Cora trailed behind as Port put the suitcases in the trunk.

"Don't look so sad!" I commanded, impulsively giving them both a hug. "I'll see you both soon." I didn't add although I wanted to, I hoped to have good news. There was no promise of that after all.

"Come back and stay anytime," Cora said quietly, smiling a little as she accepted my hug and gave one in return. She added, "No matter what happens. We appreciate what you're trying to do."

Now I was the one almost crying. Porter's hug was a strong one from a man who looked almost frail. He nodded without saying anything, which was his way of agreeing with Cora.

"It's possible Douglas could come home any minute," I reminded them. "He did say so in that last note. I'll call you tomorrow sometime, probably in the morning."

They stood in the front yard and watched me drive away.

Chapter Sixteen

When I arrived at the hotel where George was staying it was six-thirty. I was a little early but Andy was already there. He had come in Douglas' jeep.

"Just as well we're all here," he said without preliminaries as soon as George opened the door to his room in answer to my knock and we were all inside. "It's about a forty-five minute drive to Griff's. I thought we could start there with something to eat."

George and I said that was fine with us and without further ado we went out to the jeep. They waited for me to properly lock up the Beretta. George said he had paid for his room for another night and both of our vehicles should be fine parked where they were. Both men seemed to take it for granted I would sit in the back and they would sit in the front. For a second I wanted to argue the point, but I squelched it. Andy would drive of course, and it would be awkward for George to pack his six foot two frame into the rear seat.

Although this jaunt has been my idea, Andy was the one on familiar territory. He started to talk just minutes after we were on the road and I leaned forward between the front seats to be able to hear everything he was saying. He inclined his head slightly to the right, glancing at both George and I from time to time to make sure we were listening.

"Griff's is a pretty decent sports bar and has good food so I think they'll be busy tonight. The locals and the tourists go there.

If we see anybody who's an acquaintance of Doug's or mine they'll probably say hello. If people have met you before they're pretty friendly." He took his eyes from the road for a second to glance at me specifically. "Did you want to go to all of the places Doug hung out?"

"How many are there?"

Andy considered. "I know of five he's been to, but some not that often, and one isn't anywhere near where we're going. I don't think he'd been back there for a long time."

"Then it isn't practical to try to the place that's off the beaten path tonight," I decided. "If need be that will come later. Do you think we have time for the other four?" You are including The Dug Out?"

"Yeah, I figured you'd want to go there," Andy's said.

"We have to," I said firmly. "I'm hoping those creeps who instigated the fight that night will be there, too."

George and Andy looked both surprised and amused.

"May I ask what good that would do?" George asked the question.

"It would be helpful to know if they're still holding a grudge against Douglas."

"Oh," George mused, "rather like a Hatfield and McCoy kind of thing?"

"Something like that. They sound like the type. If they are, would they be satisfied with the sentence Douglas got?"

"What are you planning to do?" Andy asked. "Walk up to one of the Keeler brothers and ask him?"

"Their name is Keeler? I didn't know that. But to answer your question, no, probably not. There are more subtle ways to go about it."

Andy opened his mouth, and then closed it again. No doubt he was about to ask me what subtle way I had in mind, then decided not to. I didn't enlighten him because I wasn't sure myself. That was a bridge to cross when we got there.

"If we happen to find other people who know about what happened," I went on instead, "or maybe even someone who was there that night, if they recognize you they might want to talk about it. That's what people in bars do don't they? Talk a lot?"

"That's one of the things," George agreed.

There was a lapse in the conversation with the sound of the jeep engine making the only noise as Andy drove. The traffic on the two-lane road was light.

"Am I right in thinking you wonder if Douglas had another run in with the Keeler boys since he left jail?" Andy sounded skeptical. "I find it hard to believe Doug would come back up here to hang around."

I presented an idea. "It's always possible they found out when Douglas was getting out, and were waiting for him."

Andy frowned at me, then at George. "Is she always like this?" he asked George.

George shrugged. "It's worse when she's hunting."

"Make fun if you want to," I said, just a little indignant. "I notice you both volunteered to come along."

"Yeah," Andy had to admit. "I must be hard up to fill my time away from the garage." He grinned. "But I'm glad I came. Your friend here seems like a nice guy."

"I am," George agreed modestly."

Summer weather up north can be very unpredictable. Sometimes the temperatures never go very high and everyone will complain the summer passed them by that year. Other years there can be days of record heat with humidity to match. That night a cooler wind was blowing, as I had noticed from my guest room window that afternoon. I was wearing blue jeans, a long sleeved Henley, and brought along a light jacket, and my choice worked out well. I doubted summer campers dressed up very often and that proved to be true. George and Andy both wore jeans and casual shirts. We fit right in.

The place was packed. We stood at the entrance for ten minutes waiting for a table in the dining room. Loud raucous laughter was coming from the large bar to our left. I thought Douglas couldn't have come here for peace and quiet, but then he had a lot of that at home. I remembered that Dena Janascik said she had never heard of Griff's, but she was right, it was not in the same county.

"I don't suppose you'd be interested in seating in the bar?" the hostess asked hopefully.

"We wouldn't mind at all," I assured her without consulting my companions. We all knew we would be more likely to find someone who knew Douglas and Andy in the bar. I preferred a quieter atmosphere for eating, but this was business.

We were shown to a corner booth. Since whoever faced the wall couldn't see much, I knew it made sense for Andy to have a seat with the full view of the bar and beyond. He gallantly motioned for me to get in ahead of him so I had the same view. George took the other side, which gave him a side view of the end of the bar and a frontal view of a number of copies of prints of John Wayne movies.

We were all hungry. The men both ordered barbequed ribs and I decided to try the grilled trout that was advertised as a local specialty. My mouth was salivating. The smells coming from the kitchen and surrounding tables were tantalizing. As for beverage Andy ordered the brew on tap, George coffee, and I asked for water, deciding to wait on anything stronger as this could be a long night, with three stops to go. No one would think it odd to come here just to eat. I asked Andy if he recognized either one of the bartenders and he said no. Apparently the regular staff had the night off.

The food was good and since it was too noisy to converse without almost yelling we made small talk and enjoyed our meal, taking our time. Andy's eye often surveyed the bar and entryway. Once he spotted a former customer of his but the man didn't see us, and since he wasn't what we were looking for Andy didn't draw his attention. The man disappeared into the dining room with his three companions. After finishing our food we dawdled. Andy and I both ordered coffee and George took a refill. Between eight-thirty and nine one of two men who sauntered up to the bar nodded at Andy and gave him a small wave.

"Hey dude, it's been awhile," he called loudly.

"Any prospect with him?" I murmured, close enough to Andy's right ear that he could hear me.

"Maybe," he allowed, acknowledging the greeting with a friendly salute and a "How's it goin' Zeke?"

George turned to take a look and Zeke gave us all a friendly grin. His companion showed mild interest then turned back to order his drink. Zeke said a couple of words to the bartender and to his friend before walking over to our booth. His weathered face and muscular arms told the story of outdoor living, and his rotund

149

belly of a liking for beer. He held out his hand and Andy shook it. He nodded at George and myself but did not ask for an introduction.

Zeke and Andy jawed for a moment about their prospective lines of work. Zeke logged, trapped and did fishing tours. Business was fair. Our visitor glanced over to where his beer was sitting on the bar and his friend was deep in conversation with someone else.

"Bring your brew and visit for a few minutes?" Andy suggested lightly. "If your friend doesn't mind?"

The local man decided he would. George pushed over to give him a place to sit. There was an ashtray on the table and after asking my permission, very gentlemanly I thought, both George and Zeke lit up a cigarette.

My heart actually skipped a beat as Zeke said, "Haven't seen your pal Doug for a while, either."

I sipped my coffee and sat back to be a casual but alert observer.

"Neither have I," Andy admitted, just as casual. "He left town for awhile. I guess you may have heard he had some trouble up here last year."

"Yeah," Zeke said, "I heard. Some of those Keelers are always trouble."

George and I exchanged glances. Zeke didn't notice.

Andy nodded his agreement and asked, "You had any run-ins with them?"

"No, thank god," was the sincere reply. "Anybody with any sense stays clear."

I was never one to stay quiet forever. "How many of these guys are there?"

Zeke leaned back in the booth, not averse to being the center of attention. "If you include two in-laws and three cousins and maybe three of the women who like to get into it whenever they can, probably a dozen."

"It must be hard to avoid all those people," I commented, impressed.

"They aren't as bad if they're not in the mood for boozing," he allowed. "And sometimes they keep to themselves when they do their drinking. They make a little hooch of their own, too."

150

"Would hooch be moonshine?" I asked politely.

Zeke nodded. "Hooch, moonshine, white lightening, take your pick. They keep the operation small and I hear you can only get it if they know you. I wouldn't trust the stuff myself."

I was wondering how to keep Zeke on the subject when George helped me out.

"I've been taking most of my fishing trips in Minnesota," he said. "I had no idea there was so much action up in this part of the country."

Zeke guffawed. "Yeah, fishing by day, bar brawls and illegal liquor at night. A wild crowd!"

"I don't believe it's all like that!" I protested. "The people in here all look normal to me."

"It's early yet," Zeke said, grinning at me specifically, but then he relented. "Naw, Andy here can tell you there's trouble to be had if that's what you want, but mostly it's respectable around here."

Andy was still deliberately nonchalant as he asked, "Was there much talk last spring after that fight Doug was involved in?"

Zeke leaned forward and rested his massive arms on the table. "Not so much, which is surprising. News travels fast in small towns up here, especially bad news. The Keelers usually let everybody in three counties know if they think they've gotten a raw deal about anything. One of the guys in the bar that night is a buddy of mine is how I know. But he didn't want to get dragged into court so he wasn't saying much out in the open. It was the talk for a few nights behind closed doors at the Dugout and a few other local places, but things died down pretty quick." Zeke paused a minute then added, "A couple of the Keelers were arrested for something else since the night of that fight. They weren't in jail long, got out on bail, I guess. I'm not sure what for, I've heard different stories."

Listening to Zeke I had an idea. Zeke wouldn't know that George and I knew all about what had happened at the Dug Out, or that we knew who Douglas White was. I leaned forward in supposed innocent curiosity and asked, looking from Andy next to me to Zeke who was straight across, "So who is Doug, and what happened anyway?"

George and Andy did well. They exchanged a quick look that

in no way gave away the game and Zeke willingly went on to give me the facts as he knew them. It didn't seem to occur to him that Andy might want to tell me, which of course he didn't.

"Andy here's friend was having a couple of friendly beers at a local spot oh, I guess it was about May, wasn't it?"

Andy nodded. "Early June to be more accurate."

"Anyway, it was just his rotten luck that a bunch of the Keelers, four or five from what I heard, showed up. They not only showed up, but showed up already liquored up. Doug got in their way. Sonny, that's the one who died, was a little twerp with a big mouth. Everybody who ever knew him said that. When he was drunk he was just as mouthy but meaner. The brothers usually kept him in line some but not always. My friend said Sonny asked Doug why he was in such a hurry to leave. Doug tried to ignore him which Sonny didn't like so he made some comment about maybe he had a woman waiting." Zeke took a swig of his beer and said pointedly to me, "He didn't say it like that but I am giving you the edited version."

I thanked him.

"Anyway, my pal says the guy saw red and just lost it. He was close enough to hear the whole thing. It happened so fast only a couple of people ever saw this guy Doug throw that punch. A few more saw Sunny fall back, hit a chair with his head, and hit the ground. Everybody was so surprised for a few seconds nothing happened. Then one of Sonny's brothers started cussing and went for Doug but two or three of the guys in there had their head on straight. Two of them, one my friend, grabbed his arms and another got in front of Doug so none of the other boys would have a clear go at him."

George whistled. "That's quite a story. Seems like a nice thing to do, standing up for a guy they hardly knew."

"Two reasons," Zeke declared. "First, the owner of the bar is a cousin to my pal. He put everything he had into that place and a brawl could have closed him down. The owner, Jerry, is a motorcycle dude, big hearted as they come. He was over the bar by that time and the Keelers were finding themselves shoved out the door when somebody realized Sonny was still in there passed out on the floor."

"What was the second reason?" Andy asked, which surprised

me. I thought he must have heard the story a hundred times.

"Nobody in there liked the Keelers that much, especially Sonny," Zeke said, his tone making it obvious we should have guessed. "A couple of the bigger boys picked him up and were carrying him outside when somebody noticed he didn't seem to be breathing."

"Oh no," I said, "You don't mean...."

Zeke nodded soberly. "Yep. Dead as a doornail. Jerry and your buddy Doug started the resuscitation thing on him and somebody called an ambulance but he was gone."

"From hitting his head on that chair?" guessed George.

"Guess so," Zeke surmised. "The word was at the bar a couple nights later was Sonny had some kind of aneurysm, I think that's how you say it. Some kind of weakness in a vessel in his head. They say you shouldn't speak bad about the dead, but if you ask a lot of people Sonny was sick in the head anyway."

I looked innocently at Andy. "How did your friend take it? What happened?"

Andy tried not to frown at me only partially succeeding. "He wasn't too happy," he said shortly. "It went to court but he got off pretty lightly."

"Glad to hear that," Zeke said heartily. "It sure was an accident."

"How did the bar owner make out?" George wanted to know. "Still in business?" I thought he was rather enjoying the game.

"It turned out okay," our narrator said. "Two days closed to investigate then the cops pulled out and let him re-open, no fines or anything."

I wanted to find out Zeke's perspective on one more thing. "And you said the relatives of the man who died didn't make as big a fuss as you thought they might?"

"Not as much as you might have thought," Zeke rubbed his chin. "They simmered down pretty fast. Maybe they didn't like Sonny that much either."

Zeke's observation on the response of the Keeler family to the death of one of their own by an impulsive punch did not line up with what Andy had told me the day before. The Keeler clan sounded like the get even type. Would they scream for the authorities to take action but do nothing themselves?

There was a lull. Zeke had finished talking. I had shown enough curiosity about the event and said no more. George, for whatever reason, asked Zeke if the local law was strict about drinking and driving. Zeke said so- so. His experience was they only stopped you if your driving was suspect.

"Sometimes I wonder if my truck doesn't know its way home the way my grand dad's horse used to!" he chortled, but then allowed he couldn't afford the stiff fines or to lose his license so it didn't happen too often. "The local fuzz know me so they'll give me a break, but not if I'm plastered."

He had started to use another word rather than "plastered." With a glance at me he had decided it was too crass and quickly made the substitution. I affect some people like that. Shortly after Zeke thanked us for our company, told Andy to give Doug his regards when he saw him, and got up to join his friend back at the bar.

We decided it was time to move on ourselves. George paid my bill and his own. I wondered idly how the boys had decided to handle the checks as we moved along. Nothing had been said about financial arrangements. As we left I thanked George for paying for my dinner.

"You're a cheap date," he joked. "No drinks, no dessert."

"The evening is young," I returned lightly.

"True enough."

Chapter Seventeen

Our next stop was about eight miles away, another bar and grill but smaller. There was no separate dining room here. Half a dozen tables were lined up along the window side and several smaller ones were crowded between the larger tables and the bar stools. The bar took up the entire inner width of the building. I counted fourteen bar stools lined up in front of it. Candles on the tables and lights strung outdoors were the main lighting featured and it was getting dark. The other source of light was from the two wide screen television sets mounted on either end of the bar. I wasn't sure how the bartender could see well enough to know what was going into the glasses.

The place was less than half full and most of the customers were seated at the tables. Only three people were sitting at the bar, and the three of us joined them, leaving two empty stools between.

"Business is slow on Sunday evening here," I mentioned to Andy as we waited to be served.

"Looks that way," he allowed. "I expect the place is full if there's a good game playing. The campers help to keep it open this time of year, they get tired of their own cooking. You can get a great roast beef sandwich in here and the burgers are pretty good."

"You seem to know your way around in this area," I noted. "I thought it was Douglas who had the idea of escaping to the north for some space."

"Who do you think gave him that idea?"

The bartender took our order, a glass of cold wine for me, another beer for Andy and now one for George. I decided to keep a mental count on how much was being consumed and be the designated driver if it was necessary. I knew how to drive a standard shift. The last thing we needed was a ticket for drinking and driving. The cops up here didn't know us.

"Would you care to elaborate on that remark?" I asked Andy, after we had been served and the bartender moved away.

He shrugged. George was sitting on the other side of me. I learned back slightly so he wouldn't be left out.

"I wasn't being entirely truthful, just messing with you a little. I never told Doug to come up here to relax in the local taverns. But I do get north whenever I can myself, to do a little fishing or hunting. I've been coming up here for years and know the area pretty well. Doug has a small camp up in the northwest so he's better known there. When he wanted some privacy he asked me where he could hang out up here once in awhile. Like I said before, I came with him sometimes. I just wish I'd been around the night he had trouble."

I wondered if that would have changed anything for the better. "Did he find out about The Dug Out from you, too?"

"No, he stumbled onto that one somehow. I've been there only twice."

"But you remember how to get there?"

He said he did.

We sat on those stools and sipped our drinks. I idly listened to the country western music from the jukebox. The television sets were turned all the way down so it was odd to watch the picture on the screen with Willie Nelson singing in the background. All of the conversation was in low decibels. The three of us said almost nothing at all for about ten minutes.

"This hanging around in a bar is very overrated," I complained. "I don't know what people see in it."

George tried to look injured. "Andy, I don't think she likes our company."

"Anne's morning conversations over blueberry muffins have been more thought provoking," I retorted, but not with malice.

Andy eyed both of us without comment.

"I hung around a couple of bars after Jill left," George volunteered. "It didn't last long. It was too easy to spend too much and drink more than I meant to."

"Lots of people just come for a little company and a couple of drinks." Andy decided to defend the system and maybe to see what I would say. "I hear in England the pub is as accepted as a fast food place over here."

"So I understand," I had to admit, with a memory of my brief experience in England the year before. "It's rather like the local diners, like Lillian and Marion's place, a local hang out so to speak, sometimes for the whole family. But the taverns in the states aren't always like that are they?"

"If we ever find this guy, Douglas, he might agree with you," said George.

"Taverns are just like any place else," Andy put forth his opinion. "Some good places, some not." He further philosophized, "Alcohol is just like anything else in life, too. You can use it wisely or abuse it."

"It's awfully easy to abuse," I stated.

We continued along that line, bantering back and forth for a little while until we had finished what we ordered. Since Andy hadn't seen a soul he knew we decided to leave. On the way out the door we passed a couple coming in.

"Andy Weller as sure as I'm over forty," crowed the woman. She wasn't bad looking, I thought, although her blond hair could have used a better coloring job.

"Hey, Brenda," Andy acknowledged her. His tone was neutral, not rude but not warm.

"Where ya been?" she asked jovially, coming to a dead stop in the entryway so her companion had to wait outside. Since Andy was leading our group he was facing her and took the rest of the doorway with George and myself trapped inside.

Andy paused and gave her a small smile. "Just busy at home." He made a move to keep going and nodded in a friendly fashion to Brenda's date.

I thought Brenda might have had a little to drink already. On the other hand she might just be the friendly type, but she wasn't going to let Andy get away quite yet.

"Les, you know Andy don't you?" she beamed at Les.

"Afraid not," Les said with civility. He held out his hand and introduced himself. There was no help for it. Besides, someone else wanted to leave and we were blocking their exit. All five of us moved outside. Andy introduced George and myself as friends visiting from Indiana.

"You're not leaving?" Brenda said in disappointment. "Come and have a drink with us." She was still focusing on Andy but did glance at George and me to include us in the invitation.

I have no idea why but both men looked at me for permission to stay. It was ludicrous.

"Oh well, if you're an old friend of Andy's" I said nicely, "Maybe we could stay for just one."

Brenda beamed and Les didn't look too unhappy. We moved our group back inside and took a larger table in front of the windows. Someone had turned the television sets off and the jukebox up. Johnny Cash was taking his turn. Andy and Les took our orders and went to the bar. I decided to let Andy buy this round, serve him right. Since I was feeling just fine I had ordered a second glass of wine but decided I would sip it very slowly.

Brenda sat down slowly and I was sure it was because her jeans were so tight. She smiled brightly at us. "First trip up here?"

We admitted it. She thought we were a couple and I saw no point in enlightening her. She asked politely where in Indiana we were from and we told her. The mindless talk didn't go on very long as there had been no wait at the bar. Les and Andy returned with our beverages.

None of the rest of us had too much to say so Brenda chattered on. "It's been so long, you hadn't even met Les," she reproached Andy. "We've been seeing each other for months." She gave Les a playful little nudge with her shoulder. Les seemed to like it.

"Happy for you," Andy offered politely and even asked where they had met.

Brenda was happy to tell us but I must admit I no longer remember those details. A covert glance at my watch told me it was going on 10 o'clock. I hoped we could make good our escape in a few more minutes, but it was here Brenda got my complete attention.

"Whatever happened to that friend of yours?" she asked Andy, her non-stop cheery demeanor still firmly in place.

Andy took a swig of his beer and considered. "You mean Doug?" he asked off handedly.

"You know, that tall guy with the nice physique, kind of shy."

"Didn't know you knew him," Andy shrugged. He was pretty good at this.

"I don't know him," Brenda admitted. "I just saw him with you a couple of times." If Brenda knew of the trouble at the Dug Out she didn't say so or act like it.

Andy told her Douglas had been out of touch for a while.

"Oh well," Brenda sighed. "I was lucky there was still at least one good man left," this with a suggestive smile for Les. "Since you weren't interested, Andy." There was an emphasis on the "you." Andy gave her a small grin, maybe to show there were no hard feelings. "Besides, my friend Ruth saw your friend Doug around a couple of times and she would like to have gotten to know him a little but said he obviously wasn't looking."

Brenda turned her attention to me and added in a girl-to-girl approach, "Ruthie is the type you just notice. Really good looking, tall, a figure to die for. Everybody notices her."

I wondered how such a fem fatale stayed available.

Brenda shifted in her chair and took a sip of her own drink. She wasn't done chatting and no one else had much to say. I was glad of it when she said, "Ruth saw him at the grocery in Little Falls a few weeks ago but he acted like he had never seen her before."

Neither Brenda nor Les seemed to notice Brenda's statement had a bombshell effect on the three of us. I felt my jaw sag and quickly rectified the situation. George, who was sitting to my right, gave me an involuntary glance, and Andy's beer glass stopped for a second on the way to his mouth.

"Funny," Andy, bless him, said, "I didn't know he had been up here this summer."

But Brenda was losing interest in continuing that line of conversation. She said simply that he must have been and excused herself to go to the little girl's room. She inclined her head inviting me to join her but I declined. I didn't need to go. A quick mental recall of the past ten minutes made me regret it. Perhaps I could have taken advantage of that time to ask her a little more about Ruth's sighting of the elusive Douglas White. But I decided no, she probably didn't know anymore and as far as Brenda was concerned I had no reason to care about Douglas White.

Brenda took her time, probably to do her makeup, and we decided it was time to move on. I told Les how nice it was to meet them both but we really needed to go. George backed me up and started to get to his feet. The three of us, after polite remarks and an apology to Brenda for being gone when she returned, made it out of the door this time.

As Andy left the parking lot the atmosphere was thick with contemplation. About a mile down the road he pulled over into a small roadside rest area. The jeep engine idled as we considered what Brenda had said.

"Do you think she's reliable?" I asked Andy.

"I think so. Have you seen what Doug looks like? He's pretty hard to mix up with anybody else. I think he was up here when she said."

"I thought about following her to the ladies' room to pin her down to be more specific as to the time line, but it's almost a sure thing she doesn't know."

"'Little Falls, a few weeks ago,'" quoted George, hoping to be helpful.

I asked Andy another question. "Do you know this Ruthie person?"

"I know who she is," answered Andy, "but no, we're not friendly, never have been. But I do know that grocery store and there's an old guy who runs it I'm pretty friendly with. He's been there for years. He would remember Doug. Like I said most people do, and Doug's been in there with me more than one time."

I said wistfully, "I don't suppose this store would be open and this old gentleman be there himself at this hour on a Sunday night."

Andy didn't think so.

"I'll have to come back in the morning," I said decisively. "Right now there's nothing else to do but continue with our bar hopping. Two more to go." As Andy put the jeep in gear and

160

headed back onto the road I added on a positive note, "Our night hasn't been a washout so far. Zeke remembered the whole incident, and Brenda gave us a lead we didn't have. If she was right Douglas came up here after he was let out of prison."

Andy voiced the questions for all three of us. "Yeah, but why? And why didn't he let me know?"

I thought there was something else very significant. If Douglas White had been back to this area since April, it didn't look like he was going back to his old hangouts. A visit to these last two taverns should confirm or deny that.

In my opinion our third stop was the nicest. It was a small bar attached to a remodeled old hotel in the tiny town of Little Falls, the very place where Douglas was spotted by Ruthie. We passed the grocery on the way into town and it was indeed closed for the night. We found a place to park in the almost full hotel lot. It looked like the only public building around with the lights still on.

There was a separate dining room I would have loved to patronize another time. It closed at nine. The bar had been restored to continue to look as it had in the 1920's when the hotel had been in its first prime. A brass plaque in the middle of the bar proudly told the year of establishment. I know because Andy led the way and we walked right up to it. This time he knew the man behind the bar and recognition was mutual. The bartender looked about forty, with a full head of prematurely gray hair and a wide smile. He was very thin and dressed to fit into the look of the establishment, with a white shirt and striped garters above the elbows. The guy even had a handlebar mustache. He held out his hand and shook Andy's heartily.

"Well, well! Look who's here? Get bored and come to the big city for some excitement?"

"Something like that," Andy said, with the biggest smile I had seen on his face yet. "Have you got any?

Without waiting for an answer he turned around slightly to include George and me, introducing us both to Randy Eastman. The affable looking man greeted us with a "Welcome to Little Falls. I expect you haven't been here before, because I haven't seen you before."

He gestured for us to sit down and we obliged. Raspberry ice tea was advertised on a colorful old-fashioned poster on the wall and I ordered some. I expected both of the men to order another beer but they surprised me.

"Hate to be a light weight," George said with an apologetic grin, "but I've had a couple already. Would you throw me out if I ordered a coke?"

"Not at all," Randy assured him. "No where else to go in town on a Sunday night and we get all kinds of customers. I've even got some fresh coffee. How about you, Andy?"

"Count me in for the coffee," Andy said. "We've got one more stop."

While waiting for our order I looked around appreciatively. The bar was made out of a heavy natural wood, perhaps oak, and it was beautiful. No one else occupied any of the old fashioned stools but there were customers at several of the tables, all of them chatting, sipping various beverages and snacking. A menu printed to one side of the ornate mirror offered nachos, chicken wings, fried mushrooms and potato skins. There were plates of peanuts in the salted shell on all of the tables and two at the bar, plus an old-fashioned popcorn machine off to one side; the popcorn only fifty cents a bag, leave the change on the bar. All of the tables had large honey colored candles and there was adequate but discreet lighting from a chandelier in the middle of the high ceiling of the room, and from a soft light above the bar.

"Nice place," George commented and I nodded agreeably. This looked more like the sort of place the Douglas White I was getting to know would patronize. There was no television screen but jazz played softly in the background from an overhead music system.

"Your friend seems nice," I commented to Andy, who had the stool to my left.

"Very nice guy," Andy affirmed and added, "He and his wife own this place. They bought it about six years ago and renovated it with a little help from the state historical society."

"They've done a fantastic job from what I've seen," I said sincerely. "It must have taken a lot of work."

"That would be an understatement," Andy replied mildly. "They put their heart and soul into it."

"Is it paying off?"

"I think so. They got some good publicity and the rooms

were booked almost before they were completed. It's the only, what would you call it, fine dining, this side of Green Bay and on weekends you need a reservation for the dining room."

"Have you eaten here?"

"Once," he said, almost as an admission of guilt. "Doug talked me into it. Not exactly my style but the food was good even if I wasn't sure how to pronounce it."

Randy brought our beverages and we enjoyed about twenty minutes of his time, interrupted occasionally by customers. Andy was candid with his friend and told him why we were there. He included the fact no one had seen Douglas since he had served his sentence at the penitentiary. We found out Randy knew about the death at the Dug Out and what the outcome had been. But he had not seen Douglas White.

"But let me ask Carol," he offered. "She's usually at the desk on weekday mornings. She didn't mention it but she might have seen him." He disappeared briefly behind a door to the left of the bar.

He was gone about five minutes. When he returned someone asked for a refill, then two more customers walked in. Before he could get back to us a woman with long brown hair braided into a French twist came in the way Randy had gone out. Her pleasant features lit up in a smile for Andy as she walked around the bar and gave him a hug. She was almost as tall as he was, wearing a colorful peasant skirt and a bright blue sleeveless blouse.

"Where you been, stranger?" she asked him after the hug, giving him a friendly cuff on the shoulder.

"Busy," he replied in his usual abrupt manner. But there was a little smile on his face and he gave her own shoulder another little squeeze before letting her go. Carol - of course that was who this had to be - turned to George and myself expectantly. She did not wait for Andy to introduce us.

"I'm Carol Eastman. It's about time somebody brought Andy back to see us." She held out her hand.

I shook it, introducing myself and returning her pleasantry. George did the same.

"We didn't bring Andy," I clarified, "he brought us."

"I take it you're looking for this friend of yours, Douglas?" Carol said, looking at all of us but longer at Andy.

Andy said that was so.

"Would you know anything that could help us?" I blurted out. Carol did not seem to mind my impulsiveness. She leaned against the bar and the three of us stood around her, holding our various beverages. Randy was now free and stood behind the bar just behind his wife.

"He was here," she affirmed, "just once that I know of. He came in for an early lunch. It was weeks ago, in the spring and still cool. I was hostess in the dining room and remembered it when Randy asked me just now."

"Do you remember anything about him?" I asked her eagerly. "Anything unusual in his manner or how he looked?"

"He seemed just fine," she answered. "He was friendly, asking me how I was, how Randy was, how the business was going, you know, pleasant conversation. I had heard of his troubles but didn't want to bring it up. We know him but not as close friends as we would consider Andy, so I thought it would be rude."

She looked at all of us curiously. "Are you saying no one has seen him since he was here?"

"If anyone else has seen him since we haven't heard about it," Andy said shortly, excluding the sighting by Ruthie. Since none of us knew if he had been spotted in the grocery store before or after having lunch here at the hotel it was possibly accurate.

Randy put a thoughtful finger to his mustache. "Have you considered going to the cops with this?" He looked at George and added, "Would you two be relatives?"

George waited for me to answer.

"No," I said truthfully, "but we know some of the relatives. They're getting concerned about how long he's been out of touch."

"And now, so am I," Andy said rather grimly.

All five of us were silent for a moment.

"It is possible," Carol ventured, "he was headed further up north and just stopped in for lunch." She opined further, "It's a long time not to get up with anybody. If it was my brother or a close friend, I'd certainly be wondering."

"You know," she added conversationally, "Laura Keeler works for us here."

I jumped right in. "Would that be a relative of Sonny Keeler?"

"She's married to his brother," Randy gave the answer. "But Laura's all right. She's been here almost from the start." He looked at Carol for confirmation, and she gave it.

"I don't think Laura has an easy life but she doesn't say much. She's one of our housekeepers."

I thought I would like to talk to Laura Keeler and ask her if she or her husband's family had seen Douglas White since his incarceration. Then again, maybe it should be the police who should do that.

"We appreciate your help, man," Andy said before Randy got called away to wait on his customers again. "We may have to take your advice about going to the law."

George and I thanked him also and I told Carol, "This is very good tea, by the way. It is also a good diuretic. I need to ask the way to your ladies' room."

Carol led the way personally and I left my companions for the facilities located off the lobby. I was not disappointed in the bathroom décor. It totally blended in with the look of the rest of the hotel with only the modern plumbing to indicate it was no longer 1920. When I stepped out three minutes later George and Andy had left the bar. They were waiting for me in the lobby.

"I take it we're leaving?"

"Your tea was almost gone," Andy pointed out, which was my answer.

"We're on our way to the Dug Out then?" I asked as we all got back into the jeep.

"Randy says everything closes at midnight in the whole county," Andy replied, "and I have come around to your way of thinking. We need to visit the Dug Out."

"Might as well make it a clean sweep," I agreed. "So far, doing this has been worth our while. How far away is it?"

It was about a fifteen-minute drive. Getting a little hungry again, I should have munched on some peanuts or popcorn while we were visiting with the Eastmans. I wondered if our last stop would have any munchies and if so if they would be edible.

Chapter Eighteen

No further conversation took place in the jeep. Until now, my guess was Andy had thought this was essentially a waste of time and had only come along as a shot in the dark. George had come out of gallantry, bless him, plus a little curiosity. Now we knew a little more and unless I was completely off in my impression, Andy was worried.

The Dug Out was so stereotypical I laughed out loud as we approached. On the outside it was rather a dump with an unpaved parking lot and no landscaping whatsoever, although I had to admit there wasn't much trash lying around. I never did understand why Douglas had been here at all. When we entered all conversation inside lulled as everyone looked at us. The place was almost full and we stuck out like sore thumbs. There were only two other females and my mother would have said, "They've been around the block a few times." The younger one, an overweight blonde dressed in a tank top and shorts, hung on to a guy twice her age. He was dressed in leathers with tattoos covering both of his arms and a gray ponytail hanging down his back. I couldn't see the other woman very well but she was much older and sat with a man in a dim corner booth.

The man with the ponytail disengaged himself from the blonde and walked behind the bar to wait on us.

"What can I do for you folks?" he boomed in a loud baritone. He needed a loud voice to be heard above the jukebox. This time it was The Belamy Brothers.

There were only two barstools empty and Andy gestured for me to take one. I didn't argue. If he was going to take the lead again it was all right with me. He indicated George should take the other and George also did as he was bid.

Standing between and slightly behind us Andy said pleasantly, "We saw you were open and thought we'd have a late one."

"Sure," said the bartender. "What will it be?" He may have looked rough but his voice and his eyes were friendly.

Of course they wanted me to order first and I didn't have a clue as to what I wanted this time. "Do you have some sort of wine cooler?" I asked desperately.

I was given a choice out of four and chose peach - two beers this time for my companions. I thought idly some bartenders were women and we hadn't run into one all night. Something else occurred to me.

"Could this guy be the owner, the man Zeke was talking about?" I asked Andy, putting my mouth close to his ear so he could hear me.

"That's him," Andy said, still the man of as few words as possible.

"But he doesn't know you?"

"I doubt it. I've only been in here once or twice before and never with Doug."

"Why is it so popular?" I spoke into his ear again. "This is the last place I would pick of all the places we've been tonight."

"Sort of a local hangout I expect," Andy shrugged. "Besides, the drinks are reasonable."

Everyone else in the place had gone back to their own drink and their own companions and ignored us. Our order came and we sipped quietly. I was wondering how we would bring up the subject we had come here for. The only thing that came to me was, excuse me, but do you remember that little incident last year where a guy named Sonny Keeler insulted another customer who then socked him, knocking him out and accidentally killing him? I had not given in to making an impulsive announcement at Lill and Marian's café, and suppressed the urge again. As a conversation opener it still seemed like a bad idea. Maybe Andy had a better one.

"How are we going to bring up Sonny Keeler?" I leaned up and to my right within three inches of Andy's ear again. I would now know that ear lobe anywhere.

"I'm thinking about that."

We kept sipping or I sipped, George and Andy swigged. It was George who spoke this time but he didn't have to lean as close to Andy. His voice carried better.

"Maybe one of these guys was here when it happened," was his comment.

Andy thought it was possible, even likely. A little more time passed. I tried to remember what Zeke had said the owner's name was. John or Gene or Jerry, I wasn't sure.

No problem. Just seconds later a voice boomed, "Hey Jerry, bring another round will you?"

The biker dude saluted the voice and started pouring draft beer into a pitcher. There was heavy smoke in the air and I wasn't used to it. It was making me a little dizzy, or was it the wine cooler? Some of the conversation that drifted our way was laced with profanity. I wasn't used to that either. Even when my husband had been in the military and we had gone to the functions expected of us, the conversations had been light on the coarser language around the wives. Michael had thought a man with any intelligence should be able to express himself without gutter language. In my book that went for women, too.

While Jerry was delivering the refill another bartender wandered over to our end of the bar. I wondered where he had come from. He looked past retirement age. "You people doing all right here?" What he meant of course, as even I knew was, were we ready for another drink.

Andy gave George and me a glance and nodded civilly back at the man. "We're good," he said, and the second barkeep drifted away

We were getting nowhere, I thought glumly.

George must have been reading my mind. He leaned to his left and asked me, "Just what is it you hope to find out?"

"I'd like to know if anyone here has seen Douglas, either in this place or out of it. I also wish there was a way to know if any of the Keelers saw him when he came back through here. And, I wouldn't mind knowing if any of these people think the Keelers are carrying a grudge."

"Is that all?" Andy asked, with more sarcasm than was necessary.

"For a start." I ignored his tone.

Jerry was working his way to our end of the bar with a rag wiping spills and Andy decided to act. He leaned over to indicate he wanted a word and the owner paused obligingly. Because Andy was leaning between our two stools George and I were able to easily hear what was said.

"I hear you've owned this place for a year or two," Andy expressed it more as a statement of fact than as a question.

Jerry nodded. "Almost two years," he clarified. "It was a dump when I bought it but I always wanted a little business and I thought the place had potential." He looked more closely at Andy. "Have you been in here before?"

"Just once or twice. I saw you but I didn't know you were the owner." Andy glanced at the small crowd. "Looks like you've done okay. I've got an old buddy, Zeke Dietzer, who mentioned you."

Jerry grinned. "Zeke, huh? The old rascal gets around. But I'm doing okay, thanks. Once the profit margin gets a little bigger I plan to pave the parking lot and do a little remodeling."

Andy nodded. "Good for you. I remember hearing it used to be a rough crowd who hung around in here."

I suppressed the urge to reach over and squeeze Andy's hand. What a great lead in question, never mind my opinion that if the crowd was any rougher than this, I didn't want to experience it close up and personal.

Now Jerry leaned his elbows on the bar and got conversational. "There was a time you wouldn't have wanted to bring the lady in," he admitted. "But I won't put up with any s…. and the customers know it. You cause trouble in here once you get a second chance. Twice and you're out for good. Otherwise anybody's welcome here."

George decided to get into the conversation. He held out his hand and introduced himself. The friendly owner gave George's hand a strong one-time shake with his own huge paw. Andy introduced me simply as Sally, a friend. Bravely I held out my own hand and Jerry gave me a gentler version of his handshake. He said it was nice to meet us, invited us to come back anytime, and asked if he could get us a refill. Since I had over half of my drink left he was not asking me personally.

Andy made his move. He glanced at his watch. "Like to, but it's close to closing isn't it? We need to move along." Then before Jerry could leave us Andy looked around and said conversationally, "I sure don't want to cause any offense but I'd like to ask kind of a personal question."

Jerry looked wary. "Okay, he said, "shoot. But if I don't like the question you don't get an answer."

Andy nodded. Now there was an empty stool next to George and Andy took it. That didn't make me very happy as it put me on the outside where I could still hear Jerry but might not be able to hear Andy. I leaned in as close as I could, huddled up next to George. Since his attention was totally to his right he didn't acknowledge it. The current music playing was Reba crooning a love song and it wasn't as loud. I silently thanked Reba.

"I know there was trouble in here over a year ago," Andy said, looking straight at the Dug Out's owner. "I know it had nothing to do with you but it did have a lot to do with a buddy of mine."

Before Andy could go on Jerry grimaced. "I'm no brain," he said shortly, "but it doesn't take a great intelligence to figure you aren't on drinking terms with the Keeler boys. You mean the guy who gave Sonny the punch."

It was encouraging to know Jerry didn't have that kind of excitement in his bar very often. He knew what Andy was talking about.

Andy nodded. "He went to prison for it, not for long, maybe three or four months. Did you hear?"

"Seems to me I heard something about that," Jerry admitted cautiously. He looked at the three of us curiously. "If the three of you are cops they got a new way of doing things now."

"We aren't cops," I assured him. I would have explained who we were but Andy spoke up again.

"Not cops, friends. Or I am. It's a long story how these two got involved but it's beside the point. The thing is, the guy did his time, got out the end of April, and never came home."

Jerry didn't look too impressed and Andy held up a hand. "I know, I know. He's a big boy. But it's a little more complicated than it sounds. Tonight we find out he was seen in Little Falls in May. Meanwhile nobody we know of has heard from him; family, friends, nobody. I thought the same thing you're thinking until just lately. Now I'm not so sure."

"I haven't seen him if that's what you're wondering," Jerry said noncommittally.

"You would remember him?" I asked.

Jerry nodded definitely. "I liked him. He came in here a few times before the trouble, sat at the bar, made small talk, nice guy."

"Do the Keelers still come by?" Andy asked.

Jerry gave him a keen look. "Now and then," he admitted. "I'll admit I don't care for 'em much but they keep a lower profile since that night. Sonny was the noisiest one anyway."

"Would you care to give an opinion as to how they took Sonny's accident?" Andy was still looking Jerry straight in the eye.

The biker dude leaned back against the counter behind him and rubbed the gray stubble on his jaw, but he did not look away from Andy.

"They didn't broadcast it in here," he said finally. "They probably know better. But I have heard they didn't take it too well. That is the two brothers and Sonny's oldest boy, Hank. I'd say they didn't think your friend got what was coming to him. The rest of 'em probably don't care but they'd be too chicken to say so, at least where it would get back to the rest of the family."

The bar was suddenly quieter. A large group of people had left and the music had stopped. Jerry looked over my head at someone or something. I resisted the impulse to turn around to see what it was. He leaned forward directly in front of George.

"There's a couple of guys sitting at a table over there who know the Keelers, they might even be relatives," he offered. "They come in here pretty regular but I haven't heard them talk about Sonny for a long time."

Not one of us turned around to look. We all kept our focus on Jerry. He added, "You might ask if they know anything. Can't see it would do any harm."

It just goes to show how wrong somebody can be.

171

Andy took Jerry's advice. George and I stayed put but we did turn around a little so we could watch. The men Jerry had pointed out to us to were sitting at a table with three others. Jerry told Andy the first names of the men he should ask for, and as he approached their table all five looked at him curiously. Or rather four did. The other had his back to us, was in the middle of a story, and only stopped when he noticed he didn't have the attention of the group anymore.

Andy gave them all a friendly nod before turning his attention directly to one of the two men who had been pointed out to us.

"You're Gus?" he asked politely.

With a nod the man indicated he was. Andy introduced himself and asked if he could have a word. Gus may have been curious or simply friendly. He shrugged and said sure. He picked up his beer and followed Andy to a more private end of the room where they sat down together. Since it was too far away for George and me to overhear we had to be content to wait, but we didn't have to wait long. Within a few minutes they both got up. Gus returned to his friends who were back to their story telling. If his expression was any indication the conversation had not put him off. Andy came back and set his glass on the counter.

"Ready?" he asked.

"If you are," I said.

He nodded and without further ado the three of us left. Jerry was already occupied elsewhere. The girl who had been keeping him company earlier was nowhere to be seen. I glanced at Gus's table as we walked out. If Andy's questions had bothered him you couldn't tell. He was laughing at something someone had just said and was reaching into his shirt pocket for a cigarette. The other man Jerry had singled out did watch us as we left.

We were sitting in the jeep again and Andy didn't reach for his keys right away. He knew we wanted to hear what Gus had to say but it wasn't much. Gus had known who Douglas White was, said who didn't? He remembered the fight all right. He had been there.

"Gus and the other guy, Gene, were both there when it happened," Andy explained, "and he didn't mind talking about it. He told me they're both cousins but not close ones. They work with the others sometimes, seasonal, in construction. My guess is they know about the moonshine too but I didn't get into that." He stretched and yawned before going on. "The bottom line is he hasn't seen Doug and said he would have recognized him, not a doubt. He thinks Gene would have mentioned it if he had, and if Sonny's closer relatives saw him they haven't said so."

"Dead end," George surmised gloomily. "Do we have enough to go to the sheriff?"

"I don't know," I answered slowly. I told them about my visit to the sheriff's department earlier in the day, which neither one of them had known about. "That last note Douglas sent his parents might make them hesitate to put much effort into it yet."

I leaned back against the seat. "Is it possible Gus was lying?"

"It's always possible," Andy didn't bother to turn around. His hands were clasped behind his head and he was staring out of the front windshield. "My impression is no."

"But if the brothers and the son saw Doug White they might not have told anybody," George suggested.

"We can guess until the cows come home," I said sadly, "But that's all we're doing, guessing. The one thing we have found out tonight is pretty important. We know after he got out of prison Douglas was seen in Little Falls. I might discount what Ruthie told her girlfriend, but not Carol."

"And you think you can do something with that?" George asked skeptically. "I mean, I know you can be stubborn but what's left?"

"Talking to the old gentleman who runs that store, and I wouldn't mind talking to that housekeeper at the hotel, what's her name, Laura, wasn't it?"

They both thought it was. We talked together for several minutes. I was definitely planning to come back in the morning and was telling them so when a long bed pickup truck pulled into the parking lot. It got our attention when it abruptly left again, spitting up dirt and gravel as it pealed out of the parking lot. Maybe they hadn't realized it was nearly closing time.

"Kids," guessed George. There was no way of knowing. There were no lights in the parking lot and the window glass of the departing truck was tinted.

173

Chapter Nineteen

Andy dropped us off at the motel and said he had to get home. He had a long day coming up and was not as young as he used to be. If he was going to make it he had to get a little sleep. We thanked him for chauffeuring us and he told us not to worry about it

"Something isn't right," he said. It is always nice to have some confirmation. "I'll give you another day but after that I think it's time to come out with all this."

"Agreed." As I climbed out, I paused before shutting the door on the passenger side to add, "You were a big help tonight. Thanks."

He gave me a nod of acknowledgement. "Call me at home tomorrow night if you don't get back until after seven. Otherwise I'll be at the shop, and you have both of the numbers. I want to know if you find out any more."

He grinned at George and said, "Nice meeting you. If we don't see each other again come back and do your fishing up here sometime. I'll show you around."

George was appreciative and responded in kind.

If I believed in luck, I would say I got lucky. The motel had only two rooms left, both of them suites, and the desk clerk was willing to let me have one for regular room price if it was only going to be for one night. It was only going to be in use for about nine hours, so it was a fair price. George offered to get my bags

174

out of the car, but the only one needed was small so I him I'd fetch it. We agreed to meet for breakfast about eight-thirty. Before we parted George made it clear he was coming with me again in the morning and I didn't argue. His company was most welcome.

My stomach was growling shamelessly. The Dug Out had offered pork rinds and hot wings, neither of which appealed. I found some plain pretzels and bottled water in the vending machine in the lobby and munched while soaking in the large hot tub in my bathroom. I filled it full enough to use the jets and sank into mindless oblivion for about five minutes. After that my mind started kicking in again, going around and around with facts and impressions, and I groaned out loud. The evening had not been a washout, but there were still so many questions and few specific answers. Getting nowhere, my best option was getting some sleep.

Since I knew the Whites woke up early I called them as soon as my eyes were open and focusing. It was almost eight o'clock. Cora answered. Giving her a lot of specifics would require a lot of explanations, so she was only told my inquiries were turning up some points of interest, and I'd get back to her soon. My one question for Cora was predictable and the answer had not changed. Her son had not presented himself.

With that settled I finished my morning toilet, packed my bag again, and went to the dining room for breakfast ten minutes late, but beating George by five. He looked a little haggard and I told him so.

"You didn't drink enough to have a hangover," was my greeting.

"Thanks, and you're looking well yourself," was his retort.

I raised an eyebrow, said nothing, and sipped coffee while he went to get some of his own.

"Sorry." George sat down on the opposite side of the square table and faced me. "The bed in my room is too soft. After two nights on that mattress my back aches."

"I could have said good morning a little nicer. Want to start again? Maybe we both need some breakfast."

His face cleared. George was never surly for long.

After eating of the generous fare offered we went to my room

175

to call Anne.

George looked around and whistled. "Nice digs."

He took a slip of paper out of his wallet and handed it to me. Without argument I took it and dialed the number. It was still a local exchange and without any snags the phone at the other end of the line rang almost immediately. After three rings an elderly female voice answered and obligingly summoned Anne.

"Sally!" she said, and there was an excited lilt to the high pitch of her voice that let me know she had something to tell. George has stretched himself out on the floral print divan and I gave him an encouraging nod. "I'm so glad you called. I've been waiting to hear from you. I almost tried George at his room this morning, but he promised someone would call so I waited."

"You have news? George is here with me. Go ahead." In the background, I could hear dishes clattering and distant conversation.

"Just a minute," Anne said in a rather conspiratorial tone of voice. "Let me move out to the porch. This is a cordless." That done, she continued. "My cousins know those people you have on your list, the Farmers. And what's more they know who Douglas White is too."

"Small world," I commented.

"Well," she amended just a little bit, "they don't know Mr. White well, but certainly would recognize him or know him to speak to."

Nothing too odd there as Douglas and Ingrid had at one time lived in the area for a number of years, and Douglas White was a man people almost always remembered. It was a mild coincidence.

As it happened, Anne's cousins and the Farmers had worshiped at the same church for many years, but after going for several months without a minister, Anne's relatives had moved their membership elsewhere. With the loyalty and also the reluctance elderly people often have to make such a drastic change, the Farmers had stayed.

"So," Anne summarized, "because of the change in church membership and because the Farmer's don't get out very much anymore, Percy and Edie haven't seen them in awhile.

It seemed to me Anne was rambling more than she usually

176

did but I held my peace and listened.

"I told them I had a friend who knew the Farmers. I said my friend knew they were getting on and wondered if they were still living in the area, still in their own home."

More white lies I thought with a smile.

"Well, Edie thought they were, with a little bit of outside help for what they can't do themselves anymore. Then without any hints from me Edie suggested that we stop by! She said late afternoon would be good, after they had time for a nap, but early enough not to interfere with their meal. She called first of course, right after church, and they were happy to have visitors. I think Edie and Percy felt a little guilty for not making time to see them earlier."

"How did you manage to explain the mutual friend you were supposed to have?" I butted in.

"Dropping the names of Porter and Cora, of course," Anne said glibly. "And that wasn't much of a stretch, you know, because we have met and spent time visiting together. That's how I broached the subject of Douglas. Percy and Edie never met Douglas' parents, but they knew quite a lot about Douglas and his wife; small town talk."

"That started Mr. Farmer reminiscing the relationship he and his wife had with Douglas and Ingrid. He shared some very nice memories, and eventually told me what I wanted to hear. He said, 'Doug hasn't been by here since winter. He came for a nice visit that day after Christmas, remember Nita, telling us we wouldn't see him for awhile, he was going away for a spell."

"I said just casually you know, it was a long time since Christmas, and Mr. Farmer said, 'yes, I thought maybe we would hear from him by now. He said it would be about six months. First there was business to attend to and then he was going on a sabbatical. That's the word he used, sabbatical. I can't think what he meant by that. Maybe some kind of retreat or something but that's what he said,' and I am quoting Mr. Farmer almost word for word," Anne finished.

"Wonderful," I breathed. "Anne, you are wonderful!"

George was sitting straight up on the couch, his backache and fatigue forgotten. He had to wait a few more minutes while I told Anne about our own discoveries. She considered it progress and was delighted to hear about it. Then there was the matter of confirming when George would come for her the next morning. I almost got away when she wanted a promise we would get back to her after dinner with an update. By the time I hung up George was like a kid waiting to open his Christmas presents. I glanced at my watch.

"Let's check out. We need to get started for Little Falls. I'll tell you all as we drive and we can stay in the lodge there tonight. Maybe they have a bed with a firmer mattress for you. If you want some extra strength Tylenol to give you some relief, there's some in my overnight bag."

Because we would be farther away, there would be some difference in the time needed to go back for Anne in the morning, but George was usually an early riser and didn't mind. In any case he said he intended to get to bed early. Then there was the little matter of having two vehicles. I could hardly talk to George as we drove along unless we rode together and it seemed silly to take them both.

Again the hotel was accommodating. Their parking lot was large and if we understood they could in no way be responsible for the vehicle we left, it would be all right to do so. George was still determined to take his truck and do the driving so I put all of my things behind the seat in the extended cab and we were on our way.

"Don't you see?" I said to George after telling him what Anne had told me. "Douglas got out of prison, which he described as the business trip, and went north to spend a bit of time alone somewhere before going home. He decided to be totally reclusive about it, but he did ask Marian at the diner if she had ever gone to a retreat, and he mentioned it again to the Farmers. Now we know he must have spent that time in the general vicinity of Little Falls."

"Too bad he didn't tell them what and where," George said laconically. He had not been as excited about Anne's news as I had. He assured me he had been paying attention the night before and knew his way back but he was keeping his eyes on the road as we talked.

"That would simplify things. But it must be somewhere up north, and I think something happened to him while he was there.

178

He planned to be home by now."

"He wrote a note to his folks less than two weeks ago," George pointed out unnecessarily. "He got delayed. This could still be a wild goose chase."

I was silent. There was no denying the truth of it. But somehow, it didn't feel right.

"Why such a plain little note?" I asked aloud. "Why just a plain little note to his parents, but nothing to his brothers, the Farmers, Andy, anyone? Why not a phone call, for crying out loud? The man everyone describes to me would not drop out like this."

George had no answers.

****

The elderly man at the convenience store in Little Falls was not what I expected. Instead of a thin stooped old gentleman with a shock of white hair and a merry twinkle in his eye, he was the complete opposite. He was short and very fat with an oxygen cannula in his nose attached by a long tube to an oxygen tank on wheels sitting on the floor. Under the short-cropped gray hair and bushy eyebrows, he glared at us as George and I opened the screen door and entered.

"If you don't buy anything you can't use the bathroom," he barked.

"I don't need to use the restroom but I will buy something," I said sweetly, looking around. It was a small store, loaded with supplies ranging from fish bait to bread. The sound of voices coming from a room in the back of the store indicated mister personality had some help unloading supplies.

I picked out a bottle of water, a roll of hard candy and a small package of tissues. George selected a bag of peanuts, which I confiscated.

"All in the line of duty, George. This goes on the expense account. And that reminds me; let me put some gas in your truck, too."

While George went outside to pump the gas I paid for our purchases. There was no one else in the store.

"I don't need to go to the bathroom," I repeated pleasantly, "but I wondered if you could answer a question for me."

The proprietor gave a wheezy sigh.

"Would you remember that accident a year ago where Sonny Keeler died in The Dug Out?" My questions came after careful consideration about how to word it. I wanted it to keep his attention and curiosity without raising the storekeeper's ire any higher than it seemed to be on a daily basis.

"Of course," he said shortly. "Everybody who lives around here knows about that."

"Would you know the man who gave him that punch if you saw him again?" So okay, that was two questions.

He looked at me guardedly but nodded. "I know who he is."

Now I would give him some information. "We're friends of Andy Weller's" I said, knowing it was a bit of a stretch. "You know Andy too, don't you?"

I got another nod but my reluctant interrogate was getting impatient with me. Someone else had come in and would want to take my place at the counter any minute.

"Andy wants to know and so do we," I said more urgently, "if you remember seeing that man lately. It's rather important."

I had to move aside for the other customer to pay but I stood my ground. When the way was clear again I impulsively held out my hand and said, "You're Henry, aren't you? Andy said he's known you for awhile."

After a little hesitation Henry held out his hand and let me give it a shake.

"Andy's been coming up here since he was a kid," he admitted grudgingly.

"His friend's name is Douglas White if you didn't know. Andy says they've been in here together but we heard Douglas was here not so long ago by himself. Do you remember?"

"Has he done something else?" the old man demanded, heaving his bulk onto a padded stool.

"No, but we need to get in touch with him. We think he came up here for the summer but he didn't leave an address."

George came back in to settle up on the gas and behind him came three teenage boys, boisterous and cheerful. Henry watched them suspiciously as he swiped the credit card I gave him. I signed the slip and looked up at Henry as I laid down the pen.

"He hasn't been here but once that I know of," was the verdict. "That was at least a few weeks ago."

"Did you notice anything unusual about him?"

"No," Henry said.

That was all we were going to get out of Henry. I thanked him.

"So we have a third person who saw Douglas and they all may have seen him on the same day." I related the latest information to George as we walked back to the truck.

"What's next?" George asked.

"I want to see if I can talk to that housekeeper who's married to Sonny Keeler's brother"

There was only one way to do that. We drove back to the hotel where we met the Eastmans the night before. George waited in the truck while I went up to the desk in the lobby and asked for Carol. She appeared momentarily, recognized me, and smiled pleasantly.

"You were with Andy last night. What brings you back?"

Thinking how nice it was of her to make it so easy for me I told her. Was Laura Keeler working today, and did Carol think she would see me?

"She is here, and we can ask her," Carol said easily.

"I certainly understand she has the right to refuse," I assured Carol. "We're running out of options here. If anyone has seen Douglas White around here since you did, it seems to me somebody would have told the Keelers."

Carol agreed. "Some people love to stir things up. Follow me."

I followed her up a staircase to the second floor. There was an elevator but Carol had assumed I wouldn't mind walking up one flight and she was right. We went down a carpeted corridor and turned left. There were four more rooms off of this hallway and a cart with cleaning supplies stood in front of an open door.

Carol introduced me to the middle-aged woman who was stripping the bed. She had shoulder length brown hair, bangs, a neutral expression and light eyes. She was about my own height but heavier, a bulging waistline showing underneath her blue tunic. I thought she was a woman like so many others, one you wouldn't particularly notice or remember. But then the same

181

could be said for myself, although I don't have a bulging waistline - not yet anyway.

The mild curiosity on her face turned to a blank mask as soon as Carol explained what I wanted. I felt the need to add some reassurance.

"I'm not from the police or anything," I said quickly, looking directly at Laura. "To be honest, Douglas White's family is getting concerned about him so they've put out some feelers and we found out he was in this area, actually right here in this town, earlier this summer. I know how news gets around and how people talk in a small town, I'm from one myself. Because of what happened last year it occurred to me if people noticed Douglas, someone would mention it to a member of your family."

There was a pregnant pause. Laura glanced at Carol and then looked back at me. She shook her head. "I haven't seen him," she said in a low voice. "If Bud has he didn't say so to me."

"Would you ask him when you get home?" I asked politely. "Perhaps he just didn't mention it." Unless you and your husband don't talk to each other, I thought.

Laura nodded. "I'll ask him."

As tempting as it was to ask her about the death of her brother-in-law and glean some more impressions, Laura wasn't likely to cooperate. Her guarded look and short answers told me that. I asked Laura to let her employer know if Bud or anyone had seen Douglas White and turned to leave, following Carol.

We were several steps down the hall and ready to turn the corner when a voice called out, "Ma'am?"

Laura was standing in the doorway of the room she was cleaning. When I turned around she asked, "Do you know exactly when it was, when your friend was seen here?"

"I don't," I said regretfully, "not the exact date. May sometime. He was seen in the dining room of this hotel"

Laura disappeared back into the room she was cleaning. As we reached the staircase I said in a low voice to Carol, "please don't be offended but do you believe her?"

Carol sounded pensive. "I don't know, I really don't. I wouldn't swear she's telling the truth. If push comes to shove I don't know her well enough to say for sure."

We were both old enough to know very nice women would

do a lot of things they shouldn't to protect their man. Whether he was worth it or not didn't always enter the equation.

I thanked Carol but she lingered a moment, leaning on the large post at the bottom of the elegant stairwell.

"What will you do now?"

"Darned if I know," I admitted, giving her a rueful smile.

"Maybe you could use a cup of coffee while you sort it out," she suggested. "Our dining room is open. It only closes from two thirty until five."

"What a wonderful idea. I'll collect my friend from our vehicle and we'll do that."

George didn't think it was such a bad idea either. The hour was right between late breakfast and early lunch and the dining room was almost empty.

Since Carol had insisted the coffee was on the house we both ordered a Danish. As our server went to warm and fetch the pastry I had an idea.

"Be right back," I blurted out to George. He probably thought I had to make an emergency call to the lady's room.

But I dashed back up the stairs to the second floor, slowing my steps as I reached the turn to the left. The cleaning cart in the same place it had been ten minutes earlier and the door to the same room was still open. The sound of a low female voice could be heard through the open door, but before I could get close enough to frankly, eavesdrop, Laura raised her voice. Even so, the only word I could clearly hear was, "stupid," before she slammed the phone back onto the receiver. I was too late to catch anymore of the conversation.

I backed quietly away and retraced my steps. The wooden floor underneath the carpet creaked slightly but Laura didn't come out to investigate.

Returning to my seat in the dining room I informed George in suppressed excitement, "We may be here nursing our coffee and killing a little time, or, we may have to beat it out of here in a hurry." I told him about the interview with Laura Keeler and the end of the phone call just overheard.

"She knows something," I was certain. "She may not have when I asked her but she does now, and she's not happy. When she leaves we're going to follow her, even if we have to wait until the end of her shift."

George was incredulous. "You want to sit here for three or four hours? Then you want to tail her vehicle? I have no idea if I could pull that off. They don't train people at the phone company for that."

"She doesn't know you or your vehicle," I argued in a low voice. "All she'll see is a guy in a truck following her down the road. I'll slump down in the back."

We were served mouth watering cherry Danish, butter melting on the side of the plate. We sipped our fine tasting coffee, enjoyed the treat, and talked some more. I knew George was right. There were certain problems. It was not acceptable to hang around in the dining room until two thirty, although Laura could not see us sitting here unless she came right in and that didn't seem likely. The staff probably parked their vehicles somewhere in the back. Laura Keeler wouldn't notice us, but we wouldn't know when she left.

We saw Carol again. She gave a little wave as she skirted the other end of the dining area on her way to the kitchen.

"How's the coffee?" she asked cheerfully.

"Wonderful," I said without hesitation, and George echoed my sentiment.

"Could we bother you one more time?" I added humbly, and with no hesitation she sauntered over to our table. Today she wore lightweight jeans and a peasant blouse, her hair braided so it hung over her left shoulder. If she was annoyed at these interruptions in her busy day she hid it well.

I asked her where the employees parked, what Laura drove, and if she would know if Laura left early.

Before answering Carol's mouth quirked into an amused little grimace. "I take it you think she knows something?"

"I do," I said firmly, and told her about my trip back up to the second floor. "Are your housekeeping personnel in the habit of making phone calls from the rooms they clean?"

"No," Carol frowned. "It isn't strictly forbidden but they have a lot to do and a tight schedule. There isn't time for being on the phone except during breaks. If anyone is on the phone too much it's noticed and the staff member is reprimanded. I've never known Laura to do it."

"It could be a coincidence," I allowed, "but that's a reach don't you think?"

George and Carol both thought it was.

To answer my next question Carol said, "I think one of their vehicles must be down because Bud has been driving Laura in to work for several days. He drops her off and someone else comes to pick her up. Sometimes she has to wait for her ride."

Laura's normal shift was seven to two thirty, five days a week. If she wanted to leave early she would be asking permission from Carol. Carol was very agreeable to letting us know if and when Laura left and even told us we were welcome to wait where we were, which we declined to do. I should stay well out of Laura's sight but George could move his truck to a place on the side street where the employee entrance could be seen.

"You want to follow her home?" Carol ventured, her puzzlement showing. "Will that help you?"

George gave her a look that clearly said he was of the same mindset.

"I want to know where they live or if she doesn't go straight home, where she does go," I insisted. "We have to have as much as we can for the police to take notice and be willing to follow up. You wouldn't happen to know where she lives, would you?"

Carol considered this. "Not exactly. I know they qualified for and bought a double- wide trailer about two years ago. They put it on a piece of land out of town, north of here somewhere. I know she has about a twenty-minute drive to work."

Carol said she hoped we would keep her and Randy informed on our progress, and excused herself.

"If her husband and his brothers have a mean streak in them," George waited until she was almost to the kitchen, then looked at me sternly, "we don't want to be messing with 'em. I like to think I can hold my own with the next guy but I don't go looking for trouble."

"We aren't going to confront them," I soothed. "We'll stay well out of the way. Maybe there won't be anything to learn but we have to try."

I leaned forward and put my chin in my hands. "I admit this could be a long day. You remember last night that cousin at the

Dug Out said the Keeler brothers often do construction work in the summer? If Laura has no way to leave here, even if she wants to, we'll have to wait until her ride comes."

We didn't have to wait that long. Ten minutes later, as we were about to move George's vehicle to the side of the hotel, Carol came back. I hadn't seen her leave the kitchen but she walked back in from the lobby. She sat back down in the chair she had vacated before and leaned forward, her elbows on the table, clearly with something she wanted to share. George and I moved the chairs we had been about to get out of closer to the table to maintain privacy.

"You were right about Laura, Sally," she said softly. "Something is up. She's upset. She just beeped me and says there's a family emergency. Another housekeeper has agreed to lend Laura her own car so she can leave. She wants to go when she's finished with the room she's cleaning now, and will come back later to return the car. I asked if it was anything serious, and was there anything I could do. She said no, her granddaughter was sick at daycare and she had to go get her and take her to a niece's house for the rest of the day. Normally I wouldn't think anything about it, but I asked at the desk if there had been any calls for Laura since she came in. There haven't been."

"Carol, you are wonderful," I breathed. "Can we leave here without Laura seeing us go back to our vehicle?"

She said we could if we left through the front lobby, the way we had come in. Laura had a little work left to do and would leave through the employee workroom. Carol also suggested we leave George's truck where it was and just wait. Laura would leave town going east on the main street before turning north and we should see her go.

Chapter Twenty

So it was George at the wheel with me crouched down in the extended cab as we waited for Laura to leave. Fifteen minutes later she did. It helped that another vehicle pulled in right behind her, putting someone between us. It also helped that for several miles the object of our interest stayed on the main highway. When she finally took a right turn the road was not deserted and she gave no indication she noticed the white pickup truck that took the same turn. George did not follow too closely, but I ducked even farther out of sight.

"There's construction going on out here," George informed me. "There was a sign at the turn off about lots for sale. She must be going to visit her hubby."

George nicely continued to keep me informed.

A few moments and a few miles later he added worriedly, "The traffic is thinning out. If this is a dead-end I don't know how we're going to stay inconspicuous."

"Keep driving right past where she parks if you can," I directed. "Just act like you're curious, maybe like someone who would be interested in buying."

For a second I risked lifting my head enough to peek. Close to the end of the paved road Laura pulled her borrowed car carefully into a graveled driveway.

"The road keeps going but it's not paved any further," George said. "I don't see any way we can stop here without somebody wondering what we're doing. If they come up to the truck you're going to look pretty silly hiding in the back. I'll keep going."

When I could feel our truck pulling off pavement and into dirt I asked George if I could sit up safely and he thought so. Turning around, I spotted Laura walking toward a house in the making. The frame was up and she disappeared inside.

"You've got to stop. If you go any further we won't be able to see anything."

He obligingly turned around and slowly drove back the way we had come. The workers must have been used to curious people coming around. No one paid any attention to us.

"Pull in here," I said, as we came to the unpaved driveway of the house next to the one Laura had entered. The only vehicle already there was a panel truck with an electric company logo on the side. "Can you get out and look interested in the house? I'll stay here."

George pulled in to the left of the panel truck, and with no comment as to what he thought of our shenanigans, he did as I asked. For several minutes he moseyed casually about, eyeing everything from the foundation to the roof. No one approached him. I had a clear view of Laura's vehicle and the upscale home in progress she had entered.

I almost cheered when Laura came out of the house with a man walking next to her. He slowly walked her back to her vehicle in what appeared to be an attempt at having some privacy for their conversation. When George spotted them he stayed casual. With his hands in the back pockets of his jeans he wandered off to the side, peering under a cedar deck.

If Laura and Bud – and this had to be Bud - noticed George or his truck, they ignored both in the heat of their low voiced but intense discussion. From my vantage point it was obvious Laura was angry. George had left the engine running so I carefully lowered my back window a few inches. Mercifully the skill saws and nail pounding inside receded into background noise and I could hear a little, catching words like, "idiot," and "always trouble," from Laura, and "worry too much," from Bud. The engine noise kept me from hearing any complete sentences. When Laura raised her hand to give her spouse a smack Bud grabbed her arm and glanced around. Now he noticed the truck with its engine idling and George about sixty feet away with his back to them. Quickly ducking down I was almost positive he hadn't seen me.

George's truck windows had a light tint, which gave me a little advantage, but I didn't dare to look out of the window again and stayed sitting on the floor until I heard Laura start the engine of her borrowed car and the gravel's crunch as she backed out of the drive. As soon as I heard her pass behind me I took another look, just in time to see the back of Bud Keeler as he went back into the house and supposedly back to work. George was no where to be seen so I guessed he had gone around to the other side of the house, still feigning interest in purchasing or building such a home.

It was about two more minutes before he returned, giving me a little time to consider what to do next.

"Nice act," I complimented as he climbed into the driver's seat. "There's no reason for Laura or Sonny to think anything suspicious was going on."

"Not entirely an act," he said with a smile. "I didn't think it was a good idea to be too interested in those two or leave as soon as she did, but that is a nice house." The smile disappeared replaced by a look of contriteness. "She's mad about something. If you wanted to follow her again we're a little behind."

I shook my head. "I don't think so. I mean, we could catch up with her but we won't. I've been thinking about whether we should stick with her or with him. It's silly to think the Keeler boys have Douglas White hogtied somewhere and she's gone to let him loose."

"What then?"

"We should see where Bud Keeler goes when he's done working today. What if one of those cousins at the bar told him about being approached last night? Now, just hours later, his wife is asked about Douglas. Don't you think he must be getting a little nervous himself? From what I saw just now, as little as it was, Bud has something to hide all right." I shifted in my seat and took a swig of water from the bottle I had bought at the grocery. "Which reminds me. What did you hear?"

Before he started to tell me we decided we should leave. It

might draw unwanted attention to stay much longer. George agreed to proceed down the dirt road as though we, or he, were curious about what there was further on. We hoped if we had been noticed we would soon be forgotten. As he moseyed casually along and out of sight George told me what he could hear of Bud and Laura's conversation, which wasn't much to be sure, but added to what I heard and fuel to our suspicions that Bud had seen Douglas White since his incarceration. George had heard a few more words, such as, "I wondered why you…" this from Laura, and "I knew you'd just…" from her husband.

About half a mile farther on, George put the truck in park and we talked about how to proceed. This took about fifteen minutes. George repeated what he had said before, that following Bud Keeler could be tricky. I agreed but argued we had to try. If there was any indication we were drawing unwanted attention we would abort the endeavor and move on.

"If we can't find out anything else today we'll go to the sheriff with what we have. We'll have to take the chance they'll be interested."

I looked at my watch.

"It's lunch time. These construction workers should be breaking for lunch soon shouldn't they, and I would think they're too far away from anything to leave."

George agreed it was likely the workers would break out lunches and stay put. I surveyed our surroundings. It was a pretty lush spot and there had been surveying done to mark lots for eventual further development. But for now all of the action was behind us. We were alone for the time being. The unpaved road continued on, far enough so we couldn't see the end of it. When you looked more closely there were also rough trails meandering through the woods.

"How about a little hike before lunch?" I suggested brightly. "Let's see if that path over there leads us back behind the construction sites."

"I keep reminding myself I came up here willingly to lend you a hand," George remarked, his only comment as he pulled the truck off to the side of the road and turned off the ignition. I pulled my sneakers and some socks out of a suitcase and changed from my sandals.

It was a pretty summer day, the warmth off set by a good breeze and the partly cloudy sky hinting of possible rain by late afternoon. The trail was rough, obviously not often used anymore, and I was glad of my long cotton slacks that kept my legs from getting scratched with wild berry branches. As intent as I was on the issue at hand, I was not oblivious to my surroundings. There were tall gorgeous firs, pines interspersed with shorter maples and other varieties, the shrubs, and a splattering of wild flowers so yellow they looked freshly painted. The smells of leaves, wild grass, and faintly of honeysuckle permeated the air.

"It's beautiful out here." George was holding yet another branch out of the way to keep it from slapping me in the face. "I wonder if it's all private land."

"If it is it's not posted," he noted. "Nobody should nail us for trespassing."

That was a comfort. We didn't converse much more, both of us intent on finding out if our path would lead us behind the houses under construction. It did, but came up short at a deep culvert and behind the third house from the end of the paved road. There was enough overgrowth that no one could see us, but we were a good distance away from our objective. I asked George if he thought we could get through the overgrowth of vegetation and move farther right. He said we could if we didn't mind the inconvenience.

In was an inconvenience to say the least. The culvert had a few inches of water sitting in it. Mosquitoes and tiny black gnats materialized from the stagnant water, harassing us. Then there was long wild grass and brambles to get our feet tangled up in, which I did more than my share of, and three times more often than George did. Once he had to catch me or I would have gone sprawling. It was a good moment to thank him for being there. He smiled slightly and nodded. George didn't seem to mind our situation very much in spite of his reluctance. He may have been enjoying it a little, not that he would admit it.

We moved slowly to gain our objective of being directly behind the home Bud Keeler was working on. We followed the line of the gully, which put us closer. Still the drainage ditch presented a barrier, and even if it had not, we could not have left the cover of the edge of the forest without being noticed. As it was, if anyone had been watching they might have wondered if there was a herd of deer in the thicket. We were counting on nobody paying attention. The noise of band saws and hammers had abated; lending credence to our theory everyone had stopped for lunch. But even if we had been close enough to hear conversation someone had a boom box going strong, tuned to a hard rock and roll station. No one was in sight.

"So where are these guys eating their lunch?" I wondered out loud but keeping my voice down.

"You must have noticed the vehicles parked along side of the road," George reminded me. "That's probably where they are."

"Great," I huffed. Now what?

But as long as we weren't being eaten alive by the bugs we decided to stay put for a little while and see what happened. It was a good decision. Making small talk about home building to pass the time, George was pointing out to me the difference in the floor plans when he stopped abruptly. I turned from following the direction he was pointing in to see what had drawn his attention. Three men were casually wandering around the side of the last house and down to the edge of the property. They stopped just short of the culvert, roughly fifty feet from where we were hiding. By the time they got that far we had backed off a little more and crouched down almost to our knees into the wild shrubbery and long grass. One of the men was Bud Keeler and I thought one of the others was the cousin at the bar the night before, the one Andy had not spoken with. The third man was a total stranger. All three lit up cigarettes and we caught Bud's voice as they approached.

"I think we can trust her to keep her mouth shut," he was saying. "They can't pin anything on us."

Bud was a small man, deeply tanned and wiry. We could see all three men pretty well, or at least I could. It was no time to ask George how his view was. The man I had never seen before removed his baseball cap to wipe a damp forehead with the back of the other hand, his cigarette dangling between his fingers. He looked worried.

I caught my breath at what he said and heard George inhale and exhale in long, slow, motions. "We were fools," he growled. "We wouldn't have done it if we wasn't liquored up." He was taller than Bud, older and heavier.

192

"Yea, well," Bud rejoined with defiance in his tone, "what's done is done and he hasn't shown up anywhere has he, or his body either?"

When Bud said that I reached over and gripped George's sleeve.

Their other companion shook his head and looked at the other two as though he doubted their sanity. "You think you can keep this quiet forever? Seems to me if the law comes back around and pushes hard enough, somebody's gonna say something to make 'em suspicious."

Bud gave him a hard look. "I count eight people know and that includes you."

The cousin didn't seem intimidated. "I'm not the problem," he said mildly, "and I wasn't there. But Laura's already spooked, Joe here is nervous, and one day Hank will get good and drunk and say something to somebody he shouldn't. It doesn't take a rocket scientist to see the situation." He took a long drag on his cigarette and shook his head glumly. "Doesn't look good."

"It was only a matter of time before somebody would come looking," it was Bud talking again. "We could have figured that. You said those three last night weren't with the law. When they don't come up with anything what can they do?"

"It gave me a turn last night when I saw that jeep." The expression on the face of the man now named as Joe didn't indicate he was reassured. "I seen it a few times last year and knew it was his."

I gave myself a mental pat on the back for suggesting we use it.

"What's done is done," Bud said with finality. "There's no proof and no one knows what happened. I'll talk to Hank after work. He doesn't want to go to jail any more than we do. If we keep quiet nothing's going to happen."

He took a last drag on his cigarette, dropped the butt, and ground it with the toe of his shoe. Leaving it there, he turned to walk back to the job site. After another moment and without exchanging any words, the other two did the same.

I let go of George's shirt and took a deep breath of my own.

"Holy cow," George breathed. "It sounds like they killed the guy."

My knees were weak from crouching down and George's back must have been breaking in two. I sat down on the ground, not caring for the moment if it was moist or not. Stained pants could be dealt with later. We weren't going anywhere until we processed what had just been overheard. George gladly eased himself down beside me. He didn't say anything and the temporary silence was appreciated.

"Did I hear someone say that 'he,' meaning Douglas White, of course, 'hasn't turned up, or his body either '?"

"That's what I heard," George confirmed. "Their voices carried in our direction better than I would have figured." He picked up a blade of grass and chewed on it thoughtfully.

"That doesn't sound like they killed him, does it? I mean, if they knew they had why would they say it like that?" Before George could answer me I had another thought and exclaimed, "And there's still that third note he sent his parents!"

"He couldn't have done that from the grave," George conceded.

I drew up my knees and hugged them. "George, one thing is clear. Douglas White really is a missing person. But as of right now, is he a dead one or a live one?"

Chapter Twenty-One

We backtracked to George's truck. A couple of mosquito bites made themselves known. A damp derriere, the itching, and a sudden heavy thirst was making life rather uncomfortable. After climbing into the front passenger seat I found my water bottle and took care of one thing at least.

George fished his ignition keys out of a pocket and was going to start the engine but I put my hand on his arm. He gave me a questioning look.

"Wait a minute. I want to think about our next step."

The look turned incredulous. "Think about what? Our next step is to find the nearest sheriff's department and tell them what we just heard."

"I guess so," I conceded reluctantly. "I wish we knew what they were talking about. Did they beat him up, what? And where? Why is it they don't know where he is?"

"There are people trained to find out," George said firmly. He started the motor.

He was right of course; we had done all we could do. Feeling glum I sat mutely in my seat. There were too many loose ends. I hated to leave it like this.

Then we made a mistake. Both of us were preoccupied with the results of our eavesdropping. We were paying no attention to our surroundings as we left the dirt road behind us. Some of the construction workers were finishing their lunch break and heading back to work. Some of them were still lounging outside near the road, and one of them was the cousin who had been at the Dug Out the night before. He was standing next to a sedan that had seen better days, leaning on the driver's door. As we drove past I was only a few feet away from him with only my passenger door between us. Our eyes met and his jaw dropped.

The first word to cross my lips was one I have used only a handful of times in my entire life, as you have already heard my views on foul language. I will only elaborate by saying I did not take the Lord's name in vain.

George had never heard me use the expression before. He acknowledged it with a small amused grin, which was brief. He had seen the look on the Gene's face too.

"Oh, oh. Busted." He was stepping on the accelerator.

I wailed, "That cousin! He recognized me! How could we be so stupid? I should have gotten into the back out of sight again, or we should have waited to make sure everybody was back inside."

George glanced into his rear view mirror. "He's high tailing it back into the house to tell the other two, you can bet."

"We're heading back to the hotel," he said in a voice that left no room for argument. "We'll call the cops from there."

"Maybe no one will come after us," I said hopefully. "They can't just walk off the job if they don't want to get fired. Besides, what can they do in broad daylight, run us off the road?"

We didn't want to find out. George went back the way we had come, covering ground in half the time. But as the gunslinger in the old west might have said, our luck had run out. We pulled out onto the main road and only half a mile into our trip back to Little Falls got behind a huge hay wagon pulled by a tractor. It was a two-lane road, there was moderate traffic, and we were stuck.

"We have to get around this or out of sight," I said levelly, with more calmness than I was feeling. "If we are followed they'll be on us in a minute. I know what I said, but I don't want them catching up with us."

"They don't know we turned left to go back to town," George pointed out. "They could turn the wrong way."

But apparently George didn't like the fifty-fifty odds. There was a dirt road, little more than a cow path, coming up on the left.

There wasn't enough time to pull out and ahead of the hay wagon but there was enough time to make a sharp left without being hit by oncoming traffic, and we made the turn. As George proceeded down the rutty road as fast as he dared I turned and kept my eyes glued to the road we had left behind. All I knew for sure was I didn't want anybody turning in behind us.

It was slow going for George. The road was poorly maintained. It felt like I could have run faster, but a quick glance at the speedometer indicated we were going about 12 miles an hour. Eventually, with a bend in the road and heavy tree cover on each side, we were out of sight. No one made the turn after we did before we lost sight of the intersection.

Without asking my opinion George pulled over onto the grassy shoulder and let the truck engine idle. "We may be damn fools," he opined bluntly, "but the thought of those dudes on my tail is not appetizing."

He had my vote there. I rolled down the window, inhaled deeply of the clean country air, and let myself relax.

"I could do with some lunch," my sidekick said after a minute of his own unwinding. "How long before you think we could go back?"

"I don't know. If they don't try to find us right away it probably means they'll let it go until quitting time. That would be late afternoon, right? Construction crews try to work as long as they can when the weather is good don't they?"

George suggested we give it about ten more minutes and I said okay. To pass the time I drank more water, combed my hair, and got out to look around. To pacify his stomach George munched on some of the peanuts we had bought at the general store in Little Falls. He didn't get out but reclined his seat and leaned back.

Our time lapse was about up and I was going to get back in my seat when I heard it. With only birds, bugs, and the breeze making any noise, the sound of a vehicle was clearly audible even though it was still far away.

"Someone's coming," I told George, getting back into the truck. George had never turned the ignition off so he didn't hear the sound of the approaching engine when I did.

With only a couple of seconds to make a decision it was hard to know what to do.

"Discretion is often the better part of valor," I quoted. "Let's go on. There might be a farm or other private residence at the end of this road and it's only someone who lives there. No harm done."

George may have been listening to my rationalization but he had already gone from park into drive and put some more yards behind us. I sat sideways on the seat, bouncing with the bumps and gazing continuously out of the rear window. Thanks to the winding path, and it was little more than that, and a continuation of heavy foliage, we had good cover unless the car or whatever it was behind us got within a tenth of a mile. All I had been able to determine about the vehicle behind us was it had the distinct noise made by a diesel engine.

About a mile further on, or so I was told because it seemed like about five to me, we did come upon a residence. It was an old farmhouse with a barn and two other buildings, one housing some machinery, the other smaller, perhaps a chicken coop. All were dilapidated and weeds grew in profusion, but there were definite signs of current habitation. Half a dozen cows and a horse grazed companionably near the barn, looking up at us in mild curiosity as we approached. To the left of the house someone had planted a large garden and the corn was doing well. There was no indication anyone was at home.

After observing all this I looked at George, then behind me, then ahead. The road, such as it was, kept going and so did we. We didn't discuss it; we just kept driving. The vehicle behind us was still out of sight. Somewhere in the middle of all of this I realized Sonny Keeler's cousin could have gotten our license plate number, and at the very least knew it was an Indiana license plate. Since there wasn't anyone home at the one place we passed, we were still on our own. I thought whoever was in the vehicle behind us could hear the sound of George's motor if they had their windows down; he used diesel too.

"This cow path must be hard on your truck," I mentioned somewhere along the way. "I'm sorry."

George shrugged. "I've got it in four wheel drive. It's seen worse."

I wondered if this had been a road for a logging camp at one time because it went on and on. We decided when we found a good place to pull out of sight we would do so and see if we were being intentionally followed. The scenery got denser, with taller hardwood trees, a very small brook babbling to our right, and rockier outcroppings. It was a pretty scene but we weren't appreciating it as we might have in different circumstances.

At last we agreed it was time to terminate our flight. No ideal place had presented itself but George took a sharp left through a clearing in the forest and carefully maneuvered us across a small ravine, through a gap between some towering oaks, and brought us to rest well out of sight. We couldn't be seen but we couldn't see much either.

He turned off the engine as soon as we came to a stop. We both lowered our windows and listened.

"Will your tire tracks show where we got off the road?" I asked.

"Not for long, unless somebody's really looking hard. The ground isn't wet and the grass I drove over is pretty short so it will spring back fast."

"Do you think we should get out of the truck?" I asked uncertainly.

"If we do we'd better stay close," was George's opinion.

We didn't. We stayed in our seats and listened, eventually hearing an approaching vehicle. With only our ears to go on, we both guessed it was a truck, and we listened to it approach, then drive past. When it was too far along to hear it anymore we looked at each other, the same thought in our minds. Should we back track and go on to the hotel?

"I say go for it," George said. "They're far enough ahead we should have plenty of time to get out of here before they come back." He added the obvious, "It could be anybody happening to come down this road. There might another house or two further on."

I allowed that was true and agreed we should go.

The safety of Carol and Randy's establishment looked more appealing every time we tried to get there but we were foiled again. There was no doubt about it; someone else was coming. Before George had his clutch pushed in we both heard another vehicle bumping down the road.

"Unbelievable," he muttered. "It's getting crowded out here." He turned off the ignition again. This time I got out of the truck.

"If we're going to know what to do," I announced, keeping my voice down and shutting the door quietly, "we're going to have to see who's there. I'm going to get closer to the road to take a look."

George did not say we should stay together but without a word he got out and joined me.

I glanced at George's shirt, a short-sleeved yellow jersey, and my own outfit, light olive green slacks and a striped tee. Hopefully we would blend into the environment. George's shirt was a little faded and there was no bright coloring to my top. Quietly we climbed the little embankment in front of us and peeked around the huge trees. Nothing. We could hear one of the vehicles, probably the second one, but still could not see it. I crouched down and moved closer with ferns, brambles, and overgrowth of all sorts giving me cover. One could only hope there was no poison ivy. I could hear George behind me but doubted anyone else could. The trees rustled with an early afternoon breeze. When we were in sight of the road I hesitated and George put a hand on my arm.

"Stay put and get down," he urged in a whisper.

Since George had more experience in the woods than I did, I complied. We both backed up a step and went onto our knees. We spotted a huge tree toppled on its side only a few feet to our left. I looked at George and he nodded. We scrambled. It was better cover as long as we lay on our side and there was room for both of us to do so. The giant root system of the tree had apparently given way only recently. There were branches and leaves in abundance to provide camouflage. From our hiding place we could see a large section of the rutty road.

Nothing. The second vehicle had already gone by our hiding place and the sound of the engine was only faintly audible. We lay there on the ground, our bodies against the fallen tree, and waited in mutual understanding to see if anyone else came by, or to watch for a return of the others. George mentioned there might be a campground or good fishing spot somewhere further on which was a perfectly plausible reason for traffic. I said the fishing theory was the better explanation, as a camping area should have been marked at the turn off.

I couldn't speak for my partner, but I was beginning to feel a little foolish lying there on the ground next to a tree like I would have as a kid playing hide and seek. Leaves rustled, a few birds chirped, and I heard the scamper of what sounded like squirrels. As time passed I turned over onto my back and watched the sky. The sun's rays as they escaped the clouds and shone through the trees overhead were mesmerizing. It made me drowsy.

"If you fall asleep I'll be tempted to give you a swift kick," George said mildly, breaking the mood.

"Right." I turned back over onto my left side. "It seems your guess about something worthwhile further down the road must be true. Shall we try getting back to Little Falls one more time?"

"It's either that or seeing if any of these roots around here are edible. Don't you hear my stomach growling?"

"Did you eat all the peanuts?" I stood up and brushed myself off.

"Of course I did. It was just a small bag. Come to think of it, I'm even thirstier than I am hungry." George got to his feet. He did it pretty gracefully for a fiftyish man of his size.

We sauntered back the way we had come. I offered to share what was left of my bottled water. Very nice of me, George said, but he had some lukewarm fluids of his own in a small cooler behind the cab.

As the saying goes, going back always seems to take less time than it did to get there. The rutty road really didn't seem as long as we pulled out of the forest, took a right turn, and made our way once more back to the paved local highway. George guzzled his sports drink, I finished my water, and we began to relax as we made the left turn onto the county highway with roughly twenty minutes to our destination. We agreed to eat before taking action, which made sense anyway, because we could ask Carol if she knew where the nearest law enforcement agency was. If Laura Keeler had come back to the hotel to return her borrowed vehicle, fine. I wasn't going to worry about seeing her again and George concurred. We both felt we would be safe from harassment when we hit the town limits, especially during daylight.

This time we almost made it. By my estimation we were within five miles of Little Falls, when the dark blue sedan the

Keeler cousin had been leaning against when he spotted us pulled out of a private driveway immediately in front of us, so close we had to slow down not to hit its rear end as it pulled out into the road. Bud Keeler was in the passenger seat and he knew very well who we were. Watching him glare at us through their rear view mirror was not a pleasant experience. What was even more unpleasant was what happened after he said a few words to the driver. Their vehicle slowed down but also moved toward the centerline in the road, giving us nowhere to go. Clearly we were being forced onto the shoulder or into the ditch. The driver hadn't brought the car to complete stop when Bud jumped out and walked back to confront us.

Everything happened quickly after that. There was no time for George and I to have a discussion about how we would handle this. George's instinct, as he told me later, was not to let the two occupants of the sedan meet us face to face. A red mini van pulling up behind us may have assumed we had car trouble. It simply pulled around both vehicles and kept going. There was on coming traffic but the instant the mini van had cleared George hit the gas. With tires squealing and the dust on the shoulder of the road flying he turned his faithful white truck around in a u-turn and sped back the way we had come.

The white van coming from the other direction had to slam on his brakes to let us in, and laid on his horn in protest.

"Where's a cop car when you want one?" George observed grimly.

"Keep your speed up and if there's one anywhere around he'll find us," I said hopefully.

He told me to turn around and keep watch so he could fully concentrate on the road. With my heart in my throat I shifted around to once again watch for the enemy.

I remembered my husband telling me he and George had enjoyed stock car racing as teenagers. It must be like riding a bicycle, you never really forget. By passing everything on the road in front of us, which amounted to about five vehicles of one sort or another, we immediately put distance between the Keelers and ourselves. Because of the time it took them to turn around and change directions I lost sight of them almost immediately. The power George had under the hood helped, too.

"Now what?" I asked.

He passed an older model luxury car driven by an old lady. Part of the move took place on a double yellow line, and I did not miss the glare she gave us as George swept by and pulled back into our own lane in front of her.

"We can just keep going," he suggested. "This is no cow path. It will take us somewhere. There's a curve ahead. Take a look and see if they've closed in."

I complied. George was still going well over the speed limit and for the moment we had the road pretty much to ourselves. When I looked back at the curvature in the road the only thing in sight behind us was the car we had just passed.

"They're not close enough to see," I reported. "They've got to be at least half a mile back."

"By the time we get back to where we started," George reminded me, "the road winds even more. We might not be able to stay ahead of them like we can now. All we need is to get behind another piece of farm machinery crawling along."

"So you're suggesting we find another place to turn off and try to disappear?" I kept my eyes glued to the road behind us.

"It's either that or take our chances."

"You haven't seen any signs telling us where the next town is, have you? If only we could find a town, even a large grocery store or gas station. If there were plenty of people around I don't think they'd try anything."

George remembered seeing a road sign while we were following Laura Keeler, naming two small towns within the next fifteen miles, with another, the name he couldn't remember, twenty miles further on. We had already passed one of the little burgs and it had amounted to a few houses and a gas station no longer in operation.

It was a decision we didn't have to make. Fate had determined our behavior several times that day and it intervened once more. Less than a quarter of a mile in front of us we both saw a huge semi tractor-trailer loaded with new machinery and creeping along well below the fifty-five mile an hour speed limit. There was no visibility allowing George to even consider passing this time; the double yellow line would be obeyed. Only yards before we would reach the behemoth was the very road we had

203

bounced down a short while before.

I knew my companion would take the turn and he did.

"At least you know the way this time." I was trying to be positive. He didn't have to tell me to watch our back it was the instinctive thing to do, although I had no idea what we would or could do if we were spotted and overtaken.

We made the first large curve in the road for the second time that day without seeing anyone turning in behind us. I felt only partially reassured and not even that much when George piped up, "It won't take them long to realize we must have turned off somewhere. They can't be that far behind."

"Well," I considered, not looking at him, my attention still focused on our rear "they have several choices."

"That should buy us some time," he agreed, keeping his foot to the pedal. My luggage and other supplies behind the seat and the paraphernalia George had in the truck bed were bouncing around alarmingly.

"I've thought about stopping and facing those two," he added, "but I'm not sure if they have firearms or just what they'd do. I didn't bring my shotgun, either."

This time we met someone else on the road. It was an old red pickup truck, driven by an elderly gentleman with a white beard and fierce eyes approaching us from the other direction. It didn't seem prudent to get him involved. He barely gave us a glance we passed each other. We went on and came to the dilapidated farm. There was still no sign of anyone at home and we kept going. As time passed we must have gone by the spot we had left the road the last time through, but I wasn't exactly sure where that had been. The trees, the road, the stream running inconsistently on the right side, and the shadows dancing as the trees filtered out most of the sun, became a constant pattern. We both turned our windows down again, but we didn't see or hear anyone behind us.

Once we spotted an old cabin about fifty yards from the road. It had seen much better days. Used for hunting once upon a time, George guessed. Now it was no more than a tumbled down pile of rotting boards with an old fireplace exposed on one side.

I asked George how far we had come since our turn off and he thought about four miles. It seemed like ten I told him, and asked if he thought it might connect with another major road somewhere. He said there was no way of knowing but it was possible.

"I hate to bring this up, but pretty soon I've got to find somewhere to empty my bladder. Would you believe it's almost 2 o'clock?"

"You're not the only one," he answered, with an automatic look behind us via the rear view mirror. "Can you hold on a little longer?"

"I think I'd better. I'd feel a whole lot easier about stopping if we have the road to ourselves for awhile yet."

He nodded his agreement and drove on.

Another ten minutes went by. There was no sign of another living soul. We had come across three primitive paths, barely passable for any on- road vehicle, and George took the last one. Even with his four-wheel drive he crawled along, coming to a stop well out of sight of anyone or anything on the path we had left behind. He turned off the ignition and we both sat quietly and listened. Only the sounds of the forest met our ears.

I grabbed my bag and quietly opened my passenger side door. "I'll be back in a few minutes."

I meandered ahead, took a right, and disappeared from the view of the truck. Certainly George would use the time he had to himself to attend to his own bodily function needs.

I didn't intend to go very far. It wasn't necessary and why take a chance on getting lost? This ground was rockier with slippery moss and wild grass in places where the sun didn't penetrate very much. Carefully I did what I needed to and feeling much relieved, backtracked to where we were hiding out.

George was in the bed of the truck carefully straightening out the mess we had made in our flight. He watched my approach. When he could be heard without raising his voice he said, "Since it looks like we're never going to get lunch you want a snack out of the cooler?"

"You've got supplies on ice back there?" I asked in surprise.

He shook his head. "No fresh ice. I didn't bother with it this morning. But there's some stuff back here that doesn't need to be kept cold and I've got a can opener."

He opened the container and I stood on my tiptoes and looked with interest at what he had. There were some chips,

205

crackers, and cans of beans, tuna, sardines, and fruit cocktail, as well as four cans of warm soda pop.

"Not bad," I approved. "We could be doing worse out here roughing it. All I have in my supplies are some breath mints and a couple of cereal bars. I usually have some chocolate but I was afraid it would melt."

I actually enjoyed that late lunch. We both knew we would hear anybody or anything that got close to where we were holing up so we ate perched on the tailgate of the truck bed. After retrieving the can opener, George opened the hatch for our seating enjoyment. I ate tuna and crackers and washed it down with warm root beer.

"So what's the plan now, coach?" George said glibly, munching barbeque chips and beans. He had even found two disposable spoons.

"I could do with a little input. Every time we try to get back to Little Falls we are thwarted. I'm almost afraid to try again, and yes, the Keeler's are intimidating me."

"Hard to know what they're capable of," George consoled me. "I told you already I wasn't brave enough to let them get close to us back there."

"Would you have taken a chance if I wasn't with you?"

"I might have," he allowed, "especially on the main road. Hard to say."

We talked about our possibilities. First, sitting tight for a while longer before making another attempt to back track the way we had come. Second, sitting tight for a while longer then continuing on to see where the forest road led. And third, we finish our food and move on immediately. With the third option we agreed to move forward rather than go back. Or, I suggested, we could always stay put for several hours and wait until dark. Surely they would give up looking for us by then.

"It doesn't get dark this time of year up here for," and here George consulted his watch and did a quick calculation, "almost seven hours. Waiting that long doesn't appeal to me much."

Admittedly it didn't hold much attraction for me either. I took a closer look at our surroundings. To the right and about half a mile farther than I had gone for privacy, the landscape rolled gently upward.

"If we take a walk and go up that hill," I pointed it out, "the top might give us a view of most of this area. I know there's a rough path going that way. What do you say to an after lunch stroll?"

"I had in mind an after lunch nap with you keeping watch."

"Ha, ha."

The more I thought about it, the more appealing it became to climb up that hill. In the end, when George saw I was determined to go, he went with me.

"Let's hope our enemies don't find my truck while we're gone," he said pensively.

"That could be bad. Can we hide it any better?"

So we took some precautions. George moved the truck a few hundred feet farther into the forest. I suggested we take a few of our belongings and the cooler out of the truck and hide them somewhere separately. It sounded silly, saying that out loud, and I expected to take some teasing for it. But that didn't happen.

"This whole thing is getting so crazy the idea seems reasonable," was George's response.

So we did just that. I quickly repacked my smaller carry on bag, adding to it a flashlight and a heavier shirt of George's. He took the cooler. We carried them with us for another short distance and buried them under some heavy shrubbery. We wanted to be sure we could find our cache again, and George had a few tricks from his experiences as an outdoorsman. He walked a few paces to a tall oak and motioned me over. Giving me a leg up he had me break some branches about eight feet above ground. They would never be noticed by anyone who wasn't looking for them. To us they were obvious.

I tied a sweater around my waist, drank the last of the root beer, put the empty can back in the cooler, and we set out. There was a rough path of sorts and as long as we stayed on it we weren't in danger of getting lost. Before getting started George insisted on spraying both of us with a heavy layer of insect repellant. I turned up my nose at the smell but would be grateful for the nasty stuff.

Fortified by our nourishment we set out at a good pace and made good time. Only heavy overgrowth slowed us down. George held offending branches aside for me several times but I still took a few slaps on my bare arms. The scratches were very superficial and I bravely ignored them rather than put the sweater on and sweat. As we moved further away we saw no need to lower our voices, but our conversation was sparse. We both were set on reaching the top of that hill and we finally did.

To my disappointment we couldn't see as far as I had hoped. We weren't high enough. On the positive side we couldn't see where we had hidden George's vehicle. Our view consisted mainly of trees and more trees. Three minutes of looking at that and I suggested we go back.

"Not so fast," my companion cautioned. "Wait a bit and let your eyes get used to the scenery. You may see more than you think. Besides, if we're quiet for a bit sound carries up here and we may hear things, too."

Chastised, I did as he said. George had the advantage of being over six inches taller than I am and boasted almost perfect far vision, but my hearing was probably more acute. Together maybe we could figure out which way to go.

Eventually I distinguished trickling water and heavier disturbances in the countryside that George told me was probably critters moving about. For the time being I didn't ask what kind of critters.

With the patience George had more of than I did, he eventually found the track we had now traveled down twice that day. He could trace it at intervals through the density. When asked, he said he couldn't spot any vehicles on the road, or anywhere else.

He was gazing long and hard to our right, shading his eyes from the sun, which was free of clouds for the moment. Using the sun as a gauge, I guessed he was looking southwest.

"That's the direction we'll be heading in if we keep going straight up the road," he told me, "and there is something going on up there. There's a larger clearing and I can make out, well, I think it's some sort of building."

I kept silent, letting him continue to observe without distraction.

"The road keeps going for a while, or something does," he continued, "but I can't tell where it ends."

"Too bad we don't have binoculars," I commented.

Sheepishly George admitted he had a pair in the glove compartment but had forgotten all about them.

"And I know what you're thinking," he added sharply, "but you can forget it. I am not going back to get them."

"Maybe I was going to say I would go back to get them," I said innocently.

"Fat chance," he retorted.

"Okay. Let's go back. We can decide on the way which direction to take."

We had been free of menace long enough to relax again and we sauntered back in a good frame of mind.

"Where's the water I keep hearing?" I asked. "We saw that little stream running next to the road but it wasn't big enough to make any noise."

"There has to be a larger body of water beyond where we've been. It can't be too far although sounds are deceptive."

I suspected George's idea of distance would be a lot different than mine. "How far does sound carry? I mean, I know it carries a long way when you're out on water. But in a heavily wooded area I never thought about it."

George could not give me a definitive answer. He said it depended on the density of the trees, how hard the wind was blowing, and which direction it was coming from.

"We have time, the afternoon's only half over. If you think it could be important we could follow the road a little further and see what's up there."

George's offer was very unexpected. Until now he had been focused on getting to Little Falls and a decent food supply. I considered his offer. We really needed to find a sheriff or local cop of some sort before the day was out. Time seemed surreal out here, especially since trying to get anywhere was becoming like climbing up a slippery slope. We kept sliding back to the bottom.

"This isn't part of a state or national park, is it? I'm aware it should have been posted, but except for that one residence we haven't seen anything. But if it isn't private land shouldn't there be park rangers patrolling once in awhile?"

"I looked at a county map yesterday afternoon," George informed me. "There is a national forest around here and an Indian reservation too. If that farm borders on an edge of it we may have missed the marker or it may have disappeared. It's possible. It's not unusual for private land to come up against federal or state owned property. That housing development we visited this morning can't be that far from here."

Before we could continue this discussion my ears picked up the sound of a diesel engine. It was faint but distinctive. Glancing at George I saw he heard it too. We kept walking but both strained to hear. We were within minutes of getting back to our gear when the sound, which had gotten a little louder, became faint again and died away.

"Something is worth coming and going on that cow path for," I remarked. "Considering it isn't kept up by the county or the forest service or anyone else, I still wonder what it is."

George grinned. "I told you, probably a good fishing spot." But after a bit of thought he amended, "It isn't the best time of day for it, but still, could be."

I slackened my pace. "If there are friendly locals hanging out nearby we might be able to latch onto them to get safely out of here. But if we drive up in the truck we're vulnerable. There's no way we can get close without being noticed."

George looked pained. He was several paces ahead but paused and put his hands on his hips. "You're suggesting more walking?" Before he could get an answer he went on. "I've been thinking about this. Maybe we're over reacting? By now they've got to have thought this through a little more. What's that guy's name, Bud? From what we overheard back there he's pretty nervy. He can't know we overheard anything and by now he's thinking, what's the big deal? They're looking for this guy, so what?"

"So you think we should take the chance. We should climb back into the truck and head back to Little Falls"

"That's what I'm thinking."

"What about that little stunt they pulled on the road back there forcing you onto the shoulder?"

George admitted that had been unnerving. "But I'm getting a little tired of playing cat and mouse. I say we're overreacting, and I definitely do not want to walk all those miles back to the state highway. Besides, what then? Hitchhike?"

"I am not suggesting we walk all the way back to Little Falls.

What I think we should do is find out what's farther on, but do it with our feet. What if Bud and Gene and the other guy now remember hearing a lot of rustling in the marshes while they were having their little talk, and realize it wasn't any of those critters you mention from time to time?"

We were now within sight of the pickup again. Rather than recover our buried goods we debated the issue. In the end we compromised. George agreed to hike a short way up the road to see what lay ahead. We did not establish what those parameters were. Satisfied to have gotten my way for starters I did not push it.

Before taking off again I retrieved my bag from our cache and put a few essentials into my trouser pockets. George obligingly camouflaged our belongings as he had before. I took a few swallows of another liquid from the not so cold cooler. George took a few minutes making a couple of adjustments of his own including another quick trip into the seclusion of the brush.

Chapter Twenty-Two

I did feel safer walking. We could easily hear anything before it got close and get off the path - or road if you could call it that. When I expressed these sentiments to my partner he told me that was fine during daylight hours. After dark the creatures that called the wooded area home might make me feel differently. I reminded him that was hours away yet, as he had said himself. Once more he wasn't asked to specify the forest inhabitants he was referring to. It was much nicer to envision little bunny rabbits, squirrels, and a few deer.

We walked on in silence. I knew on a regular path I could easily do a mile in fifteen minutes, but this was a little slower going even if it was pretty clear of overgrowth. Sometimes the ruts in the road were deep and walking on the side single file worked the best. George's legs were longer than mine and I suspected he was holding back a little to accommodate me.

Once more we heard before we saw. This time, no doubt about it, we were hearing human voices. The sound of running water became louder almost simultaneously. We could not make out anything specific being said, although you couldn't mistake the sound of heavy pounding. We were almost upon a sharp curve to the left in the road. Instead of taking it George, who was in the lead, jerked his head toward the seclusion of the trees.

Probably because the stream or small riverbed was to the right of the road, he had chosen the left side for seclusion. That was okay with me too. I didn't really relish getting wet again. The left side was dry but had little else going for it. Compared to our previous hikes this was the worst one yet. The spaces between the taller trees were full of brambles and berry bushes and who knows what else.

"Sorry," George said in a low voice. He hadn't been able to stop a rogue branch from slapping me in the face.

"It's okay," I replied in a loud whisper. "It's better to keep playing it safe until we know if we're among friends. It's impossible to be quiet getting through this mess."

"With all the noise they're making they can't hear us." He pointed to a spot barely visible through the density of our surroundings. Not much farther on was a small meadow lush with tall grass.

"We'll stay to the edge and work our way around to that hill on the other side," George directed. "Keep your eyes and ears open."

We did just that and saw only two small rabbits that scampered out of our way when we got too close. By the time we approached the meadow the voices and other sounds faded, but we could hear activity again shortly after we had worked our way around to the other side. If this was a favorite local spot for fishing they were mighty noisy about it. There was loud chatter, some laughter, some cussing, and someone was whistling. All of the voices sounded male.

In this area the ground took an upward slope. We continued on until we had the protection of that gentle hill. It wasn't necessary to talk about it; we both knew if we wanted to stay hidden we had to get down and crawl up to look over the top. A bath was going to be heaven when we got through all this.

The upward climb wasn't really far but it seemed to take a long time. We had to worm our way around a few tree stumps and various other impediments. I tried not to think about what might be crawling up my shirt or into my pants as I pushed myself over the ground. Twice when there was plenty of cover I got on my hands and knees to make a little progress, but I was eating grass again long before catching up with George. He had covered the distance disgustingly fast. It must have been all those hunts and that basic training in the military.

He couldn't resist giving me a broad smile as I reached his side. "Not bad for a girl," he murmured.

There wasn't any need to whisper, just to keep our voices low. We both watched. There were three vehicles and about five men below with enough distance between us to be reassuring. No one was looking up in our direction and even if they had been we wouldn't be easy to spot.

They weren't fishing; they were building a cabin. There was enough of it already up to get the picture. They were using discarded lumber, and I remembered that old cabin and wondered if these men had taken what they were using from it. One of the party was pulling old nails out of the studs before another man would carry it to the site. He deftly measured the piece and cut it with a table saw so they would all be the same size. Two others were erecting the structure and they had a large portion of it complete. There was no concrete poured as there had been at the building sites we had visited in the morning, just a sturdy wooden base sitting on large concrete blocks. The building looked really small from where I sat, but George said it would be about four hundred square feet, which was a good size camp.

"There doesn't seem to be anything going on down there to get nervous about. I feel a little silly spying on them like this."

He didn't answer but kept watching. Not having anything better to do I followed his example.

Deciding to be observant, there were a few things to observe. First the forest road, which was actually between the work in progress and the stream, did not end here but continued on out of sight. Second, I had a good view of the stream and it had grown considerably in size, now looking more like a small river. Third, most of the workers looked well over forty, but a much younger man was sitting on the tailgate of one of the pickups, just as George and I had earlier while we were eating. Blond and thickset, he was watching rather than assisting and sipping something out of a can. There were several cans strewn about, thrown out of the way of the workers. I asked George how much longer it would take to finish building the cabin and he said probably not long as it looked pretty basic. I pointed out this must be private land if they were building something on it. He thought that was probably true as this didn't look like a government job.

214

Not complicated enough, he added wryly.

"If you don't see anything sinister going on maybe we should get out of here and go back," this from me.

"Doesn't look suspicious," he agreed. "Leave the way we came?"

That was my choice, even though it meant going back through all the pucker brush. It would be awkward sliding down the hill and dropping in.

George didn't make a case for introducing ourselves to the working party, either. It was one of those things you can't explain. We could easily have stood up, walked down the hill, and told them our story. The men below looked ordinary enough, nothing overtly sinister about them. Off handedly we could tell them about hiking around and casually bring up our weird experience of the afternoon. Maybe we would all laugh about it, and the friendly locals would reassure us the Keeler boys were mostly bark, not too much bite. I couldn't make myself suggest doing that, and my friend didn't fall back on his "maybe we're over reacting," attitude and suggest something of the same sort. He led the way and we quietly backed up, going most of the way down on our backsides.

"At least now we know where everyone was going," I said. "There were three trucks down there. Are they putting that up for a hunting shack?"

"Maybe," he thought. "It looks like a shelter, nothing more. It might be for storage."

As we got back to the road once again I checked the time. "It's getting on!" I exclaimed. We quickened our pace as much as we could without risking a sprained ankle.

That July day in northern Wisconsin goes down in the story of my life as one of the very longest. Only one or two others come close and we won't go into that here.

For sure, we were both getting tired. We had the road completely to ourselves on our way back and heard nothing to make us skittish. George was pulling his keys out of his pocket as we turned onto the trail where we had left everything, and I was about to remind him we had supplies to load, when we heard noise that was unmistakably human once again, and definitely coming from the direction we were headed.

We came to a complete standstill, mute for about five long seconds before it hit me we might want to move somewhere out of sight and see who was visiting. George had come to himself about a second earlier and was already tugging on my arm.

There weren't many choices for hiding places in a hurry. I followed him to the right, down a ravine, and we skirted along until we were pretty well protected behind an area of rocky outgrowth. We moved slowly to keep from making noise. The concealment was adequate as long as no one was deliberately looking for us, but we couldn't see anything.

The voices were still audible, in fact a little louder, and as we stood motionless I could hear what was being said. The first comments were irrelevant and gave me no clues as to who was hanging around. But then,

"…Where the …. did they go? It's been over fifteen minutes. You know this is gotta be them."

"Yeah, white pickup, Indiana plate," said a male with a raspy voice.

I glanced at George with my heart sinking, and he nodded. His hearing may not have been as sharp as mine was but he recognized both of those voices, too.

"Well, they can't be far. I wonder if they walked up the road? They'd run into Hank and some of the boys building the shack."

The two of them, Bud Keeler and his nervous sidekick, Gene, came up with a plan. Gene would move their own truck back to the road, block the exit from the trail, and wait. We wouldn't be able to get around him. Bud would, little did he know, walk back up the road we had just vacated and see if we had been seen by Hank or the others.

"If they come back lay on your horn," ordered Bud. "We'll hear you."

I eased my dusty backside against the rocky hill protecting us and slid to the ground. With a deep sigh George joined me. We listened to our foes turn their truck around and park it. Only one door opened and slammed shut so the obvious conclusion was Gene stayed inside. Bud was on his way to visit the boys up the road. I wondered what had happened to the blue sedan.

This was getting ludicrous. Absurd. Suddenly, the whole day struck me funny and I had an uncontrollable urge to laugh. But I couldn't laugh too loud or Gene might hear me, probably would hear me. George watched incredulously as I smothered my giggles.

"Sorry," I gasped, the effort of suppressing my mirth bringing tears to my eyes.

"You're laughing," he whispered reprovingly.

I nodded. It would be dangerous to try to say anything.

George got to his feet and held out a hand to help me get up. I accepted and we moved cautiously in the opposite direction from where Gene was cooling his heels. The whole time I was making gasping, choking noises while George looked as though he wasn't sure whether he wanted to laugh along or help me choke. We stopped where the cooler was concealed and as we sat down the hiccoughs were going away.

"Maybe we should try to tackle Gene while he's alone, steal his truck, and make a getaway," I suggested with one last round of stifled laughter before sanity reasserted itself.

"Since I know you aren't serious I won't point out he could have that whole crew up the road high-tailing it back here by leaning on his horn before we could drag him out of the truck." My friend sounded disgusted, but the small smirk on his face spoiled it.

We sat there contemplating the fix we were in. With some clean tissues from my pocket I was able to wipe my face and blow my nose.

"Okay," I said. "We have to decide where to go from here. We don't know how long before they come back and we sure don't know what they'll do next."

We agreed it was too risky to try and get around Gene with our own vehicle. At the very least George would suffer some damage to his truck and I didn't want that any more than he did. We didn't talk about the worst case scenario.

"These guys are unpredictable. I don't know what they're capable of. We've heard they make illegal booze, but they might have killed a guy." George summed up the situation.

"It's a good thing we didn't walk into that group and introduce ourselves."

George grimaced. "Yeah. Let's not even go there."

We wondered if Bud and his companions would keep watch

indefinitely to see if we came back, or if we could wait them out. More than ever we wanted to get back to Little Falls, but as George had said earlier it would be a long walk. If someone kept watch for several more hours we could be stumbling around in the dark with only a flashlight. Better to go ahead and get started.

Quietly and efficiently, for the second time George produced our buried cache. It was still warm outside but he slipped into his windbreaker and put a can of soda pop into each pocket. I was thirsty again but resisted the urge to do anything about it. Instead I tied my own light sweater around my waist and put my purse strap over my right shoulder. I wasn't about to leave my money and my identification cards behind.

"Is there anything we have to get out of your truck?" I asked quietly. It would be risky to approach it and open a door quietly enough not to tip off Gene, but if George thought it was necessary we would take the chance.

He thought about it and decided not. It was locked and there was no indication Bud or Gene had tried to break into it. We would have to take our chances and hope they would leave it alone.

"If they decide to get nasty it's insured," George said, being the optimistic one.

We had not taken even one step toward our destination when the sound of diesel engines became all too clear. I now detested the sound of diesel engines.

"Trucks," I breathed in dismay. The sound was coming from the direction of the group we had spied on. "They're coming from …"

"Yeah," George interrupted, "Bud Keeler must be bringing back reinforcements."

I'll admit it. This time I was scared. "What do we do?" I couldn't keep a quiver out of my voice.

But there wasn't time to make any more plans. With a roar of engines Gene backed his vehicle all the way back up the path, with three more trucks following him. We were out of sight but just barely.

"Get down!" George hissed.

There was little else we could do. If we tried to leave too quickly we could be seen and if the group turned their motors off we would easily be heard. We flattened ourselves out onto the ground.

We lay there straining to hear what they were saying but is hard to hear very well when your heart is thumping like a jack-hammer. It was trying to pound right out of my chest. I remember thinking how ridiculous it was for a middle- aged woman like myself to be in such a mess.

Since at least two of the truck drivers didn't bother to turn their loud motors off we couldn't understand much of the talk. There was some laughter and I caught a few words, a lot of those foul.

"Are they having some fun at our expense?" I asked George through gritted teeth.

"Could be," he said.

Finally we heard two of the trucks pull back and leave. Now it was quiet enough to hear what was being said. That was even scarier.

"If they had engine troubles and left on foot," said a voice that was not familiar, "old Eddie may have seen 'em. Bud has a key to the house if he's too drunk to hear somebody at the door."

The dilapidated farmhouse between us and the highway; it had to be what they were talking about. I remembered the fierce looking old man we had seen earlier in the afternoon, passing us on the road. That could have been old Eddie. Probably another relative of the Keelers, I thought bitterly.

We heard the stranger and his companion as they passed us, heading up the hill we had climbed earlier that afternoon. From my vantage point, my chin in the grass, I saw one set of hob nail boots just yards away from us as they walked by. About the time it looked safe to breathe again the feet stopped.

"Gene," yelled the voice, "you and Joe look for footprints down at the creek."

Gene hollered back an okay. Soon all sounds of human presence receded.

"Do you think there's anyone left guarding the truck?" I used my lowest whisper again, almost too frightened to even move.

There was no answer. It wasn't easy because every fiber of my being screamed flight, but I waited for George to respond.

"Come on," his voice was barely audible but he got to his

feet, keeping his tall frame stooped over. "We can't stay here."

"Where?" I asked, getting off of my belly and following him.

Again he didn't bother to answer. There was no need. As quietly as the forest floor would allow he crept back to his pickup truck with me just a step behind.

For the moment, miraculously, the three trucks left there stood unguarded. We knew that wouldn't last very long. My head bobbed like a kewpie doll as I kept glancing around us for any sign of the returning of Keeler and company. George stayed more focused.

"We won't be leaving that way," he muttered.

I followed his gaze. The front tires of his truck were slashed and flat.

"Let's see if they left their keys in the ignition," I suggested. What did it matter, stealing a truck at this point? We were desperate and it would serve them right for slashing the tires.

"Okay," George allowed. "You check the red one."

I tiptoed over and peeked through the open window into the junky cab. The keys were gone. George was standing next to the same pickup the younger man now named as Hank Keeler had been sitting on watching the progress of the building project. George shook his head.

"We had better get going," this from me. "We don't have much of a head start, but what else can we do?" I jerked my head toward the left in the general direction of the farm and eventually the highway. "Let's cross the road and get onto the other side, now."

But someone's voice was getting close enough to be heard. My panicky brain noticed the tarp and the junk in the back of the pickup truck George still stood next to.

"George!" I whispered wildly. "What about in there?"

I was moving as I spoke, and probably because our options were so limited George was right with me. In a flash he lifted the tarp and with a strong hand under my elbow helped propel me into the back. I scraped an ankle on something as I climbed back as far as I could go, but suppressed any verbal reaction It was a long flatbed but it was full of gear. I crawled over something then held perfectly still. The voices were getting closer. The tarp was thick but because of the light outside I could make out George's form. He stopped moving when I did and was crouched down as low as he could between a wheelbarrow and a large toolbox. His position didn't look very comfortable but it was preferable to facing what might await us if we were caught. I was lying on my back next to the same toolbox, wedged next to some smelly hides.

It was Gene and a man I couldn't identify. Gene was not happy.

"This is b…s…," he complained. "They got spooked when they saw we were chasing them and ducked in here. My guess is they had some engine trouble, locked up their truck and headed back on foot at least an hour ago."

I was dearly hoping Gene could convince everyone else of the validity of his theory, and praying hard no one would think about looking under the tarp.

Only fear and desperation could have kept us so still for what seemed like an eternity but was probably only about ten or twelve minutes. I was getting very concerned about George and wondered if he would be able to move when it was safe for him to try.

Eventually Gene's unknown companion shouted, "See anything Hank?" and they both walked away. So one of the two men who walked past us while we were flat on the ground was Sunny Keeler's son, Hank. Extraordinary. There was no family resemblance to the "small guy with a big mouth," described by Andy. What did his mother look like? It's amazing the things that cross your mind when you're terrified.

Of course Hank's reply was a negative, and we heard him in the distance as he said so. During the time the four of them continued searching the general area George took the risk of putting himself into a more comfortable position and I readjusted my own body. Because of his height George had to lie almost flat, but he had a little space to wiggle when he needed to.

There was a whoop from one of the searching party. I was puzzled for a split second, then realized why the jubilation.

"Found the buried treasure," George murmured in confirmation.

My purse was still hanging from its strap on my right shoulder. I patted it in relief.

"This may have a plus side. Finding the cache will give the

impression we did have to abandon the truck and started walking." George said.

Chapter Twenty-Three

Our predators didn't stick around much longer. Soon we were taking a very bumpy and very uncomfortable ride. Our first stop was back at the encampment on which we had earlier been spying. I was able to keep some optimism by realizing our timing and decisions throughout the day had kept us from disaster. One of those decisions had been not to introduce ourselves to the good ole' boys building their little shack. The pit in my stomach that was getting much too familiar returned as I thought about a scenario where Hank decided to unload his truck, or wanted to get at the hides that were packed all the way in the back.

It didn't happen. The stop was brief. With the engine idling we could get the gist of what was being said over the noise of the engine. It seemed two of the men who hadn't been involved in trying to track George and me didn't know why Hank and Joe had left in such a hurry, and they weren't enlightened. As they grumbled about being deserted Hank told them to call it a day, they would finish up on the weekend.

"Come up to camp for a bottle," he placated his friends. "I'm on my way now."

Further into the lion's den I thought morosely. It was too much of a risk to even whisper my thoughts to George. He had to strain his neck to look back at me so for the most part I was looking at the top of his thinning head of hair.

Hank bounced everything in the bed of his truck including us as he led the way. Even a few miles an hour was fast over the poorly maintained track. I braced myself, thinking every muscle and bone in my body would cry out for mercy by morning. Was a good long soak in a hot tub of soapy water before this day ended too much to hope for?

It must have been worse for George. Two hundred plus pounds of him was trying to stay as still as possible so no one would notice the extra baggage. I consoled myself remembering he had chosen to leave the comfort of home and join me of his own free will. No one had twisted his arm. Well, that wasn't entirely true. Anne Carey had extended some persuasion, but not me.

The truck came to a stop so fast I was tossed forward, hit George's head with my chin, and thought surely the game was up. But no one noticed. While the boys enjoyed a late afternoon cocktail and there was no sound of anything too close by I risked whispering to George, "are you all right?" I had my mouth by his ear anyway.

He craned his neck and breathed back, "I think so. You?"

I gave him an affirmative and we went back to maintaining silence and trying to be reasonably comfortable without moving very much.

Another truck pulled up. We soon found out it was Bud Keeler and his sidekick. Instead of walking up to the camp or whiskey still or whatever it was, Bud called out to Hank, and Hank joined him for a pow-wow. We could hear someone else walking away, and guessed Bud's companion was leaving the two of them to their privacy. They sounded so close I suspected it was possible to reach out and touch one of them. I could even hear the striking of a match to light a cigarette.

They exchanged information. We already knew what Hank had to say, that there was no sign of us, but they had by chance noticed a little irregularity in the ground cover and found a few things we had left behind. Nothing worth much he thought, and wondered why we had bothered. When he snickered about flattening the tires on George's truck, I wished I could reach out and slap him. Probably George wanted to do more than that.

"Eddie didn't see 'em?" Hank asked.

Of course Eddie hadn't seen us leave although he could have

noticed us as we noticed him when our vehicles had passed each other. But Bud hadn't found Eddie so he didn't know that either.

"He's usually home by supper," Bud said. "I'll stop by there again on my way home."

"Did Laura go home?" Hank asked casually.

"She better have," Bud said, and added a couple of derogatory comments about his wife. If Sunny Keeler had been even worse than his brother it was amazing no one had bumped him off on purpose a long time ago. "She took the car she borrowed back to the hotel, and told me she was going to call her sister to get a ride home."

"Did you tell her everything?" Hank again kept his tone light.

"No more than I had to," was Bud's evasive reply. "She knows how to keep her mouth shut." He added with macho, "She had better."

It would have been so nice if someone would finally spell out what the "everything" was.

There was a pause in the conversation before Hank spoke again.

"I don't see how those two, or three if you count the third one at the bar last night, could know much since the dude hasn't turned up anywhere."

"Maybe, maybe not," Bud said cautiously. "I'd like to have a talk with 'em though, and they've got to be out here somewhere. How far could they have gotten since we saw 'em on the highway?"

Hank brought up a couple of possible ways we might have eluded their search for us. It was too bad we hadn't done that, except there was a plus to being in our current predicament. We now had more information to give the local sheriff - if we ever got the chance.

Hank and Bud sauntered away to join the others. If anyone came near us again we should have been able to hear their footsteps, but we couldn't be sure so we stayed mum most of the time. I tried to process what information we had. It was a jumble of conflicting facts. It sounded like Douglas White was alive, or at least the Keelers thought he could be. What had Gene meant during the lunch break when he said they would not have done "it" if they hadn't been drinking? It didn't sound like we were

225

being sought for some simple and polite conversation, but no one had said anything about doing away with us if we were found. Did they think they could scare us into going back to Indiana pronto? I ached to be able to converse with George about it all.

It was a miserable time staying in our hiding place. In the distance we could hear the men as they drank, talked, cursed, and laughed. There were no audible female voices. There was an odor, sweet but sickening, and another sound that was strange to me. Later George would confirm these were definite indications of an illegal still. The sound I heard was of the fires lit under the caldrons. He said it would have been much stronger if the whiskey was being made on a larger scale, and he would only grin when I asked him how he knew so much about it. Time slowly passed. We heard men coming closer and the expected sounds of engines starting and doors slamming as some of the party goers decided it was time to leave. A little more time lapsed before we picked up the sound of Bud and his companion's voices as they neared their truck. Then we could hear Hank as he approached and hollered for them to hold up a minute.

"On your way out, before stopping at Old Eddies," Hank said, "how about stopping where the Indiana truck is parked again?" He worded it as a suggestion but it sounded more like an order.

"Why don't you?" his uncle said with an edge to his voice. It was apparent he did not like being told what to do.

Hank's tone changed slightly. "I thought I'd check a few of the side trails on my way out. If they were in the woods when we found the truck they could still be around some where, and I don't think they've had time to get all the way out."

Bud Keeler didn't say anything. Maybe he nodded. "And if we don't find anybody?" His tone was lighter. "What then?"

There was a pause. I envisioned Hank shrugging, and I thought I could hear him take a drag on his cigarette. "You got any ideas? Personally, I got plans for tonight and I ain't interested in chasing two out-of-staters around much longer."

That was encouraging. Then Bud's companion, a man I thought might be Joe, had a couple of crude comments about Hank's love life. Hank didn't seem to mind. Bud let them banter for a minute, then got back to the subject of the Indiana troublemakers.

"We'll take our chances. What can they know anyway? I wouldn't have minded scaring a little sh... out of 'em, but oh well."

That was encouraging too, as long as we weren't discovered.

"We'd better get going," it was Bud's voice again. He yelled at Gene, instructing him to stay until everyone else was gone. Whether Gene liked being ordered around or not, we never knew. We could feel the weight of Hank climbing up and settling himself only a few feet in front of us. He took off without waiting for anyone else.

As long as that diesel engine was running we could now have a little conversation.

"We'd better be careful not to bounce too high or he'll notice in his rear view mirror," was the first thing George said as he carefully hunkered down even a little lower, if that was possible.

I agreed and did the same. The truck had been out of the sun but it was still stuffy in our hiding place, and the odor from the skin pelts didn't help much. Still, I was highly motivated not to be found and carefully leaned over on my side, my legs tucked in and my feet braced against the heavy toolbox.

"What now, boss?" George added lightly, managing a smile.

"Trying to keep me in a good frame of mind?"

"How am I doing?"

"Okay," I smiled back. I was very glad he could see a little humor in our predicament. "Look at it this way. If Hank finds us now we have a chance. Two against one."

"Isn't this the second time you suggested that? And don't start giggling again because I'd prefer not to find out if we're up to it."

It was true; a sudden urge to laugh was boiling up again. I smothered it.

"Right," I gasped. "This is not the time." It wasn't the time to reveal ourselves to Hank, or for me to have another fit.

Three times Hank brought the truck to a stop and although he never turned the engine off while he looked around, we shut up. Within a few minutes he would come back and go on. Trying to hold still in the bouncing truck bed took most of our energy. Our only objective for the present was to stay put until we were finally

227

free of the forest and somewhere safer.

George and I both had watches on, and they confirmed we were stuck in the back of that stinky truck for almost four hours. By then our stomachs were growling so loudly it was a miracle Hank couldn't hear them from the cab, and it was agony to maintain bladder control. Not that the odor of urine would have been noticed above the obnoxious fumes of those pelts.

Our first encouragement came when we made it back to the main road. It was heavenly not to be bouncing around anymore. "I was beginning to wonder if we would ever get out of there," I admitted. "How many times did we try?"

"I lost count," George answered. "I lost count of how many bruises I'm going to have from this ride, too."

"Did you notice which direction we turned? It was to the right, wasn't it?"

It was to the right. We were not headed toward Little Falls.

"We don't want anyone to know we're back here until it's perfectly safe. We didn't go through all of this aggravation to make ourselves known too soon. I sure hope they'll be a chance for us to sneak away before it gets dark."

George agreed.

We supposed Hank had come home to get ready for his date when he parked the truck, slammed the cab door, and we were alone.

"I think we're in a trailer park," I guessed, after listening to the sounds around us. There were children outdoors playing, a dog barked, and more noise than one would expect from a single dwelling. "Or maybe some sort of apartment complex."

George thought either one was possible. We were strongly tempted to climb out right then and there. I asked George if he thought we should, never mind how silly we would look to whoever was outdoors.

"I'd like nothing better than to get out of here, but my common sense says we wait until ole' Hank is preoccupied with his love interest," he answered, and added, "I think he might be carrying a side arm. He was pretty sure of himself looking for us without any backup."

Another unpleasant possibility that hadn't occurred to me. Hank must have taken a very quick shower because it wasn't long before our unsuspecting chauffeur came back and was on his way. Back on the road, with the added noise of the country music blaring from the cab, we were able to talk again. Now we could discuss everything we had seen and heard, which mercifully passed the time and distracted us from our discomforts.

Hank's girlfriend's house was some distance away. But as I optimistically pointed out to George, if we were getting farther away from his truck and Little Falls we might be getting closer to my rented Beretta or even Anne.

"We might also be headed for Canada," was his negative reply. I decided to ignore that. He wasn't trying to cheer me up anymore.

The girlfriend's name was Gracie. She walked out to meet Hank when he pulled into her driveway.

"Hey good lookin'," she greeted "What kept you?"

He made vague excuses, and we could hear him give her a kiss. "Nice outfit, Gracie," he complimented, which was how we found out her name. "We eatin' here?"

They went inside to discuss the matter while George and I kept using the only weapon we had at our disposal, our ears. At first it was so quiet I started to hope we could peek out and weigh our chances of slipping off. Then I heard the sound of panting, dog panting, joined by more of the same, then barking. I stared at George, willing him to come up with some sort of miracle. Of course he couldn't. The look he gave me back was of resignation. It looked like our gooses were cooked this time.

The two animals kept up the racket but did not try to jump in. Finally we heard Hank's voice coming from the house yelling at them to be quiet. They obeyed for about five seconds. Then we heard Gracie's voice. While their footsteps approached we braced ourselves. I wasn't hungry any more; my stomach was back in my throat. None of this stress could be good for me.

"Honey, Ginger, git!" Gracie ordered. "You got something back there riling 'em up."

Hank considered. "Must be those hides."

"That would do it," said Gracie. "I'll lock 'em in the back and they'll settle down."

Honey, Ginger, Gracie, and Hank left us, Honey and Ginger most reluctantly.

"Anyone who doesn't believe in the power of prayer hasn't tested it like I have today," I whispered.

"Must have been a guardian angel assigned," George agreed soberly. "That was close."

In the end, with no way of knowing our chances, we waited until it was almost dark. After the dogs were contained it was quiet again and it seemed like Gracie's house must be secluded. What little traffic or people noise we heard sounded distant, but we could not know how visible we would be from the windows of the house. The two lovebirds did not reappear so we supposed they decided to eat in. After awhile George carefully removed a warm soda from his pocket and slowly pulled the tab. The noise of that tab popping sounded like dynamite but no one responded. Rather than risk popping another one we shared the one can. It tasted good, but since my bladder was still full I dared not drink a lot of it.

Much, much, later someone had the audacity to suggest my situation that evening with George was rather romantic. I stared rudely at that person, my mouth hanging open. There had been nothing romantic about being dirty, tired, and cramped into a stinking little space with the floor of the truck bed getting more unforgiving to elbows and other prominences by the second. The only thing on my mind had been getting to freedom. If George had anything else on his mind he had the good sense to keep it to himself, but I doubt it. Only the possible alternatives kept us there so long. When our discovery had seemed inevitable, I had hoped with Gracie there Hank would not be as intimidating as he was in our previous surroundings with his relatives and pals around. But Gracie's allegiance was probably with Hank, so when we weren't exposed we didn't voluntarily surrender.

"You're closer," I finally said, meaning to the opening to the tarp. "Do you think it's safe to take a peek? He's been in there awhile and we've got to make a move sometime."

When George hesitated for a fraction of a second I hissed, "It's going to be dark soon!" This caper had proved who had more patience. Waiting for hours by a tree somewhere for a deer or turkey to show up was never going to be in my future. "I don't know how long Hank plans to stay but we need a little light to see by. Unless we stay back here until he goes home and make our escape in the middle of the night. Frankly, I cannot wait that long."

"Me either." Very slowly George eased his body the short distance to the back. If anyone had been watching they would have noticed someone or something was moving around under the tarp. He couldn't turn himself around without raising himself up slightly or without physical contact with a couple of the items we were competing with for space. I held my breath. After several seconds his feet were under my chin, his face was at the back of the truck bed, and there had not been any reaction. I moved myself in the same direction, accomplishing it without making a racket but not without bruising my knee. Once I had my face up to George's torso there was no room for me to advance any further.

We had a little relief from the darkness of our enclosure as George gently pushed aside one small portion of the cover. To keep myself from losing it I counted slowly to thirty. George lifted himself to the level of the bed of the truck and cautiously pivoted his head about as far in all directions as his position allowed. I was to number eighteen when he lowered his neck and looked back at me.

"There's no one around from what I can see," he whispered, "and I don't hear anybody. Stay still. I'm going to stick my head out and look around a little more."

I could hardly go anywhere, I thought crossly. If I could have, I should be the one to do the looking since I was smaller. Unfair, but consider the strain of the circumstances.

Popping his head and a portion of his chest out from under the tarp he swiveled onto his back and partially disappeared from my view. Nerve wracking. But this only took him a few seconds.

Sliding back underneath he whispered urgently, "Let's go! Don't forget your bag."

I put the strap around my neck and crawled after him. There was no help for making a little noise and it took a few seconds for both of us to crawl out and get to the ground. I was afraid we would alert the dogs again but that didn't happen. Gracie had put them in the back yard as she said she would. George gave me a hand getting over the side and held on to it, pulling me along out of sight. He had a spot in mind and we sped for the cover of trees

231

and a storage shed directly to our right. (It would be more correct to say we hobbled as fast as our stiff limbs would allow.) Once we made it without causing any reaction we paused.

"Thanks, George," I said, my manners back in place. He had made a good choice on the spur of the moment. From here we had a better view of everything. Hank had parked right in front of the small cabin. If anyone inside had been watching we would have been seen making our get-a-way, but the curtains were pulled. The backyard and the dogs were not visible from the truck or the side of the house we had crossed in our run for cover. No one had noticed us, at least not yet. Taking in all of our surroundings we seemed to be by ourselves about thirty feet from a small country road.

We didn't hang around to observe anything else.

"This way, I think," George guided. We limped the first few yards, but quickened our pace as soon as our lower limbs would allow it.

The light from the setting sun was visible through the trees. We were heading north.

Chapter Twenty-Four

After a pit stop in the seclusion of a copse of firs and oaks, we kept walking. It was a little cooler and a relief after the stuffiness of our hiding place. The evening rain hinted at earlier had never materialized although we could see some thunderclouds overhead. Both of us were so hungry we munched the granola bars stuffed in my pocket and swigged our last can of drink as we moved along. We passed three other dwellings and once an old Irish Setter trotted down to the end of his drive to take a look at us. From the denser brush and trees I heard some noises and once I saw a retreating deer. But no human or other creature came near. By the time it was completely dark we could see the lights of some traffic on the main road.

"We have money," I said. "If someone stops and they look all right I think we should beg a ride and offer to pay them."

We hadn't talked very much since making our escape, all of our energy devoted to getting far away from Hank and closer to some sort of civilization.

George nodded. As an after thought he asked, "Where do we want to go?"

"Anywhere with a telephone," I said with feeling. "We need to call Andy Weller, and you haven't forgotten you have a truck stranded out here somewhere have you?"

"Not hardly."

Standing at the corner of we knew not where, except now we

were on a road that was actually paved and had to lead to somewhere, I asked my long suffering sidekick to wait a minute. I pulled a comb out of my purse and ran it through my hair, dusted off my pants, and found a towelette in my purse to wipe my hands.

"You look wonderful," he offered, deadpan. "Especially in this light."

That remark did not deserve an answer.

George had only a penlight since the larger flashlight never made it out of the woods. It wasn't much but with a clear sky, a quarter moon, and the lights of fairly frequent oncoming traffic we did all right. We both remembered making a left turn here on our way to Gracie's and decided to walk in the other direction in case Hank left sooner than we expected. The shoulder of the road was usually wide enough to be safe as long as we walked single file.

"One thing hasn't changed, you know," I spoke after a time.

"What's that?"

"We still need to find Douglas White."

"Oh him. Since those outlaws don't seem to know what happened to him how can we find out?"

"A good start would be to know what they did to him. Only I don't think we can do that part."

"Amen, sister. First thing tomorrow if Hank or one of his relatives doesn't find us first, we go right to the nearest law agency around here."

During our enforced confinement I had verbalized to George something that had puzzled me. "By chasing us around and threatening us, aren't the Keelers showing their hand? It didn't sound like they wanted to do murder, just scare and intimidate us. From what we've heard do you think they killed Douglas?"

George's opinion was no to the killing, at least not outright.

"So, accepting the premise they don't know we overheard their little conference this afternoon, what do they want with us?" I had persisted. "Why not play it cool? Do they think they can terrorize us?"

"I've been thinking about that too. My guess is these are some macho bully types who usually get their way. Pushing people around must usually work for them."

"But if they want us to leave so badly there must be a reason."

"Yeah. Probably something illegal."

We were not able to draw any firm conclusions. A few more of those would have been welcome.

Finally, two teen-age boys in a souped up sedan stopped and asked if we were all right and if we needed a ride. We told them we had engine trouble while out on a hike and yes, we would be grateful for a lift. They told us the nearest town with a telephone and some amenities still available at this hour was about four miles away. They would gladly take us there.

"Nothing else to do," shrugged the driver, an engaging red head with freckles. We climbed into the back seat. The red head made a u-turn and roared off. I wondered if either one of the boys noticed the odor we carried after spending so much time next to the animal pelts in the pickup bed, mixed with our sweat. They never let on if they did.

The sign on the outskirts of town boasted six hundred and fifty two residents. This metropolis included a gas station and convenience store, complete with a dairy bar doing a brisk business. In five minutes flat we were deposited at the door. I handed the driver ten dollars and the two boys, grinning broadly, thanked us and drove off.

We had to wait our turn for the public phone and George offered to buy me a sandwich while I waited, but my appetite had waned.

"Go ahead," I urged him. "I know you feel starved. Maybe later for me, just bring me some water."

He came back to find me disconsolate. He stopped his hero sandwich midway to his mouth when he saw my face.

"What now?"

"I've tried Andy at his shop and at home. No answer. You think he's up here looking for us? He thought I'd call him hours ago."

George thought it was very possible. We found a ledge to sit on and think. The ledge was much more comfortable than Hank's pickup bed had been.

"You have to go for Anne in the morning or she'll be worried," I remembered.

235

"Yeah, and right now it looks like I might get six hours of sleep before I have to leave. That's if things finally go smoothly for a change."

There were no guarantees about that. I drank generously of the cold bottled water. "Do you think it's too late to call Carol and Randy at the hotel?" Before he could answer me I added, "But even if it isn't, I can't expect them to come all the way here to get us."

George considered this. "They may have heard from Andy. I vote you try. The bar might still be open" He grimaced. "Hindsight is always so much better. We should have offered to pay those kids to take us right where we wanted to go."

Since it was too late for that and our choices were limited, we would try to get in touch with Carol and Randy.

Some things are the same no matter where you go. The page we needed in the telephone book hanging from a chain at the phone booth was torn out. George went back inside to beg the number from the staff at the counter and I sat there idly watching the customers coming and going. I was still wary and kept an eye open for any of the unfriendly people we had seen that day.

Out there in the proverbial middle of no-where, dirty, tired, and totally unprepared for it, my ship came in. Two men very conservatively dressed, with short haircuts and driving a non-descript older model black town car, pulled into the fuel island. They caught my attention when they got out. They could have been military personnel in civilian clothes except their bearing was a little different. One of them attended to pumping gas and the other went into the store, unintentionally bumping into a young man who was hurrying out.

"My apologies, brother," he said in a low, courteous tone of voice.

I was a little intrigued. Perhaps they were priests. They certainly did not fit in with the local color. My interest heightened when an employee came out to aid a customer at the pumps and greeted the other man.

"Hey, brother." The employee was an older man himself, almost bald. He warmly grasped the possible priest by his free hand and gave it a good shake before attending to his errand.

They must be some type of clergy. Maybe they were going to

236

Green Bay. I am always interested in people.

George appeared with the phone number we needed and an apology for taking so long. They had been busy at the counter and he had to wait his turn.

"Would you mind doing the honors?" I asked him nicely. "If Carol answers I'll take over if you want me to."

He said okay and I continued my people watching. The employee and the unassuming man were conversing again and I could hear them pretty well. My ears had been well trained through the course of the afternoon and evening.

"….you have everything you need out there?" and the reply being, "of course, brother. You know how we are always provided for…"

It wasn't much you may think, but a sudden idea was taking shape in my mind.

"Sally!" George hissed. "I've got Carol here. Andy has been in touch. I think you should talk to her." George was always shy with women he didn't know very well.

Putting my budding inspiration to the side I took the phone.

Carol explained what was going on while we were trying to get back to civilization. Andy Weller called and spoke to Randy at the hotel in Little Falls a couple of hours earlier. He had been working all day on a heavy piece of equipment for the county and the job turned out to be more involved than planned. Catching a burger at Lill and Marian's café just before they closed, he remembered my promise to call him.

From there it had all gotten very complicated. When Andy couldn't locate us at the hotel he decided to try our former lodgings. He was told my car was still there and another lady was trying to get in touch with us. Would Andy like her number? She was an elderly lady and obviously worried: Anne, of course. Andy did call her, so now four people were wondering what had become of George and me. The joint decision was to wait until midnight before calling the sheriff's department. Meanwhile, somehow, Anne had talked Andy into coming to get her and taking her with him to Little Falls. They were on their way now.

Someone else was impatiently waiting to use the phone and there was no way we could condense and explain everything. I asked Carol how far away we were. About an hour.

"I could wake Randy to come and get you," she hesitated, "but he has to be up at the crack of dawn tomorrow morning."

I assured her we were all right and please not to worry about us, and please, please, not to wake up Randy. Deep down inside, contrary to what Carol heard, I was wishing she would insist. My fatigue was weighing heavily on me.

"Have Andy call us when he gets there," I went on, trying to shake it off. I gave her the name of the store and the telephone number of the phone booth. "If we haven't found a way back to Little Falls by then we'll answer. Otherwise just wait for us to come to you. I really am sorry for all this trouble, Carol, and for keeping you up so late."

"Monday through Wednesday we take turns being available until eleven," she said with good humor. "And you can make up coming in so late by spending the night here. We have two rooms open."

"They're taken," I promised. "I think you can count on us for two nights."

We stood aside for the person waiting to use the phone. I asked George to stay close to wait for our return phone call, hoped the pay phone would be free by then, and went into the store. The car I had been watching had pulled away while we were talking to Carol. I wanted a word with the convenience store employee who knew them.

The sign on the door said closing was in fifteen minutes, hence the last minute rush. Like George I had to cool my heels and wait. You would think waiting would get easier, but it was getting harder.

My turn finally came with two patrons still behind me. I had deliberately chosen the line that led to the man I wanted to speak to.

"I have a personal question," I told him. "Could I have a word when you're finished waiting on customers?"

He had no problem with it. I got out of line and waited some more.

When the customers were gone I introduced myself.

"I'm Bill," the clerk said in a friendly way. He had come around the counter and we moved away a few steps.

"I saw you speaking to that gentleman in the town car out

238

there. Sorry, no eavesdropping intended, but I did hear some of what you said. Were those two men from a private facility of some sort?"

Bill came through.

In the meantime we had gotten our return phone call. When I rejoined George he saw the instant change in me.

"What did you get in there, a supercharged espresso?"

"Something better," I beamed. "But you first. Did Carol call back?"

"Nope, someone even better. Miss Carey." He grinned, looking a little rejuvenated himself, probably a combination of talking to Anne and eating the sandwich.

Andy and Anne had appeared at the hotel only minutes after we connected with Carol. Our rescue team was on the way.

George glanced at the thinning number of cars in the parking lot. "Closing?"

"Yup. We'll have to hang around. Maybe a squad car will come along and ask why we're loitering."

"We haven't seen a cop all day, the one time we wanted to. If they do show up what should we tell them?"

"Only that we had a flat tire in the woods and are waiting for a ride. The rest is going to wait until tomorrow."

For a while after the convenience store closed we had company. Two of the four employees left within minutes but the other two stayed for half an hour to clean up. One of them was Bill, who gave us a little wave from inside while he pushed his broom.

I took my wrinkled sweater from around my waist and put it on. The temperature was dropping. Intermittently we sat on the ledge or strolled around. While we sat I told George what Bill had told me, plus the possibility that came to my mind. This time he was impressed.

"Definitely worth checking out," he agreed, "although it still leaves a lot of questions."

"I think Douglas White is the only one who can answer all the questions," I replied. "And my instincts still tell me he is still breathing oxygen."

As Bill and his co-worker locked up he asked if we were okay and we assured him our friends would be arriving shortly.

Then we were alone.

"They should be here in ten minutes or so," George said comfortingly.

It was a little eerie being by ourselves again. Even the traffic had thinned out to almost nothing. Better than being stuck in the bed of a pickup truck under a tarp or found by the Keeler bunch.

We had to have one more complication before the end of our ordeal. Since it would be a long drive back after Andy and Anne came for us, I decided to take advantage of the public restroom. It wasn't locked up, which was a surprise, and it had been recently cleaned. I wondered if vandalism to public restrooms must not be a problem in this little community, or whoever cleaned up had forgotten to do it. I had about finished my business when there was an urgent hiss coming from outside the door.

"Stay put! Don't come out until I tell you to!"

This bathroom was not nearly as nice as the one at Randy and Carol's establishment. On the other hand it was roomier and cleaner than the space I had occupied most of the evening and featured running water, a commode, and plenty of paper towels. I waited obediently, knowing George was not in a joking frame of mind, and he knew I certainly wasn't. Unwanted company must have stopped at the gas pumps. Two of the pumps were open for business with a credit card twenty-four hours a day. It could be awkward if someone else wanted my spot, but that didn't worry me very much. The only female Keeler who knew us was Laura and I wasn't afraid of her.

It was only a three-minute wait, but it was a long three minutes.

"Come on!" the voice outside said urgently.

I unlatched the door and found myself propelled willy-nilly the short distance to Douglas White's jeep. I caught sight of Anne's serene face behind the steering wheel, no Andy in sight.

As George pushed me into the back and climbed into the passenger seat he said, "Go, Miss Carey," and before he had the door completely shut she obliged.

Chapter Twenty-Five

George repeated the events of those few minutes in my presence three times to three different audiences so I feel confident they are being related accurately here.

When I left to use the bathroom he decided it wouldn't hurt to do the same. He was finished before I was and came around the corner of the building to see a pickup truck gassing up. All of our experiences of the afternoon had made him cautious so he paused to inspect the occupants before revealing himself. He recognized two of the men we had seen building the storage shack in the woods. They had never seen us so they might not know who we were, but why take a chance? What if the boys had described us to everyone while they were having their drinking party? If they were hostile, what chance did we have? After telling me to stay in the ladies' room he had kept watch, once having to retreat even further when one of the men decided to use the men's room himself. When George peered around the corner again it was to see Anne pulling cautiously into the service station, driving right up to the door of the convenience store. She was handily right between the gas pumps and George.

As we drove away the two men gave us a curious look. A gray haired elderly lady peeling out of a parking lot arouses some interest. But they didn't follow us.

Driving cheerfully back to Little Falls, Anne may have been up way past her usual bedtime but you would never have known it. Slowing down to a sedate five miles under the speed limit, she clucked maternally over us. Of course she wanted to know what had happened. We wanted to know where Andy Weller was.

"The poor man is all in," Anne said. "It was very nice of him to call me, and when I asked him to please let me go with him because I wouldn't have slept a wink, he came and got me, as you can see. But I insisted he let me be the one to come for you because I do know how to drive a standard shift and he has to go back to his shop in the morning. When he heard you were all right he sat down in a chair in the lobby and went to sleep."

I thought he must have been completely exhausted to let an almost octogenarian he had met only once drive his friend's vehicle. It was such a relief to know we were finally going to reach Little Falls, and we were both so worn out, that neither one of us enlightened Anne to much of what had happened. She seemed preoccupied enough with night driving on a road she was unfamiliar with not to press us.

"You got here pretty fast," George did comment. His math was telling him Miss Carey hadn't kept to the speed limit on her way to rescue us.

"Did I, dear?" she answered innocently. "That's good".

As Carol let us into the door of the front lobby, Andy roused from the chair he was slouched in and eyed us.

"You two sure look like something the cat dragged in," he said unnecessarily.

"Nice to see you, too." But after all, he had come for us and gone through the trouble of looking out for Anne as well. Besides, he was right. I gave him a small smile and rejoined, "You don't look too hot yourself."

It was a good thing he had chosen a leather chair to crash in. His work clothes were greasy and dirty. Add to that his messy hair, bleary eyes, and the stubble on his face, he looked more derelict than George and I did.

"What happened to your wheels?" Andy asked with a yawn.

"A long story," George said. He slumped into another chair. "Taking care of it will have to wait until tomorrow. I'm all in myself."

Carol was standing by. She asked if she could get us anything and told us our rooms were ready. I felt guilty keeping her up and said so, but my appetite had returned and it would be nice to sleep without the discomfort of an empty stomach.

"Just a glass of milk and maybe a piece of fruit?" I asked timidly.

We all agreed it was too late to go into our ordeal. Andy said now that he had a power nap under his belt and knew we hadn't joined Douglas among the missing, he had to go home. There was still work to be done in the morning and he needed to be there. On his way out of the door he gave Anne a peck on the cheek.

So Andy left, promising to return the next evening, and warning us not to disappear again. Carol produced fruit, milk, and cookies before hustling us off to bed. It was so wonderful to see a bathtub and clean sheets I almost cried.

****

If that Monday in late July had been one of the longest days in my life, the eleven hours after that were some of the best. When things are miserable relief is so sweet. Never before had a snack, a bath, and a bed felt so good. After being shown to our room I could see Anne was giving in to fatigue as well.

Handing me an extra nightie out of her own luggage she gave me a fierce hug and said only, "I'm so glad you and George are all right, dear. I look forward to hearing all about it tomorrow."

She was snoring softly before I finished my bath and climbed under the covers of the other double bed.

****

By ten a.m. we were all sitting down to a sumptuous breakfast. Carol had lent me some clothes; I had rinsed out my under wear the night before. She was taller than I, but a pair of Capris and a Henley fit pretty well. George was making do with his jeans, but someone had found him a clean extra large shirt. We were both rested and refreshed.

"How's your back?" I asked as Anne and I joined him at one of the larger tables in the dining room.

"I'm sore about everywhere else from being cramped up so long," he admitted cheerfully. "But my back isn't too bad. That

243

bed upstairs was just what the doctor ordered. How about you?"

My body ached in places I had never considered, but manageably. My left knee and a couple of other spots sported bruises, and I had a kink in my neck. I assured him I would live, but offered to share the ibuprofen I had left after partaking of it freely myself while getting dressed.

While we were eating Carol and Randy joined us. Between bites, George and I took turns filling everyone in on what had happened after we left this same dining room less than twenty-four hours earlier. Our audience of three listened intently.

"But you must go to the authorities now," Carol pointed out when we were almost to the end of our tale. "They saw Douglas that day he was here, surely, and did him some harm."

"Did Laura Keeler show up for work today?" I asked casually.

In fact, she had.

"I think she now knows at least part of what happened, but her husband may not have told her we followed her yesterday, and you can bet he didn't tell her about stalking us."

George eyed me speculatively. "You don't plan to ask her, do you?"

"No. Let the sheriff or police or whomever we go to around here handle that. I have another mission, and since I have already imposed upon you two way above and beyond what is reasonable," and here I looked at Randy and Carol, "I might as well go for broke and ask to borrow a vehicle." I added hastily, "There should be no danger involved. But it will take George a little while to rescue his truck, and while he's busy handling that there's something I need to check out."

I didn't want to take the time to go back for my rental, either. Before taking all of what we had to the law, it might be possible to settle the question of where Douglas White was once and for all.

Randy and Carol Eastman gave me the pick of their two personal vehicles. Since I was pretty sure the road I was taking was paved I chose Carol's little compact car with an automatic transmission over Randy's four-wheel drive truck. No one pressed for details after being given a promise they would get the entire story upon my return. Anne had been gracious when I declined her company, but she insisted on knowing my destination, reminding me of the unexpected complications of the day before. Her logic was sound.

"You are entitled to your little mystery," she said when I told her, and asked no more questions.

George knew where I was going and why, but he said nothing. Instead he consulted Randy on a good tow service and announced he would make sure he had plenty of friendly company when he returned to the secluded little spot where he had left his pickup truck. He added rather ferociously there had better not be any more damage. I hoped not, too. George had sustained enough wear and tear on this mission already. Since there was no way he could leave until the next morning he would also be a day late back to work.

The instructions Bill, the convenience store attendant, had given me were simple enough. There had been no need to write them down. Thirty miles down the main highway to the north, fifteen more on the county road to the right, a sharp left, and follow it to the end of the road. It was miles away from where George and I had stumbled over the Keeler brothers and it was approaching the Canadian border. I suspected the last road, several miles long, was sometimes impassable in the winter, but it was paved. The buildings and parking lot at my destination were preceded by acres of wooded areas, meadows, and farmland. Nothing indicated who owned the idyllic scene but there were a handful of men out in the fields working. When I came upon the open gate in front of an impressive building with a stone facade there was a small sign saying simply, "St. Joseph's Abbey."

The narrow paved drive separated and veered off in two directions. Guest parking was in the front, a spacious lot with several cars parked there. Impulsively I took a sharp right turn and went in the other direction. With no one or nothing warning me off, I slowly drove behind the main entrance and followed the driveway as it circled around several other buildings. Eventually I found myself back where I had begun, simply on the other end of the main parking area. But not before I saw a Toyota Camry inauspiciously parked under an oak tree in a smaller parking area behind a building used for farm machinery.

Chapter Twenty-Six

A very elderly man in the robe of a traditional Benedictine monk sat at the reception desk. I dutifully signed the guest register and asked to speak to whoever was in charge. In a quavering voice he said that this was Tuesday and it would be Brother David I should speak to, but he was engaged. Could I wait? He would see how long it would be. When I assented, he dialed a number on the house telephone on the desk. It would be about twenty minutes.

There was no one else in the main reception area and I wandered about looking at the beautiful room. It looked like a hunting lodge minus the hunting trophies. Instead of a moose head mounted over the mantle, there was a portrait of the Benedictine father who had established the abbey over a century earlier. There was a large bouquet of freshly picked wild flowers on the sofa table, but otherwise, the aura was definitely male. I wandered over to the largest window and gazed out at a well-manicured lawn surrounded by a well- tended garden. Two men were visible weeding and two others, these in gray robes, were deep in conversation as they moseyed down a footpath and out of my sight. The monk at the reception desk did not seem surprised to see a woman here but I didn't see any others. I turned my mind completely over to the issue at hand and how I would approach Brother David.

In almost exactly twenty minutes a short, stout, middle-aged man, wearing a gray robe with a black cord knotted around his middle, strode into the room and without preamble approached me.

"Mrs. Nimitz?" He greeted me in a clear and pleasant voice. "How can I help you?"

I shook the outstretched hand he extended to me and replied, "I believe you can help me, sir. I'm quite certain the man I'm looking for is staying here."

With only a slight alteration in his facial expression the man replied, "Indeed?"

The room, which had been deserted except for myself, burst into activity with the arrival of four men through the main entrance. They were in street clothes and carrying on a lively conversation.

"Follow me," Brother David invited. He turned on his heels and exited the room the way he had come without looking to see if I was behind him.

He led the way into an office directly behind the reception desk. It was a large room but it was full, the space occupied with three file cabinets, two desks, and three chairs, as well as a wall full of cupboards. The desk spaces were almost completely covered with a computer, books and ledgers.

"Forgive this," my host swept his hand across the expanse of the room before indicating one of the empty chairs for my use. "We have a nicer conference room but it is occupied at the moment." He glanced at his watch and added, "Lunch time is almost over. I have about ten minutes left. Tell me who it is you are looking for."

"I appreciate your directness." I sat straight up in my chair and held his gaze. "It is very good of you to see me. I'm looking for a man named Douglas White."

Brother David's face was unreadable. "Why do you think he's here?"

I told him. "It really is important that I speak with him, if that's at all possible. You can tell him if he wants to remain here anonymously after we talk, I won't give him away." I did not add he would have to be a pretty big heel or unable to comprehend all the things he was being told if he chose to do that.

"Some of our visitors do ask us to keep their stay here

247

confidential," the monk conceded cautiously. "We respect their right to privacy if we can."

"If the police get involved, and I think they soon will, that won't be possible anyway."

Brother David did not express any surprise at that remark, and he didn't ask me to elaborate. He was not easily rattled. "Will you wait here?"

Brother David picked up the phone and asked another brother to fill in for him for a few minutes. Then he left me alone. I sat there quietly, wondering where to begin when and if I finally met the illusive Douglas White.

Brother David did not come back. About the time I thought I had been forgotten, another man, this one dressed in slacks and a dress shirt, opened the door and asked me to follow him.

We walked past two classrooms. Both of them had their doors open. One was full of elderly gentleman being lectured by none other than Brother David. The other had six men of various ages absorbed in study.

Before I could ask any questions of my unnamed guide we crossed a common room, almost deserted, and he opened the door on the far side. This room was smaller, furnished as a cozy sitting room, and there was one man present, his wheelchair parked next to the brown leather couch.

"Douglas White I presume?" It seemed like such an appropriate greeting.

He looked very much like the photograph taken with Ingrid I had seen in his home, except he was thinner now. His left leg was heavily casted and elevated. There was a splint on his left wrist. The weary and slightly haggard look on his face hinted of endured pain but he gave me a little smile.

"I'm at a disadvantage, Mrs. Nimitz. I don't think we've met."

"Please call me Sally. We have never met before, but I feel like I know you."

He invited me to sit down. My guide left us but he left the door ajar a few inches. Maybe it was against the rules at an abbey to leave a man and a woman alone if they weren't married to each other. Douglas White expressed no problem with it so it was fine with me too. Without waiting for him to ask me, I went into an explanation of who I was and why I had come. He was surprised, no doubt about it.

"Whatever I expected you aren't it," he responded with a touch of humor at the end of my narrative.

My explanation had taken a little time. There was a discreet rap on the door. "Are you all right Douglas?" asked the young man who had escorted me in. "Can I get you anything?" He included me in the invitation.

I admitted a glass of water or a cup of coffee sounded nice. My conference with the man who had finally been located would take awhile. I checked the time.

"Have you had your lunch? I don't mean to keep you from it."

He had eaten lunch and gallantly asked me if I had eaten mine. Assured I wanted nothing to eat he instructed, "Coffee and water for both of us if you don't mind, Chris."

He shifted in his wheel chair, and winced a little.

"Compliments of the Keeler boys?" I asked, watching him.

"Mostly," he admitted. "But before I decide to bare my soul tell me what else you know."

"I know what it's like to lose a soul mate. When your brother told me about your loss and how happy your marriage had been, I knew you felt completely lost, and although your family cared, they didn't realize the extent of your suffering. What I wanted to find out was how you had handled it, believing that was the key to your disappearance. You covered your tracks really well, but after spending a little time with your parents and looking through your house, I guessed you didn't want anyone to know where you had gone. Prison was about the only thing that fit, although later, I did consider a long-term rehab facility. I wasn't sure about the incarceration part until your friend Andy decided to tell me what he knew."

"You got Andy to spill the beans? You must have great powers of persuasion, Mrs. Nimitz."

"Sally. And the only reason he did was because he was getting uneasy too, and he didn't want me telling your family anything yet. Through a personal friend I found out when you had served your time, and where. But where had you gone after that? It wasn't too hard to guess you had other plans before going home but you left very few hints as to your next destination either. I found out you weren't a big traveler, especially by yourself. But you had withdrawn money from your bank accounts and placed charges on your credit card."

I paused as he looked at me incredulously. I hastily explained being given permission to look at his mail. "Your parents were getting very anxious, you know. Those little notes you sent didn't do much to make them feel better by the time July was rolling around."

"How are they?" Douglas asked quietly.

"Fine. They are amazing really, when you think about it. Your brother David sent me up here and they trusted me sight unseen."

Our beverages were delivered, and Chris lingered a moment. "Would you like me to serve?" he offered.

Douglas looked at me and I said quickly, "I'd be glad to do it."

"You're left handed," I commented as I poured coffee for each of us out of a china coffee server. Chris declined a cup and left us again.

"Yep. I can't lift anything heavy with it yet, and I haven't mastered everything with my right."

To prove his point he poured his own cream and stirred his coffee with his right hand. He managed it adequately, if awkwardly.

"How did you ever write that note your folks got last week?" I blurted out in sudden remembrance.

His lopsided grin was charming. It was not hard to figure why women did not want Douglas to stay lonely.

"I didn't. There's a guy here who's going through the process of taking the orders. He used to make a living forging documents and handwriting for spies."

I laughed out loud. "It's a good thing we didn't know that. Everyone was so sure it was you we took it for granted you were alive somewhere."

"You were hurt pretty badly," I added mildly, but Douglas was not ready to tell me his side of the story quite yet. He told me to continue.

Dutifully, but condensing it, I recounted the bar hopping on

Sunday night and the adventures of the previous day.

"I was wracking my brain trying to figure out where you could be," I concluded. "Unless you had ended up in some secluded spot and, well, not made it out, I believed you weren't far away. Remember, not knowing you had access to an accomplished forger, I knew you had been alive about two weeks ago to write to your family again. But no one had seen you in about two months." I stopped to sip coffee and went on, "Until I overheard that conversation at the gas pumps last night I was leaning toward my previous theory of a rehab unit."

If the reader has not noticed, I am good at jumping from one subject matter to another and now, I confess I did another turnabout. "By the way, how come all three of the notes that were sent after you left home were post marked from Chicago? That is the one thing that didn't make any sense."

Douglas had been listening to every word, his facial expressions doing interesting changes as he was filled in on the search for his whereabouts. He answered with a certain amount of smugness, "This abbey has a parent organization there. I arranged ahead of time for the first two to be delivered. Several days ago a visiting monk took the last one back with him." He added, "but you aren't too far off with the rehab idea. It just has a little different look to it."

I thought my own expression was unreadable, but apparently not. His demeanor changed. "I know. Everyone has to know sometime." He shifted his weight a little again as he had been doing every so often. "I need to stand and stretch. Give me a hand?"

He used his right upper extremity to gently ease his left leg off the wheelchair support, and I supported his weaker left side as he got into a standing position. He indicated a crutch that had been sitting unnoticed against the wall and I handed it to him. He tucked it under his left arm and crutch walked, using his strong right leg and both arms, sparing his left wrist as much as possible. After a couple of laps around the room he did not return to the wheelchair but roosted on the couch instead. Without being asked I helped him get the heavy cast comfortable. He accepted my offer of a second cup of coffee, and since I had watched him fix the first cup I added the cream before handing it to him.

"Thanks," Douglas accepted the cup, took a sip, and waited for me to take a seat and join him.

As I did so he smiled and said, "Hearing you tell about it, your adventures with your friend avoiding the Keelers yesterday sounds rather humorous, or it could to someone who doesn't know them very well. But I'm sure it didn't seem very funny at the time to you and your friend."

"Not usually," I admitted, deciding not to share my moments of hysterical mirth. "We felt rather cowardly but told ourselves we were being wise. I think it was worse for George. He was telling himself he would have confronted them on the highway if he hadn't been concerned about me."

"As you can see they know how to play rough. If you think I look beat up now you should have seen me before the black eyes and the bruises healed. You two were being smart."

After a small lapse in time I ventured, "And, you weren't?"

"Nope." Douglas readjusted a pillow behind his back and clasped his hands behind his head. "Okay, here it is. " But before continuing he added, "You may be surprised to hear this is the first time I am telling anyone the whole story."

"Really?" I was surprised.

He nodded. "You heard me right. But we'll get to that. It isn't such a long story and you have guessed a lot of it already. I did have lunch at the hotel in Little Falls that Tuesday in late May. It was the week before the holiday. When I left the hotel and headed for my car I came almost face to face with Bud Keeler. It was a surprise to both of us. He was talking to a woman, but she had her back to me and never saw me."

Laura Keeler, almost certainly. Bud must have gone to see her over the lunch hour. Douglas was going on and I was the listener now.

"Bud didn't notice who I was until she walked away. I was standing next to my car ready to get in, but for some reason I just stood there. We stared at each other for a long minute, then I walked over to him. We had never said a word to each other before, but he had been with his brother at the bar that night, and he was in the courtroom."

"Now, by that time I had been here for several weeks. I had gotten a tremendous amount of peace and had no hard feelings toward anybody. In that frame of mind, of well-being toward my fellow man, I wanted to square it with Sonny's family. So I walked up to Bud, man to man, and told him I was glad to have the chance to personally tell him how sorry I was for what had happened."

There was a pause for another sip of coffee and a side note. "This is going to sound really naïve."

"Hindsight is always better," I comforted.

"Yeah. Well, he stared at me hard. When I started to walk away he said, 'It would be nice if you had the guts to say that to his boys.'"

"I turned around and told him I would be only too glad to do that. He said how about right now, I said okay, and I followed him like a sheep to the slaughter."

"He led the way to their still in the woods, the place you and your friend never saw from your hiding place. When I got out of my car I was pretty sure I was in trouble. Why would Bud Keeler want me to see what they were doing illegally? But it was too late. There were two other guys there already and I was no match for the three of them. It wasn't too long before one of Sonny's sons came and now it was four to one.

Douglas White's voice was steady but there was a slight tremor to the hands holding the coffee cup. He set it down gently, and continued. "They played with me for awhile and I can say I probably took it as well as anyone. They forced me to drink with them. It was strong moonshine and as I look back I often think it was a good thing I did have some of it in me, although I tried to not to drink much."

I have never liked graphic violence. As Douglas went on it was as though I was watching, and my own hands weren't too steady, either. I set my own cup down and clenched my fists in my lap. This was wicked.

"As they drank it turned into a small mob. They fired each other up until the first one took a punch at me. Just like I had Sonny, they said."

Douglas smiled at me painfully. "No need to give you all the gory details. It went on for a while, I don't remember how long. I threw a punch or two of my own at first but figured out that only stirred them up more, so I took it after that without resisting. They might have killed me I guess, but a couple of them were sober enough to know they had already gone too far. Then they left."

"They left you there?" Of course they had, and it was a stupid thing to say, but it was a gut reaction.

"They must have. I passed out and when I came to it was dark and no one else was around. Everything hurt when I moved and I lost consciousness again. When I came to the second time I was able to think a little better. I noticed things, like my car was still there, and except for the sound the still was making, the noises were all normal for the forest at night. No one had come back."

Since Douglas was a hunter he would know that. The knowledge must have been helpful.

Telling his ordeal seemed easier for him now. He steadily reached out for his cup, took another swallow, and moved his injured leg farther up on the pillow before going on.

"In different circumstances it would have been better not to move too much but I didn't know if they would come back in the morning and finish the job. I decided I would get in my car and get back here if I died trying." He grinned that charming grin. "At the time, dying didn't look like such a bad alternative. It was almost daylight when I made it about a mile from the abbey and managed to pull along side of the road before losing consciousness again. I knew someone would find me."

"You traveled at least sixty miles," I calculated, "You were injured, half conscious, your driving must have been terrible, but no one stopped you. Are law enforcement personnel that sparse around here? We didn't see anyone yesterday."

"As I recall, three squad cars appeared at The Dug Out pretty fast," Douglas commented dryly.

There was a polite knock on the door and Chris re-appeared. He was obviously concerned for his friend and I gave him a smile as he repeated his previous performance, asking if he could do anything for us. He also pointedly asked Douglas if he was getting tired and needed some rest.

My companion's response was to formally introduce us. We shook hands.

"Are you all right?" I looked straight at Douglas and repeated Chris' concerns.

"Haven't done so well in a long time," Doug said promptly. "It was time for this. Come back in about thirty minutes, okay?"

I can condense the rest of it. The badly wounded man was rushed to the emergency room of the nearest hospital and from there he was transferred to a higher level of care medical center. He had bad contusions, a bruised liver, a badly fractured leg, a concussion and a fractured bone in his wrist. The leg had taken the worst of it, largely because it had been moved so much after the breaks.

Before I could ask the question foremost on my mind Douglas beat me to it. "You're wondering why I haven't taken all of this to the local law by now," he said. "At first I was half out of my head with pain. After getting through surgery I was still out of it with painkillers. Since no one knew me at the hospital and no one knew what had happened to me, I supposed that was why no one filed a complaint. It was pretty obvious to the doctors and nurses I had been beaten and a deputy did show up to question me. I lied. I told him I couldn't remember anything. No one came back. The prior believed me when I told him I had not hurt anyone or been an instigator. There are strict policies here for respecting privacy if at all possible, and since no one has filed a complaint, the brothers let me decide when and if to tell my story." He smiled a little again. "Until now they were still waiting."

"Why?"

"That's a little harder to explain," he proceeded carefully. "I was in the hospital about five days. By the time of discharge I was in my right mind and the prior agreed to my recovering here. Over the next couple of weeks I managed to withdraw enough money to help pay some of the expenses without leaving a paper trail, and I gave the hospital and the doctor the abbey as my home address.

"At first I waited to contact the folks because I didn't want them to see me all beat up, and I didn't want to go into the whole story until I looked and felt better. I didn't think they would be worried yet. But there were complications. I got an infection and my leg didn't heal right. I spent a couple more days back in the hospital and I've been here about three weeks longer than expected. A guy about fifty doesn't heal so fast as he did from football injuries in high school."

"This is certainly a good choice for privacy," I remarked. "No one I have met in the past six days ever mentioned the abbey being here. If we believed in coincidences or luck, it was sheer luck that found me listening at a gas station to an employee talking to a brother from here. How did you find it?"

"They like to keep a low profile," Douglas agreed. "There are people living only a few miles from here who probably don't know this place exists. Those who come here for rest or for instruction are rarely local people." He squirmed and readjusted himself for the umpteenth time but waved me back to my chair when I started to get up to help him. "One night after drinking too much I got lost, simple as that. I ended up sleeping in my car and when I woke up in the morning two of the brothers were tapping on my window asking me if I was okay. Obviously I wasn't and I was vulnerable enough that morning to admit it."

"That was before or after Sonny Keeler?"

"Shortly after. It was after my first long interview with the county district attorney. If you don't believe in divine intervention you could call it luck."

I said softly, "But I do, and I think you do too."

He nodded. "I'm not Catholic, and no one here has tried to convert me. But here I was finally able to get honest with myself and with God."

The time was right for candor. "Are you getting through your grief at losing Ingrid?"

"Losing Ingrid, losing my kids, and having killed a man, even if it wasn't intentional," he answered without hesitation. "Ingrid's the toughest but it's coming. Maybe the feeling of loss will never go away completely, but the intenseness of the hurt has eased a lot."

I studied my hands for a moment and felt him watching me. "Have you wondered why your tormentors think they can get away with malicious assault?"

"Well so far they have, haven't they? I've had a long time to think about it. They're a bunch of outlaws and they shouldn't get away with this. If they came this close to killing me what else have they done, or what else are they capable of? But I'll tell you this, Sally Nimitz, there is one thing I am still a coward about, and it is not going home and coming clean with my family. Plain and simple, it is going through the whole process with the authorities again. It will be my word against the Keelers and they will stick up for each other, swearing they don't know a thing about my injuries. I'm told everything will heal completely with a little more time and only some early arthritis in this leg will remind me. The abbey has been a safe place for me. It will be hard to leave, but I do want to go home, get on with my life, and leave this whole mess behind."

"What you say may have been true before I walked through the door today, but now George and I have overheard some interesting conversations. You can't run away from facing this, but now you have more leverage."

Douglas White said nothing for a while. I got up and wandered over to the one window in the room. It had a view of a large field planted with peas, and with another crop I wasn't familiar with. The peas seemed to be thriving. It was very pastoral, just like the rest of the abbey surroundings. A brother dressed in a brown robe was driving a tractor to one side of the field. I had done what David White had asked and it was about time for me to leave. George was already going to be a day late getting home. One more day should be long enough to pass what information I could on to law enforcement, and they could contact me at home for follow up. I would book a flight for Thursday.

"If you aren't in a hurry to get off of the family payroll," said a voice from the couch behind me, "perhaps you could come back tomorrow and bring my folks?"

****

I was in a state of euphoria on the drive back to Little Falls. The trauma of the previous day had been worth it. I found Douglas White!

But I wasn't so engrossed in my own satisfaction not to the notice the flashing lights of a state trooper who had pulled a vehicle over. Oddly, they were at the intersection of the long private drive from the priory as it met the county road. There was no doubt about it: it was the beat up sedan that had been at the construction site the day before. The state police officer was

257

standing next to the driver's window talking to Bud Keeler.

Had Bud followed me out to the priory, and had he been waiting for me to leave? I would never know for sure, but knew if he had ever gotten close I would have spotted him before this. He was now being detained long enough for me to get safely back to the hotel in Little Falls, return my borrowed car, and finally, with Douglas White's blessing, contact the law myself. I pulled around them and looked back to see if Bud Keeler was watching me, but the body of the trooper blocked my view.

Was it luck, a state police officer finally making a timely appearance? Only if you believe in luck.

Three Months Later

It's October and my favorite time of year is almost over. I'm sitting out on my little patio, basking in the late afternoon sun and enjoying some private time. There hasn't been so much of that in my life since I left Douglas White at the Priory that Tuesday afternoon. Ten months earlier when the matter of the death of my neighbor Amelia Marsh had been settled, I had escaped the legal rigmarole. Not so this time. I've had to make the trip back up north twice. Since Douglas' evidence is much more conclusive than what George and I had to share and other people are beginning to talk, I may not have to go back again. Some of the Keeler family are beginning to co-operate with the authorities. One is Laura, Bud's ever long -suffering wife. Apparently going to jail for her husband's family is one step she isn't willing to take.

I am sipping some sugar free lemonade and being wonderfully lazy. The ringer on my phone is turned off. For an hour or so I can sit here uninterrupted and recall everything, and I don't mind saying it brings quite a bit of satisfaction - not that there were not frustrations at first. The local deputy we went to initially seemed quite put out to have to deal with anything more serious than traffic violations, acting very reluctant to move when outsiders presented him with a larger problem. When the name Keeler was mentioned the response was even chillier. I ended up placing a call to Officer Vrieze at the sheriff's office in Waupaca county. That, plus Douglas' brother David moving from his end did the trick. By the end of the week fur was flying, so to speak.

Douglas had to give several interviews in the reception room at the priory. Happily he had a lot of support, and not just from his friend Chris. The reunion of the White family was all you can imagine it would be, a real tearjerker. As their son requested I delivered Porter and Cora personally, but I stayed out of it after that. Occasionally someone would try to pull me back in and when I refused even resorted to the "but if it weren't for you..." sort of pressure.

But it would have been only a little longer before Douglas would have reappeared anyway, which I remind the White family when they try to get too sentimental with me. It is true my investigating, if you want to call it that, did result in accumulating more evidence to stop the members of the Keeler family who had decided they were a law unto themselves in northeastern Wisconsin. The whole affair is becoming quite a local scandal. There is illegal booze, drug running, even poaching, coming to light. It is likely at least two local law officers, one in the forest service, were paid to stay clear. Old Eddie, the fierce old man who lives alone in the house on the solitary road into the woods, is a great uncle and an alcoholic. I expect he's lost the source of his free whiskey.

Please don't think the White family and myself aren't on good terms; we are. In fact, we had a visit here in Hanley in late August by none other than Douglas himself, chauffeured by Andy Weller. Douglas was hobbling with his leg in a soft supportive boot and his wrist in a splint, but he looked fit and relaxed. Since there was plenty of fish and George hadn't had his promised fish fry yet, they accepted an invitation to join us. The previous night they took David out for a very belated birthday steak dinner. David and his family were invited to the fish supper too, but they had a prior commitment. About nine o'clock, after the neighbors had excused themselves, the five of us remaining, Anne Carey being the fifth, talked about the events from May on. I think both Andy and Douglas were amused at how enthusiastic Anne and George were in their part of the whole affair. For myself, I was relieved George held no hard feelings about the damage to his vehicle, nor about the extra time he had to spend in Wisconsin. I was generously reimbursed for all of my expenses and more, so I insisted on paying for two new tires for George's truck.

"The three of you make a pretty good combination," Andy remarked.

"They're the best," I praised my friends. I had thanked them both sincerely for their assistance several times, but it didn't hurt to say it again.

There have been other matters keeping me busy, too. I still have a job. My daughter is being married at Thanksgiving, in Massachusetts. She has done a lot of the planning herself, but anyone who has done it knows how much there is to getting ready for even a simple wedding. Everett and his family are going with me and my mother is making the trip from Arizona. Janelle's one surviving grandfather is too frail to make the trip so Everett will give his sister away and Judy is going to be the maid of honor. Joel is so excited about getting to ride on an airplane he is driving us all to distraction. I still need to find my dress. It is all crazy and wonderful.

A book could probably be written about the crimes committed, the investigation into them, and the trial. But my task was to find Douglas White. That was my story. The best part is, even as his brother was sitting in my living room that day in May, unknown to us, Douglas was finding himself. He's going to make a full recovery.

Made in the USA
Las Vegas, NV
02 July 2022

51009829R00154